The Silver Spoon

D1384244

The Silver Spoon

K.T. ARCHER

iUniverse, Inc.
New York Bloomington

The Silver Spoon

iUniverse books may be ordered through booksellers or by contacting:

iUniverse
1663 Liberty Drive
Bloomington, IN 47403
www.iuniverse.com
1-800-Authors (1-800-288-4677)

Because of the dynamic nature of the Internet, any Web addresses or links contained in this book may have changed since publication and may no longer be valid. The views expressed in this work are solely those of the author and do not necessarily reflect the views of the publisher, and the publisher hereby disclaims any responsibility for them.

ISBN: 978-1-4502-3204-3 (sc)
ISBN: 978-1-4502-3203-6 (dj)
ISBN: 978-1-4502-3205-0 (ebook)

Library of Congress Control Number: 2010907552

Printed in the United States of America

iUniverse rev. date: 06/08/2010

This is dedicated to:
My mother and sweet little grandmother
who gave me the courage and strength
to be the woman I am today.
Also to author Jill Conner Browne
whose books have given me insight and inspiration
to write.
Thank you all!

Prologue

"Lab, call holding on 103."

After finishing the blood draw, I bandaged the patient's arm, wished him well, and went back to the office I shared with respiratory to pick up on 103.

"Lab, this is Lizzy."

"Busy?"

"Hey, Momma. Yeah, I think everyone in Montgomery has been in today." I'd spent most of my life in and around the hospital, so it was only fitting that I'd wind up with a career in the medical field. My mother had been the nurse manager in our hometown emergency room, but I had taken a different path; I worked in the lab. When I moved from my hometown to Montgomery six years ago, I accepted a job in the emergency room of this massive trauma center. It was always busy. "I have a minute, though. What are you up to?"

"Not much," she replied. "I just had a question. How long does it take to get direct donor blood?"

She never called me at work, and, sure she already knew the answer, I laughed. "Seventy-two hours from the time the donor donates until it's ready for the recipient. Is this a test?"

Her tone was serious. "No, just a question. I know you're busy, so

I won't keep you. Will you call me if it slows down or when you get home?"

"Sure. Did you get the answer you needed?" I couldn't imagine why she'd be asking such a question.

"Yes. Call me as soon as you can. Love you, little one." I could hear her voice shaking.

"I love you, too. Is everything okay?" Instead of answering my question, she hung up.

The beeper on my hip began to chirp. I looked at the screen: *Trauma Alert. Car accident. Multiple victims.* I wanted to ignore it and call her back.

"Heads up, girl!" Spencer said as he entered the office, "Dr. Allen said he wants as many emergency-release blood units as you can get." He gathered his respiratory supplies for the incoming traumas. We had met through work but had become really good friends. Normally he could read me like a book but I was grateful he was too distracted with the emergencies coming in to notice my concern.

"How far out? How many?" I asked.

"Three minutes on the first victim. Eight was the last count, but there will be more. Church van and carload of teenagers. See you in trauma two."

I knew my call to Momma would have to wait. I called blood bank instead.

"Blood bank, Vanessa."

"Vanessa, it's Lizzy. I need the emergency-release coolers. We've got eight and counting coming in from a car accident. Dr. Allen wants as many as you have."

"You need backup?"

"That'd be great. I'm on my way."

I dropped my collection tray in trauma two and then ran down the hall to the main lab. Everyone in blood bank was working feverishly to log the numbers from each unit of blood and pack the coolers. As I assisted in packing, I kept thinking of Momma.

"Hey, direct donor is seventy-two hours, right?" I asked.

"Yes, and it has to go to Birmingham," Vanessa replied. "Not something we can do for a trauma."

"Oh, no, just verifying something I was asked earlier."

She smiled. "Good! I thought you were about to complicate things."

"And I thought we were going to have a good night," Kay said, pulling a cart into blood bank for us to load the coolers onto.

"You wish!" I replied, passing her the full coolers.

Once we had the cart loaded, Kay and I returned to the emergency room. The first victim was rolling through the ambulance bay doors.

I grabbed two of the coolers and then instructed Kay, "Put two in each trauma bay. Don't forget to armband everyone for blood bank with as much information as you can."

As I ran toward trauma two, she yelled, "You owe me a drink after this!"

"I'll be your designated driver. Thanks for your help!"

Over the next three hours, patient after patient poured into the ER from the wreck. Kay and I worked well together. It had taken medics time to get the surviving victims cut from the wreckage. While we waited for the next patient, we got caught up on the walk-in patients who needed lab work. I had to make another trip to blood bank for more bags of blood. As I passed units of blood to the nurses, I was drawn back to my conversation with my mother.

After the last patient from the wreck was brought in, I looked for Kay. She was in the office, restocking her tray.

"We're out of the woods," I told her.

Throwing her hands up, she said, "Hallelujah! I'll take my floor work over this any day. This is too intense."

"Before you get too relieved, I have a favor to ask."

"What's that?"

"I need to call my mother. Will you stay for a few more minutes?"

"I will, but you'll owe me drinks, plural." She laughed.

"You got it! I'll have my pager if you need me." I hurried to grab my cell before something else happened or before Kay changed her mind. I tried the house first, but there was no answer. *Workaholic.* I dialed her emergency room number.

"ER, this is Sandy."

"Hey, Sandy, it's Lizzy. Is Momma around?" I asked.

"Um, yes, but she's not down here. Let me transfer you." She sounded stressed, but if she was having the same kind of day as I was, I could completely understand. The phone rang a couple of times before Momma picked up.

"Why did you need to know how long it would take to get blood?" I asked.

"Well, I needed some, and I knew we were the same type," she replied. I waited a beat to see if she was going to elaborate, but she said nothing.

"What do you mean *you* needed some?" I felt a lump in my throat.

"Are you still at work?"

I took a deep breath. It didn't help. "Yes, but I'm on break. What's wrong?"

"I think we need to wait until you get home to discuss it." Her voice shook. She was crying. Mom never cried in front of other people.

"I think we need to discuss it now. Please tell me what's wrong," I said. My mind was racing; I was not prepared for what she was about to tell me.

"Lizzy, I have a grapefruit-sized tumor on my cervix, which is causing me to lose blood. I've been admitted to the hospital while they do more testing. They think it's cancer."

Chapter 1

"Lizzy?" a voice whispered.

I opened one eye. It was still dark outside, so I closed it. I thought that if I didn't open my eyes all the way, it wouldn't be real. The tumor had been diagnosed as cancer ten months ago, and treatment had not gone well.

"Lizzy, I need you to wake up." The voice was still soft but more adamant. Rhonda, my mother's best friend, needed me, but nothing good was going to come out of her mouth.

Now Rhonda was standing directly over where I was lying on the couch. She was a tall, lean woman with a boyish haircut and lime-colored eyes. I could see dread in those eyes this morning.

I'd cried myself to sleep last night, and I was still in the same position. I prepared for the worst and tried to stall by asking, "What time is it?"

"It's a little after five."

I pulled myself off the couch. A dull ache in my muscles reminded me that I hadn't slept much in the last few weeks. I looked over at Rhonda. Dark circles under her puffy eyes told me she hadn't slept much, either.

She was trying to be gentle. "Lizzy, her breathing has changed. I think you need to come and take a look."

Fear churned in my gut. My hands shook, and I took a deep breath to calm my nerves. Watching her the night before, I'd known her journey was coming to an end, but this didn't make it any easier. Although I was twenty-five years old, I'd never truly been on my own. My mom had always been my rock, and I was about to lose her.

I followed Rhonda down the hall. Mom had raised me to be strong like her, and I couldn't get scared now. I'd promised her that she would die at home, surrounded by people who loved her. No ambulance, no heroics, no sterile hospital environment—just home.

"You can do this!" I had meant to say this to myself, but as Rhonda turned around, I realized I had said it out loud.

She took my hand. "Yes, you can," she said. "You are your mother's daughter, and she wouldn't have asked this of you if she thought you couldn't handle it. I'm proud of you, kiddo, and I know she is, too. She's always been proud of you."

As we entered the room, I could see only my mother, lying in the hospital bed and struggling to breathe. I took her cold hand; her breathing was obviously labored. This was it. My mother was really going to die, that morning, and there was not much time.

Stroking her hair as she had stroked mine so many times, I whispered in her ear, "Momma, I love you. You've been so brave, and I love you so much! Thank you for being my mom. I'm not scared, so please don't you be scared. We're all here for you." My words were slow as I fought back tears.

As I looked at her, it is hard to remember the strong woman she'd been. Her body was tired from fighting this battle. She'd never been a thin woman, but now there was added weight from the fluid her body retained. Her dark brown hair was extremely thin, a side effect of the last round of chemotherapy. Closed eyelids covered her chocolate-brown eyes; I wished I could look into them one more time. Her skin, once olive, now had a sickly yellowish tint. Just five foot two, she looked like a child in the oversized hospital bed.

At the foot of the bed, Rhonda, Patricia, and Sandy held hands as they watched over us. Each woman had a different link to my mother: Rhonda had been her childhood friend and had been there for my birth; Patricia had met Momma in nursing school; and Momma had taken Sandy under her wing after an ugly divorce and had mentored her through her nursing career. Each one loved her almost as deeply as I did.

As if jolted by an electrical shock, I was snatched out of the moment. Someone wasn't there who needed to be. Although Grandmother was sleeping in the next room, it was by the grace of God that she hadn't gotten up. I wasn't sure she'd understand what was going on since she had Alzheimer's. It was Momma's sister who also needed to be with her when she drew her last breath.

Calmly I said, "Momma, I need to call Aunt Tanya. If you can't wait, I'm sure she'll understand, but I need to call her. I won't be gone but a minute. I love you." After kissing her cheek, I turned to face the three women at the foot of the bed. My statement seemed to stun them.

Patricia asked, "Are you sure?"

Ever since Momma had slipped into a coma a week ago, I hadn't let negativity slip into her room. Now it was important that she not be anywhere near this conversation. "Not in here," I said as I walked past them. Patricia and Rhonda followed me out of the room, both regarding me quizzically.

I could understand and respect their concern about Aunt Tanya's presence. Tanya had been unsupportive of the idea of Momma dying at home and had told me several times to send her to the hospital. I believed she felt that way only because she was scared. However, I hadn't forgotten why I'd asked her to leave in the first place. Seeing her go through Momma's china cabinet, laying claim on things even before Momma had died, had been too much for me. My mother may have been in a coma, but she was still alive. Her life should have taken precedence over a box of silver forks, knives, and spoons. I demanded she leave and wait for me to call closer to the end.

"Lizzy, why don't you just wait until it's over?" Patricia asked with concern.

"I can't. This will be the last time she sees her sister alive, and I have to give her that opportunity regardless of what's happened. I know this will make all the difference in the world, and she'll do the right thing." I was trying to convince myself more than them. I walked toward the phone.

"Then let one of us call." Rhonda managed to reach the phone first. "You don't need this right now." She'd become a protective momma bear since my own mother had gotten sick.

"Rhonda, I have to. I was the one who put her out of here and told her I'd call when the time came."

"But Lizzy, it will only hurt more if the silver is more important than your mother."

"That's true, but I have to believe she loves Momma and will make this right."

Patricia asked, "How can she make it right when she doesn't see how wrong it is?"

She was probably right, but I wouldn't be able to live with myself if there was even a slight chance that Aunt Tanya wanted to be there for her sister. There had to be some good inside her, not just selfishness.

Rhonda reluctantly placed the phone in my hand. "I'll be here if you need me," she said.

"You always are." I dialed the numbers.

The phone rang a number of times. *You have to do this*, I told myself. *It's the right thing.* As hard as it would be to tell her the end was near, I still envisioned her being by our sides, being the big sister and aunt she should be. But as the phone continued to ring, I also thought about just hanging up.

Halfway through the next ring, she picked up. "Hello?" Her voice was rough from sleep.

"Aunt Tanya, it's Lizzy. I need..."

She interrupted me sharply, now wide-awake. "Lizzy, what do you want? It's five-thirty in the morning!"

"Yes, I know what time it is, and I'm calling to let you know it's almost over," I replied, trying to stay calm. "Momma's breathing…" My throat was burning as I tried to fight back the tears.

"What are you talking about?" I could hear her alarm clock start to wail in the background. "My alarm is going off, and I've got to get ready for work," she said in an even harsher tone.

"It's Momma, Aunt Tanya." *Please don't make me say it,* I thought. "I don't know how much time we have left, and I promised I'd let you know when…" I trailed off because I couldn't say, "My mom's about to die."

"You really need to stop being so melodramatic, Lizzy. I don't have time for this."

In my mind I could see the stance she'd taken with me numerous times throughout my life. Back arched, shoulders back, stern, her angular face harsh, and her body stiff. *That bitch!* "You need to make time. Momma is dying."

Rhonda grabbed at the phone, but I wouldn't give it up. Taking several steps back, I mouthed in her direction, "I'm fine."

Because of the distraction, I barely heard Tanya say, "when I get there." I couldn't believe what I'd heard, so I asked her to repeat herself. With even more venom, Tanya said, "You put me out four days ago for no good reason, you deny me what's rightfully mine, you hire an attorney to oversee your own cousin, and now you want me to stop everything and run to you! Why, Lizzy? Are you just tired of dealing? Do you see you've messed up and think this will make everything better?"

I couldn't take it, and I knew it wasn't the time, but my anger broke loose before I could stop it. "I put you out because you were walking through this house telling people, 'She said I could have this when she died, and that's going to be mine, too.' How did you expect me to react? I was trying to be with my comatose mother, and you were shopping through her worldly goods like this was Macy's!"

Following Rhonda's lead, Patricia began moving ferociously in my direction, hand outstretched. "Hand me the phone! Give me that phone!" she commanded.

God, what was I doing? My mother needed me. This had to stop. I held up my hand and took a deep breath. In a calmer tone I said, "Aunt Tanya, if you want to be with your sister before she dies, you will get on your way. If you don't, then don't rush. I really have to go. Good-bye!" I clicked off the phone and began to cry.

Rhonda took me in her arms. "It's okay! She's not worth it! All that matters is that you did the right thing, Lizzy."

After taking several deep breaths, I knew I had to put Tanya out my mind. My mother needed me as she drew her last breaths, and this was not going to change. She'd warned me. Momma had known long before this moment what her sister was capable of, so I shouldn't have been surprised.

Quietly, Rhonda asked, "Are you okay? Why don't you take a minute or two?"

Pulling away from her, I said, "What was I thinking? We don't have time for this. Being there for Momma is all that's important now."

Wiping away the tears, I said, "I suggest we all put our game faces on. Let's go help Momma on her journey."

In Momma's room, Sandy was at her bedside, taking her pulse. "Pam's breathing is a little more labored, and her pulse is weaker. It could be any time now."

We all gathered around her bed, laid our hands on her to show our support, and waited for the end to come.

Chapter 2

Just fourteen days ago, the family had gathered around a table at the hospital to listen as Dr. Elliot explained what we were about to face.

"The tumor has metastasized again and is wrapping itself around Pam's ureters, preventing the elimination of toxins from her bladder. While we could begin treatment in that area, she'd grow increasingly sicker, and the outcome will be the same." Dr. Elliott spoke softly and avoided eye contact with any of us. His original diagnosis of the cancer made this even more difficult for him. Mom had been not only his patient but also his friend before he'd found the first tumor.

We all sat quietly as he continued. "Our testing shows it's a fast-growing tumor that will cause renal failure. As her blood levels increase, Pam will slip into a coma. I'll do everything humanly possible to ensure that she's comfortable."

"Why not try the treatment?" Aunt Tanya asked Momma.

Momma touched Tanya's hand. "If it would make a difference, I would. But the treatment won't cure me, and my quality of life will be terrible. I can't put you all through that." She turned to look at me.

My eyes full of tears, I nodded to let her know I understood, although what I really wanted to do was beg her to try the treatment. I couldn't, though. Since her diagnosis, the cancer had metastasized three times. The treatments seemed to make it worse. There was no getting ahead of it.

After our meeting with Dr. Elliot, I drove Momma home. Neither of us spoke. My mind raced with the efforts we'd made over the last few months, and I wondered how it was all going to end.

Momma broke the silence. "Lizzy, I want to ask you something, but I want you to be honest with me."

"Okay."

"Will you be okay if I die at home?"

"Is that what you want?"

"I've thought about this a lot. I don't want to put you through it, though, if it will be too much on you."

I thought about it for a moment and then said, "After all you've done for me, I'll find a way to handle it."

"You won't be alone. Patricia and Rhonda will be there to help. I'm sorry for talking to them first about this, but I wanted you to know you wouldn't be by yourself."

"I know you and Aunt Tanya have had your issues, but don't you think she'll want to be there, too?" Momma and Tanya had a love/hate relationship, but they were still sisters.

"I hope we can put all that behind us, and yes, I do hope she'll be there for you as well. But Tanya is who she is."

Knowing my mom was going to die gave me hope that Aunt Tanya would be there. I truly believed it would bring them closer together. I wanted it as much for Momma as I did for Aunt Tanya.

As I pulled into the driveway, I saw Patricia and Rhonda waiting for us on the porch. The women were complete opposites. Rhonda was always stylishly dressed and perfectly coiffed, while Patricia was always in jeans and a T-shirt, hair pulled back in a ponytail. Momma was somewhere in the middle on style and fashion. Each woman complemented the other, and I could see why they were such good friends.

Rhonda went to Momma as she got out of the car, while Patricia came to me. She took me in her arms and whispered, "We're here for as long as you need us." As I cried, she pulled me in closer. That night would begin the many nights of worry and sleeplessness.

The next morning, Ivy Medical Home Care arrived with Dr. Elliott. I was taught how to run the pump that would deliver Momma's morphine. Dr. Elliott gave me his personal cell phone number so I could reach him at any time with questions or concerns. The morning seemed to fly by.

News spread quickly through my small hometown. Well-wishers began calling to see if we needed anything and if it would be okay to stop by. Momma was well known and loved in the community, so it didn't surprise me that people wanted to help.

During the first week, my mother accepted anybody and everybody who came by—as long as they weren't coming to say good-bye. People brought food, flowers, and Bibles; preachers and pastors came; and someone even brought a clown to lighten the mood. There were many conversations about old times, as well as prayers, tears, smiles, and laughter. Momma accepted and welcomed all of it. I always stayed close during the prayers; the pain medication made her so sleepy that she was prone to nodding off. While heads were bowed and eyes were closed, I would prop her up with my shoulder and listen for the rounding words that signaled the approaching "amen." I always made sure she was awake before the prayer ended. If anyone knew, they were polite enough to keep it to themselves.

While my mother visited with friends, co-workers, and neighbors, I looked after my grandmother. She'd come to live at our house shortly after Momma was diagnosed with cancer. As if cancer weren't bad enough, Alzheimer's was eating away at Grandmother's mind. I always wondered if the disease was accelerated by seeing her baby girl diagnosed with cancer and watching the torture of chemo and radiation therapy. By the time we learned of Momma's fate, Grandmother had forgotten that cancer even existed—which, in a warped way, was a blessing in disguise. While our lives were spiraling downward, life remained just the same for my grandmother. Maybe it was God's way of looking out for her.

Although my mother was the younger of two children, her older sister, Tanya, was very hands-off when it came to family responsibility or crisis. Occasionally during my childhood, I'd seen Aunt Tanya retract like a crab into its shell, closing herself off until Momma or Grandmother had dealt with the situation. As soon as the problem was resolved, she'd reappear.

When my grandfather died and my emotions overwhelmed me, I lashed out about Aunt Tanya's absence. Momma seemed to know that one day I'd notice. "People handle things in their own way," she told me calmly. "Withdrawing is Tanya's way of dealing."

"But she should be here!"

"Lizzy, you may not like it, but sometimes you have to accept people as they are, faults and all."

I may not have wanted to accept it, but that day I learned a valuable lesson, one of many Momma would teach me as I grew into a young woman.

Our current situation hadn't been much different. But this time Aunt Tanya wanted *me* to handle the crisis.

Tanya popped in only for brief moments during Momma's last week of consciousness. She never had time to help Grandmother eat or to contribute to Momma's care, and she obviously timed her visits for when she knew the most people would see her. Most people worked during the day and would flood in after lunch or in the late afternoon. Aunt Tanya never stopped by on her lunch hour, never called during the day to see if we needed anything. But right around the time the house filled up, she always called to "check" on us and ask who all was there. Shortly after what I deemed "roll call," she would arrive.

One afternoon, Grandmother was napping, as was Momma, who'd suffered a vomiting spell. Aunt Tanya called to "take roll," and I gave her a handful of bogus names. Believing she was timing her visit for maximum exposure, she came over. Once she arrived, I asked her if we could talk for a moment. Rhonda and Patricia immediately remembered something they needed to do in another room. Both of them knew what was coming.

For too many days I had explained Aunt Tanya's absence by saying, "Everyone handles grief differently." With Momma and Grandmother both involved in this family crisis, maybe I could convince her we needed to work together. Facing her across the table, I asked, "Aunt Tanya, do you know what happens in this house when you're not here—or, for that matter, even when you are here?"

"I'm not sure I know what you mean," she replied innocently.

"Schedules for daily life. Linens that must be changed due to Grandmother's incontinence, toilets that must be scrubbed after Momma gets sick. I can hardly get Momma to eat, but I have to bargain with Grandmother like a child. A lot goes on in this house that I don't think you're aware of." I felt I was trying to sell her on the idea that cancer and Alzheimer's were terrible things.

"You could always let Pam go into the hospital," she replied.

"There are reasons I'd never do that. Do you know what Momma's dying wish is?" She looked at me blankly. I knew she didn't know because she didn't *want* to know. "To die at home. She spent so many days and nights working in the hospital that she just wants to keep some dignity. Plus, if Momma went to the hospital, where would Grandmother go? With you?" I knew no one was going anywhere, but the idea was helping me get to a place I needed to be. I needed Aunt Tanya to step up.

"I have my own life, a husband, a job, and those will be here after this is all said and done. I can't neglect them," she said defensively.

I was shocked. I needed much more than extra hands—I needed my aunt's love. Our family was small, and I hadn't talked to my dad in years; soon, she'd be the only family I'd have left.

I'm sure I sounded cold. "You don't think 'your life' could carry on without you for a couple of weeks while you spend some time with your sister before she dies? Or with your mother, for that matter, before she doesn't remember any of us?" *Or with me,* I thought.

"Lizzy, I won't make any promises. I can't! But I'll try and come by tomorrow evening for a while if that's what you want."

Was this what I wanted? No. What I wanted was for her to talk with me, cry with me, and tell me we'd get through this together. But if this was all she had to offer, then I guessed I'd just have to take it, sad as it was. I didn't want to drive her to stay away altogether.

Looking at her watch, she said, "I have to leave, but I wanted to ask you about the silver." I knew the silver all too well; my grandmother had been so proud of it. It had been a gift from my grandfather on their tenth wedding anniversary.

"What about it?"

"You know it's mine, right?" This time I was the one with a blank look. She continued, "I just wanted to clarify whatever misconception you might have of it being yours when all this is over."

"I know the question of who gets the silver has been a running joke between you and Momma for years. But why don't we concentrate on the task at hand?" I was unnerved and didn't want to show it. She couldn't have meant it the way it sounded.

"Why don't you let me just take it with me?" she asked. She pushed away from the table and looked around the room, trying to spot the beautiful box that held the silver.

"Aunt Tanya, you can't be serious. Are you really thinking about that now?"

Slowly she turned her gaze back to me. The look on my face surely gave away the disgust I felt. She replied, "I didn't mean it the way you're taking it. I was just thinking how valuable it is to all of us. With everyone coming in and out, I didn't want something to happen to it."

I wasn't sure I believed her. I couldn't find a response.

"Lizzy, really. Now that I see that it's not out in the open, there's nothing to worry about, right?"

Again, I didn't respond. Maybe I was being too sensitive. At another time I might have been receptive to her reasoning. Now, however, I could feel my anger rising, and I knew I couldn't let it get the better of me. I let out a deep sigh before I spoke. "What time do you think you could be here tomorrow?"

"I won't commit to a specific time, but if I can come, it won't be long after I get off work."

After a few more pleasantries, I walked her to the door. I replayed our conversation as I watched her get into her car. Something wasn't settling well, but I didn't have time to dwell on it.

As I turned the corner, I saw little Grandmother making her way up the hall. At one time, we'd been the same height, which didn't say much—we were both five feet three inches tall. Now, however, she barely came up to my shoulders. Her small hand, knotty with arthritis, gripped the cane she used for balance. The dark brown hair she'd once had was now silver, styled in the same roller set she'd worn for years. Her eyes seemed to smile when she saw me. Just her presence, so beautiful and innocent, brought a smile to my face, washing away all thoughts of my conversation with Aunt Tanya.

Chapter 3

The following day, Aunt Tanya unexpectedly followed through and arrived late in the evening. Momma's visitors had left, Patricia and Rhonda were taking a coffee break on the back porch, Grandmother was in bed for the night (I hoped), and I was preparing Momma's next dose of morphine when she walked through the door. Her first words were, "I can't stay long. Where's Pam?"

"In her room," I replied. "Thanks for coming." I was glad she'd shown up. Maybe I had overreacted to our conversation about the silver.

Since she'd never visited this late, Aunt Tanya didn't know the routine. Meds, quiet conversations, and, inevitably, sleep. Having so many visitors really took its toll, but Momma wouldn't have it any other way. As I left the kitchen, Aunt Tanya fell in step behind me. As we entered Momma's room, Momma caught sight of her sister. I could see the confusion in her eyes. Tanya sprang into action.

"Hey, Pam, how are you?"

Momma answered, "I'm a little tired today but grateful to still be here."

At this point, the only medical equipment we had in place was the IV pump that delivered the meds, so she was sleeping in her own bed. I went to the pump and administered the medication. Tanya sat at the foot of the bed. Momma was watching me. Quietly she asked, "What would I ever do without you?" I could only smile at her because I was wondering the very same thing, but here we were, faced with that reality. "Who's going to be here for you?" she continued. "To tell you happy birthday, do your Santa gifts at Christmas, help you make the decisions you already know to be the right ones?"

Tanya chimed in, "I will, of course, Pam. You don't worry about her."

My mother's eyes moved down to the foot of the bed to Aunt Tanya. "You? How will you take care of my precious girl?"

"Well, Pam, it's not like she needs twenty-four-hour care. She's a grown woman now, but I promise to be there for her anytime she needs me. Don't you worry!"

"Oh, but I do worry. And do you honestly mean you're promising me right here and right now, with my life coming to end, that you're going to be there for Lizzy?" Momma asked.

Please, please, please, Aunt Tanya! Don't make false promises now, I thought.

"Yes, of course, I promise!" she replied.

Maybe I'd gotten through to her. Maybe she really did mean what she was saying.

Slurring a bit, Momma said, "Can I have some water?"

When I started to move, my mom's hand shot up and locked around my wrist. It startled me, considering how weak the morphine made her. She asked gently, "Tanya, will you get me some water?"

"Of course. I'll be right back." She smiled and headed to the kitchen.

As soon as Tanya was out of earshot, my mother spoke. "Lizzy, this is important. I've always done the best I could raising you. I hope I haven't raised you to be too independent, because you need people in your life, but sometimes you can be too trusting. That was my mistake. I shouldn't have shielded you so much from the ugliness in people. I've made mistakes along the way, but I want you to listen to me now."

I looked down at her hand on my wrist. "Okay. You definitely have my attention."

She loosened her grip, and her eyes became clearer than I'd seen them since we started the morphine days before. "Lizzy, don't trust the people you think you can trust the most. Sometimes things are not what they seem. Do you understand?"

She was frightening me. "Momma, I don't understand!"

"I, too, have put too much faith in people. The last few days have shown me how wrong I've been."

Tanya appeared in the doorway, carrying the water like she was carrying the Hope Diamond.

I stared down at Momma, waiting for more explanation, but her attention was on Aunt Tanya. Was this the morphine talking? Momma only sipped at the water and then leaned back into her pillows. Her eyelids were heavy now.

Tanya asked, "Pam, can I do anything else for you?"

"No, but thank you." The slur was back in her speech, and it wouldn't be long before she succumbed to sleep.

"Aunt Tanya, let's leave her alone now. She needs to rest." I brushed a few strands of Momma's hair off her forehead. "I love you."

"I love you, too," she replied.

Following Aunt Tanya out of the room, I heard a soft "Lizzy?"

Returning to Momma's side, I asked, "Do you need something?"

In a whisper she said, "Remember what I told you."

"I will. You sleep sweet." I stood for a moment, taking it all in. How relaxed she seemed now! Her sleeping breaths were slow, deep, and rhythmic. From the low light in the hallway I could see the crinkle in her forehead fade away. The pain was subsiding.

While she would never complain, I knew the pain was fierce at times. I'd spent a lot of time studying her since she'd started chemo and radiation; it had become my own science. That science came in handy when she wouldn't express how she really felt, and it would become vital when she couldn't express it later on.

I went to join everyone in the kitchen, and as I rounded the corner,

I could hear Aunt Tanya bragging that Momma needed her. I almost burst into laughter when I saw Rhonda and Patricia's faces. They were not impressed.

Rhonda asked, "How's Pam?"

"She's sleeping now. The crinkle is out of her forehead." She knew what I meant.

"That's good. You're a wonderful daughter," she replied.

"Thanks, but I wish I could do more." I wanted to cry, but if I let myself, I might never stop—and I couldn't do that to Momma. She'd worried so much about me throughout all this and had stayed so strong, not even admitting when she was badly hurting. I couldn't let her down. It just wasn't the right time.

"Well, I'm going. This seems to be under control, and I'm sure you all will be going to bed soon." Aunt Tanya grabbed her keys. The three of us exchanged a look that went undetected by Aunt Tanya. We three knew there was little time for sleep—after Tanya left we'd be cleaning up, washing linens, watching for Grandmother to start wandering in the middle of the night, and pacing the floor to burn off stress.

"Yeah, Aunt Tanya, you're right. We're exhausted, but you drive safe going home." I opened the door and turned on the floodlights. After watching her back out of the driveway, I went back inside.

"And when will the Queen Mother be back?" Patricia asked. Her distaste for Tanya was clear.

"As common folk, I'm not privy to that information." I started to giggle. "You two are so bad!" We all laughed as we proceeded with our nightly chores, preparing for the next day.

As we were wrapping up, I grabbed the phone. "I'm going out on the porch for a while. I want to call Spencer and give him an update."

Patricia said, "You know, Lizzy, it's hard to believe there's never been anything between you two."

"No, it's not. I think we make better friends than we would anything else."

Rhonda threw in her opinion. "Sometimes friends make the best companions."

"Alright, you two. Stop trying to make a love match."

Both women laughed, and Rhonda said, "We're just giving you a hard time. Go make your call. It'll do you good to have some contact with the outside world."

"Please come and get me if you need me."

I settled into a rocking chair and enjoyed the stillness of the night for a few moments before calling Spencer. We'd been friends ever since I started working in the trauma center. As I waited for him to answer, I remembered how helpless he looked when I ran out of the center to come home after finding out about Momma. He'd wanted to drive me, but one of us walking out on a shift was bad enough. I hadn't cared if they fired me or not, and I couldn't wait for him to finish his shift.

"Hello?"

"Spencer, it's Lizzy."

"Thank God! I've been so worried about you. How are you? How's your mother?"

"I'm sorry I haven't called sooner. Time just gets away from me."

"It's okay. You're calling now."

I knew he understood. I told him about Momma's condition and what the doctor had told us. I told him I was keeping her at home, along with my grandmother.

"Jesus, that's a lot. How are you doing?"

My voice was shaky. "I can't say I haven't been better, but I'm doing what I have to do."

"Do you need me to help?"

"I appreciate the offer, but Momma's friends are here."

"Where's Tanya?"

"She's kind of in and out as much as she can stand."

"But Lizzy…"

I knew what he was going to say. "I know. But I have to be grateful she's here at all."

"Lizzy, is there anything I can do for you?"

"Yes, you can tell me to cool my suspicions." I told him about

Tanya's comments regarding the silver and then about Momma's conversation with me.

He listened intently. "Do you think she was warning you about Tanya?"

"That's just it—I don't know. Tanya came back into the room so quickly that I couldn't ask."

"Maybe tomorrow you two will have an opportunity to spend some time alone, and she can tell you more."

"I hope so." Little did I know it was a conversation we'd never have.

Chapter 4

Our lives had become so routine that I'd let myself fall into a false sense of security. The next afternoon, as Momma visited with friends and co-workers, I noticed a new look on her face. When I got closer, I was overcome with panic.

"Momma! Momma, are you okay?" Everyone stepped back. "Rhonda! Patricia! Momma, can you hear me?" She was having a seizure. I grabbed her behind her head and eased her onto her side on the couch. Without thinking, I began barking out orders. "Get this coffee table out of the way. Get me the phone!" Adrenaline was taking over.

Even though almost everyone there was from the hospital, I wouldn't let anyone get close but Rhonda and Patricia. Once they were at her side, I grabbed the phone and dialed Dr. Elliot's direct number. She was still seizing.

"Dr. Elliot, it's Lizzy. She's having a seizure!"

"How long?"

"About two minutes now."

"Is she protected from hurting herself?"

"Yes, sir."

"Is it still happening?"

"Yes. Wait!" I handed the phone to someone. Calmer now, I asked, "Momma, can you hear me?" She nodded. Her body was relaxed. It was over.

After what seemed like forever, she opened her eyes. I was still on edge and wanted to ask her a ton of questions, but I knew she needed time to recover. Finally, I asked, "Are you okay?"

"I think so," she replied.

"Do you know what happened?"

She looked around; tears welled up in her eyes. "Yes."

"Please don't cry. It's okay. You're okay," I said as calmly as I could. I wiped the tears from her cheeks. I knew she must have been really scared to cry in front of everyone.

She whispered back, "Lizzy, I had an accident. I'm so embarrassed." I realized what she was talking about. During the seizure, she'd lost control of her bladder. Because of the tumor it was only a small spot on the upholstery, but to her it might as well have been the size of Texas.

"You don't worry. No one can see." I glanced up at Patricia. "Can you get us a blanket? She's a little cool."

When Patricia was out of earshot, I said, "See, all better. No one will know."

When Patricia returned with the blanket, I made sure Momma was covered well. Rhonda came up behind me and whispered into my ear, "Dr. Elliot needs to speak with you."

I took the phone and instructed Rhonda to stay close and call if she had another seizure. Walking past Patricia, I whispered to her about the "accident" and asked her to kindly start ushering people out. I tried to find a quiet spot to talk with Dr. Elliott, but in the commotion people had moved all over the place. I finally found a private spot in the dining room.

"Dr. Elliot?"

"Lizzy, are you still keeping her at home?" he asked.

"Yes, sir." My voice was shaking.

"I'm going to have some Ativan sent to the house in case she has another seizure. The pharmacist will explain the doses to you. Do you have the hospital bed in place?"

"Not yet, but the equipment company is ready when we are."

"Lizzy, this is not easy. You have about six, maybe seven hours of consciousness left. She needs to be in the bed before that time comes. How's her pain level?"

Wham! Right in the throat! I couldn't breathe. Dr. Elliot hadn't sugarcoated his words. Fumbling for a coherent reply, I stammered, "What…how…but?" The room was closing in.

"Lizzy, I need you to take some deep breaths, okay?" His voice was soft now. "I'm sorry for just blurting that out. I want you to have everything you need and be informed. Okay?"

A tiny voice came from the back of my throat. "Yes, sir."

"Can you handle this? I'll hire whoever you need and come myself if you want." He was back to the Dr. Elliot I knew, kind, caring, and gentle.

"No, I'm okay. Patricia and Rhonda have been here the whole time and will be here for as long as I need them, but thank you for the offer." My words were coming a little easier now. "Can you start over?"

"She may or may not have another seizure. Her BUN and creatinine are rising due to the blockage of the ureters. The kidneys are shutting down, which is what set off the seizure today. Remember when I talked with the family, I told you she'd go into a coma?"

"Yes, sir." This was hard. My own years in the medical field allowed me to understand everything he was saying, but it all sounded different when it concerned my mother. I knew that the lab values he mentioned referred to toxins that would be lethal since her body wasn't allowing them to be discharged.

"You have about six or seven hours before that happens. I'll call the equipment company and have them bring out a bed. She needs to be in it shortly after it arrives. She won't be able to help you. I'll get them to bring everything you need. Lizzy, are you okay?" His emotion came through in his voice. "I'm so sorry."

Deep breath in and out. "I'm fine." *Be strong,* I said to myself. "Thank you for everything. I really need to go and check on her."

"Call me if you need anything. Day or night."

I got up, smoothed my hair, and walked into the living room. Momma was sitting on the couch with Rhonda at her side as though nothing had happened. She'd changed her clothes, so I knew Patricia had helped her clean up. About half the visitors had left.

"How are you?" I asked, bending down to look closely at her face. There was a slight crinkle in the forehead, not a deep one; the pain wasn't that bad. Catching a glimpse of her hands, I saw that the shakes were more pronounced. This was a side effect of the morphine, but this time I think she was scared.

"I'm better now," she said.

"Will you be okay while I make another call?"

"Rhonda isn't leaving my side. You do what you need to."

I kissed her forehead. As I left the room, I wondered if she knew. With all her years as a nurse, would she know what was happening when the bed was delivered? Would not knowing be better? Maybe she'd think she was just going to bed for the night. I didn't know. What I did know was that Aunt Tanya needed to be informed so she could be here for her sister's last few hours. I dialed Tanya's number, breathing deeply and heavily, trying not to cry.

"Hello?"

I began talking fast to stay ahead of the tears I felt coming. "Aunt Tanya, it's Lizzy. Momma had a seizure today. I've spoken with the doctor, and he said she has about six hours before she slips into a coma. He's arranging for some more meds to keep her comfortable in case of another seizure, and the hospital bed will be delivered shortly. Can you come?"

"Lizzy, I was just there, and right now is not the best time," she said, but this time there was something in her voice. Was it remorse I was hearing?

"Aunt Tanya, what's going on?" This sounded more like a demand than a question.

"It's Brad. He's upset at the time I've been spending away from home. I can't upset him further." She did sound remorseful.

"Your husband needs to get a grip on the situation. You've hardly spent any time with Momma. Once she's in this coma, you won't get a 'do-over.' Why is everything a battle with you?" Tears were streaming down my face now, and I was overcome with both anger and fear. I felt so alone.

"I'll talk with him and see what he says. That's the best I can do. You have to understand that I can't destroy my own life over this." The cold tone crept back into her voice.

From the front window I could see a delivery van coming down the road. Anxiety kicked in. I hadn't talked with Momma yet. She couldn't see this.

"The bed is here. I have to go. Please just do what you can," I said hurriedly. I left the house from the closest door I could find, trying not to draw attention to myself.

I ran across the yard and managed to stop the van some distance from the house, away from the front windows. I instructed the driver to come around the back. If we were quiet, we could get the bed in the back door and to her room without anyone knowing. Momma thought I was still on the phone, so I was buying some time. We had to do this without attracting a lot of attention.

Sternly, I explained to the technician that we had to be extremely quiet. He just listened and nodded. He knew Momma from her years at the hospital, and I believe it was out of respect that he went along with my outlandish request.

Together we rearranged the room and set up the new bed. Momma would no longer sleep in her own bed but in one she knew all too well from the hospital. Now her bed would be used by the shifts of people who would sleep in the room with her, keeping watch during the night. In an effort to ease this sight, I took the comforter and pillows off her bed, but there was no denying that we were heading into the next phase.

After signing all the paperwork, I was caught off guard when the otherwise silent technician began to speak. "Your mother is an angel from God," he said. "Try not to be sad. Her work here is done, and it's time for her to go home. My hat is off to you for doing this for her. You have the support of everyone in this community. Just pick up the phone or send a message. We'll be here. I'm so sorry." As a tear slid down his cheek, he turned and walked away.

His words hit me hard. Once the truck pulled away, I fell to my knees and cried. My mother was dying; and my grandmother was teetering obliviously through the house, talking to people she didn't know about things that happened decades ago. I had the support of complete strangers, but what I needed was the love of family. Aunt Tanya and my cousin, Adam, couldn't be bothered. I had to get it together. I had to find strength.

I couldn't say whether I was talking out loud or to myself. "Pick yourself up off this floor! Without you, this will never be possible. Get it together! You are so much stronger than this." Then I recognized it— the voice was my mother's, loud and clear. I knew she was still in the living room; it wasn't possible for her to actually be saying this to me. Her voice rose up from years gone by, from all the support she'd given me and the hours she'd spent teaching me to be a strong woman.

As I steadied myself on the rails on the hospital bed, the tears finally stopped. I made my way into the bathroom to splash some water on my face. My eyes were red and swollen, but I hoped Momma wouldn't notice. I didn't recognize myself in the mirror. My face was drawn, and I looked exhausted. "No time for this now," I said to the image in the mirror. The cold water hitting my face felt good.

The remaining visitors were making their way out the door when I returned to the living room. My mom had even walked them to the door.

"Well, look at you!" I said enthusiastically.

With a sweet smile, she reached out and hugged me tightly. For a long moment we embraced. It felt so good to have her arms around me. I never wanted the moment to end. I knew now that I could go on with what I had to do.

When I looked into her face, I could tell she'd been crying, but I wasn't going to let that spoil the moment. "What's for dinner?" she asked. "I believe I could eat something."

"Whatever you want! These little church ladies have been keeping us in food. What would you like?" I said, as though I were going to fix a meal for a queen. I knew she wouldn't eat much, but the fact that she wanted even a little made me happy.

Rhonda and Patricia made us both sit down at the table. They wouldn't let me do a thing. I could tell by the looks passing between them that Rhonda had talked with Dr. Elliot before giving me the phone, and I assumed she'd shared his comments with Patricia.

Grandmother joined us, and, remarkably, she ate without having to be coaxed. Everything felt very normal, even though it was no such thing. I knew I had to tell Momma about the hospital bed, but before I could bring it up she said, "Is everything ready?"

Reluctantly I said, "Yes." My already weak appetite disappeared. She knew. I thought we'd been so quiet, but I should have known she'd find out. When I was a teenager and young adult, I couldn't hide anything from her. She knew everything I did, probably before I even did it.

When we finished pushing our food around our plates, my mom asked to sit on the porch for a little while. If what Dr. Elliot had said was true—and up until that time he had been correct in everything he'd said—we had a few hours left. I believed this was her way of holding on as long as possible. We sat on the porch in the rocking chairs, listening to the insects singing.

Eventually she said, "I'm ready."

Grandmother was sitting on the couch, nodding in and out of sleep in front of the TV. With a very gentle voice, Momma said, "Mother, why don't you let me put you to bed?" Without resistance Grandmother got up, and the two of them headed down the hall hand in hand. As I watched them go into my grandmother's room, my heart broke. Momma was fighting through the pain and the morphine to share a final moment with her own mother. Rhonda and Patricia put their hands on my shoulders. It was almost too much to bear.

A little while later, Momma came out and told us Grandmother was asleep. "My turn," she said, standing in the doorway of her own room, looking at the hospital bed. "Will you give me a minute with Rhonda and Patricia?"

"Of course," I replied, holding back tears. I wanted to run to her and plead with God not to do this. *Please don't take her from me!* I wanted to shout. But it wasn't meant to be.

About thirty minutes later, they returned to the living room. "She wants you to sit with her for a while," Rhonda said. They had both been crying.

I immediately went to my mother's side. There was a chair by her bed, and I took a seat. Holding her hand out to me, she said, "Lizzy, I want you to know how much I love you, and I know how hard this has been for you. If you get scared, or if it all gets to be too much, please know it's okay if you have to stop."

"It won't, but if it does, I'll step back, take a breath, and continue. You've given so much of yourself to help me be who I am today, and I love you for that." It was getting harder and harder to hold back the tears.

"I'm sorry your dad missed out on knowing such an incredible person." She seemed to be reminiscing about things she had no control over. My dad had chosen to be an absentee father since their divorce, and that was not her fault.

"I don't think I could have had a more wonderful life," I assured her. "I had everything I could have wanted and was truly loved." I didn't want to think about my dad right then. He would be there after she was gone—if the relationship could be mended.

"Lizzy, I'm so tired," she said in a slurred voice.

I could see her eyelids getting heavy. "Just rest. It's been a big day," I said, even though I didn't want her to go.

"I love you, little one."

"I love you too, Momma."

With that, her eyes closed, and her grip on my hand relaxed. For a long time I just sat there watching her chest rise and fall, periodically squeezing her hand to see if she would squeeze back; but there was no response, just the rise and fall of her chest. She had fallen into a coma six hours and thirty-five minutes after the seizure.

Chapter 5

Once Momma was deep in the slumber of the coma, her stream of visitors tapered off. The church ladies still brought food, asked for updates on her condition, and updated everyone else. Under normal circumstances, this nosiness might have bothered me, but it cut down on the number of phone calls and the people coming in and out of the house. Now that Momma was in a coma, our healthcare duties had intensified—now she could do nothing for herself. Turning her, bathing her, changing the bed linens with her still on them—it was all difficult. The harshest task, however, was cleaning her up after the release of her bowels.

Grandmother couldn't understand why Momma was in bed all the time, but she sat with me while I read to her. One day, looking very serious, she said, "Lizzy, I think Pam is sick. Do you think we need to call the doctor?"

I wanted to be honest with her, but I couldn't. I couldn't put her through that pain, even if she wouldn't remember what I told her for very long. So instead I replied, "No, Grandmother, I think she's just really tired." Luckily for me, this answer satisfied her.

During the day, Rhonda, Patricia, and I played music, talked about things the three friends had done together in the past, and tried to stay positive. I've always heard that hearing is the last thing to go, and if Momma could hear us, then I wanted her to know we were all prepared for her fate. She'd spent so much time worrying about me and everyone she was close to—I didn't want her to have any doubts.

When Mrs. Shelley came in to drop off some food and check in, she asked to speak with Patricia before she left. "Is Lizzy okay?"

"She's doing well, all things considered."

"Do you think it's fitting for her to be playing music and carrying on the way she is?"

Patricia was confused. "Carrying on?"

"You know what I mean. Pam's room should be quiet and peaceful. Lizzy talks to her just like she would to you or me."

"Mrs. Shelley, please don't take this the wrong way, but Lizzy is doing what she feels is best. You make it sound like Lizzy is losing her mind."

"I didn't say that!"

"I know you didn't. But really, I don't want to think Lizzy is doing anything but the best she can."

Mrs. Shelley's voice betrayed her irritation. "I'm sorry. I was only trying to help."

She must have walked away because I could hear Patricia calling after her, "Mrs. Shelley, please don't..."

When Patricia came back into the room and sat next to me on the bed, I leaned into her and said sarcastically, "Too bad party lines no longer exist. It would be a whole lot easier to spread this piece of gossip. You know she's going to say you gave her a tongue-lashing when all she was trying to do was help."

Patricia replied, "You heard all that, huh?"

"Every word. Do you know what size straitjacket I wear?"

We both laughed loudly—it was just what we needed. Thank God for that comical break; the next few days were about to get rough.

Though Aunt Tanya failed to show up the night Momma went into the coma or the next day, for some reason she started to come around more often. Her husband, Brad, and my cousin, Adam, often came with her. They spent very little time in the room with Momma, but at least they were in the house. Part of me thought this was a blessing, but something just didn't seem right.

Aunt Tanya had been married to Brad when his own mother passed away. I'd always found it odd that he didn't go to her when Aunt Tanya told us she was sick. I'd only seen pictures of her, but it was easy to see that Brad was her spitting image, with thick red hair, small beady eyes, and a long, thin nose. If I hadn't known she was his mother, I may have believed she was his sister instead. Both carried their ages well and had very few wrinkles. Brad had also inherited his mother's height, which put him eye to eye with me. More than once I'd seen him tilt his head back in an attempt to look down his nose at people, but his eyes always had to look up. He made me uneasy.

"It's like he's up to no good," I once told Momma. She agreed.

Adam was Tanya's son from her first marriage, and he looked nothing like any of us. He was tall, with sand-colored hair and translucent blue eyes. He probably could have been a model, but Aunt Tanya had raised him to be her clone. He skirted around responsibility; most of the time, he felt someone owed him something. Adam was book smart like Aunt Tanya, but neither of them had attended college.

When Aunt Tanya married Brad, there was talk in the town that she was only after a promotion at the mill—he was her boss. Years later, I found out that Aunt Tanya had actually been the cause of Brad's divorce from his first wife. This made sense; Aunt Tanya's appearance switched from frumpy housewife to corporate vixen after Brad became her supervisor.

Patricia and Rhonda took turns staying in Momma's room with me while Aunt Tanya and her family was there. Someone always kept an eye on Aunt Tanya; neither Rhonda nor Patricia trusted her. Now that the whole family was involved, they shared my unstated concerns. It was undeniably strange that they were here so often now when they hadn't been before.

By now, only Momma's closest friends visited every day. We made a schedule to guarantee that someone was with her twenty-four hours a day. Dr. Elliot checked in often to assess the progress of the coma. He told us that she'd last no more than seven or eight days before her blood levels got so high that her body would shut down. She was still on the morphine drip, and I watched her face to determine whether she was in pain. I was grateful that I'd spent so much time watching her; now it was the only way I had of assessing her pain level.

During the third day of the coma, I called several of Momma's friends and invited them over for dinner. My mother loved entertaining, and I needed some familiarity for an hour or so. I wanted to make sure everyone had an opportunity to sit with her if they wanted to, and I wanted her to be part of our little gathering. Everyone who came had been a part of regular card tournaments at our home, and when dinner was over, the guests asked me if they could hang around for a while and play some cards. I was tickled and welcomed it. When Aunt Tanya showed up with Brad and Adam, I welcomed them in. We rotated out in pairs to sit with Momma, and Grandmother sat at the table with the card players. Everyone was having a good time—just what the doctor ordered.

Everything was relaxed, and my stress level was low. For the first time in ten days, I wasn't focused on death and dying; instead, I was letting Momma know that she was important to everyone there and that they loved the things for which she used to bring them all together.

Because it had been quite a few days since I'd been so relaxed, I sent Rhonda out to play cards so I could sit with Momma. If things hadn't been so lively, I could have laid down beside her and slept through the night. Eventually, Patricia joined me at her bedside, and we talked about how wonderful the evening had been.

I told her, "Only Momma's sitting up and joining us could have made it more perfect." But I spoke too soon.

As the saying goes, all good things must come to an end, and when this gathering came to an end, there was nothing good about it.

Chapter 6

Rhonda appeared in Momma's doorway, staring at me in horror. Heaviness fell over me. I didn't have to ask, but I did anyway: "Rhonda, is everything okay?"

In keeping with our pact to stay positive in the bedroom, she only shook her head. Patricia said, "I'll go."

Rhonda told her, "You can't. Only Lizzy can handle this one."

When I walked out of the bedroom, Rhonda grabbed my elbow. I heard a voice coming from the dining room, where everyone was gathered—Aunt Tanya. Fear crystallized in my stomach. What was she doing now? I couldn't make out what she was saying, but Rhonda was guiding me forward and closing every door we passed through. We went into the guest bedroom. Finally, Rhonda said, "Lizzy, Tanya has lost her mind. I don't want to upset you, but you really need to be prepared."

I could tell by her tone that what I was about to face was truly bad. We walked out of the guest bedroom and continued down the hall until I was standing in the dining room doorway. Now I could hear Tanya's voice clearly. "Isn't it just beautiful! I hope she remembered to put in her will that she said I could have this. Oh, it doesn't matter. I hope

Lizzy remembers her telling me one time that she wanted me to have this if she died first."

My stomach twisted with anger. Her earlier mention of the silver had portended this. Looking into the room, I could see the appalled faces of my mother's friends. Most of them knew Tanya from high school or through Momma, but they were clearly shocked by what they were seeing. Tanya had always been selfish and ruthless, but this was over the top!

She was standing in front of the china cabinet. Most of the doors and drawers were open, and she'd removed several items and placed them on the table where people were playing cards. In the center of the table was the beautiful box of silver, opened to expose the serving pieces inside. Brad and Adam were standing at her side, holding other things in their hands. I couldn't focus on anything but their faces. How utterly pleased with themselves they looked!

Everyone saw me but Aunt Tanya, Brad, and Adam; they were too involved to notice me or to see that everyone was quietly escaping the room. Someone helped my grandmother to her room behind the closed doors. I waited until she was out of earshot before I began. When I spoke, my voice didn't sound like my own. It was a deep, guttural growl, like a dog warning an intruder to back off.

"What the hell are you doing?"

They all turned to look at me. Brad's sly grin made him look like the Grinch that stole Christmas. Adam, always a handsome man, now looked ugly with greed.

Before anyone could speak, I fired off another question. "Are you all insane?"

"I was only collecting the things Pam wanted me to have." Tanya sounded so innocent as she arched her back and straightened her shoulders.

"Lizzy, there's no reason for this. You don't need to speak to your aunt that way," Brad piped up. His grin was gone, and his face reddened with what appeared to be anger.

"Brad, you are so right. There's absolutely no reason for any of us to behave this way. Who do you think you are, coming in here and disrespecting my mother's home and life like this?" I refused to be intimidated. I'd seen him do this before with Tanya. If his face reddened, she backed down. He needed to know that I wasn't my Aunt Tanya.

"We aren't disrespecting anything or anyone. If nothing else, you are disrespecting us right now!" he said.

Ignoring Brad, I moved closer to Tanya. "I want you to put everything back just like you found it. Do you hear me?"

"I will not. Pam wanted me to have these things."

"When? When did Momma want you to have these things, Tanya?"

Picking up a trinket from the table, she said, "You were there the day she said she wanted me to have this."

Through gritted teeth, I asked again, "When did she want you to have these things?"

"She said if she died before me, then—"

I cut her off. "That's just it!" I snatched the trinket from her hand. "When she died! She's still alive, but you wouldn't know that, would you, because you've been so uninvolved throughout this whole process."

"I know she's still alive," she said dismissively, "but I'm not leaving this house tonight without—" and she went for the box of silver.

With a strength I didn't know I had, I grabbed her wrist and then looked straight into her eyes. "But see, you *are* leaving this house, and without this box, its contents, or anything else for that matter. Grandmother gave this to Momma years ago, and when the sad day comes, it will go back to Grandmother." As I pulled her closer to me, I said, "Tanya, I can't believe your nerve. Has being with this gold-digging asshole changed you so much that you can't let up even for a minute? Are you not ashamed of yourself?"

She shared my anger, so when she spoke to me her voice was low. "Whether you give it to me now or later, I will have it." She shifted her gaze to Adam, who seemed to beam at some revelation.

I tightened my grip on her wrist as she tried to pull away, but now we were on the move. I was pulling her toward the front door. "I want you out of this house! If my mother's life is no more important to you than this, then you are not welcome. If you care, I will call you when this is all over, but only because you're her family. Until that day, don't set foot in my mother's house again!"

As I shoved her out the door, I turned to Brad and Adam. "Please don't make me remove you, too." Two men from the card-playing group were moving in their direction, ready to escort them out. I don't know what or who had kept them from interceding when I grabbed Tanya, but I was grateful. I'm not sure I could have taken them on, too.

Once the three of them were on the front lawn, Tanya turned back to me. "I'll be back tomorrow for that silver, and I suggest you resolve your issues with it." As if to save face, she added, "She's been my sister longer than you've been her daughter, and you can't keep me from her."

As I closed the front door, Rhonda was already trying to erase the ugliness that had just transpired by returning everything to its rightful place.

Chapter 7

I was restless all night, trying to make sense of everything. How could she be so damn cold and uncaring? All I needed was for her to be supportive, to act like she regretted that Momma was dying, but she could focus only on material things, particularly the silver.

One thing was certain: she wasn't going to give up. She'd be back, and I had to be prepared. I couldn't let this take me away from Momma, though. Nothing was worth that. I considered just giving the silver to her. After all, what was Grandmother really going to do with it now? I quickly discarded the idea. My mother hadn't raised me to be a coward or to give in to avoid conflict. This was about principles and priorities.

I hardly slept. By seven, I knew what I had to do. When Patricia and Rhonda came into the kitchen, I was already dressed and on my third cup of coffee. They spotted the cardboard box on the counter at the same time. Rhonda spoke first. "Lizzy, no! Tell me you're not going to give that bitch what she wants!"

Patricia added, "You know as well as everyone who was here last night that none of this is about your mother. She's trying to make this about her! Your grandmother gave that silver to your mother, and your grandfather would have wanted you to have it."

"Ladies, please," I said. "Am I not my mother's daughter? Give me a little credit. I have a plan. Rhonda, do you remember what you put back in the cabinet last night?"

"I think I can remember everything once I see it," she replied.

"Will you please get it for me and put it in this box?" I handed her the box I'd gotten from the garage. "I've put some paper in there. Will you wrap what you pack?"

"What are you going to do?" Patricia asked.

"The less you two know, the better."

I made some fresh coffee. In an attempt to avoid the elephant in the room, we sat quietly. Every now and then I noticed Rhonda and Patricia stealing a glance at the box on the counter, now packed and ready to go.

I hadn't left the house for days, but today I had no choice. Around eight thirty, I went into Momma's room and whispered into her ear, "I have to go out for a while, but if you can't be here when I get back, I'll understand. I love you, Momma, and I think you're the best. You were right. I've been so naïve. This is a hard lesson to learn. I'll see you soon." I kissed her cheek.

Carefully I loaded the cardboard box into the trunk, while Patricia gently placed the box of silver on the passenger seat. "We sure wish you'd tell us what you're doing. You know we'd never give you up to her."

"I know you wouldn't, Patricia. But if there are repercussions to my actions, I'll take the wrath alone. I'll be back as soon as I can. Please take good care of Momma while I'm gone. Grandmother ate early, and she should be fine until I get back."

After I pulled away from the house, I stopped at the end of the driveway for a few minutes with the engine running. I was afraid to leave Momma, even though I knew she was with the two best friends a person could have. I could see no other way. I'd be damned if Aunt Tanya was going to take anything from my mother while she was still alive. The sooner I left, the sooner I'd be back.

When I returned, everything was still calm. Patricia was watching

TV with Grandmother. Rhonda was looking through a photo album she'd found and talking to Momma about the pictures. The rest of the day was routine. No one asked any questions about my errand that morning. I felt guilty for leaving, though, even if it had been only for an hour. I brought Grandmother back to Momma's room with me, and we stayed there for most of the day.

Later in the afternoon, several of Momma's friends stopped by, and a couple of them had overnight bags. They'd stay the night so Patricia, Rhonda, and I could try to rest. Even with the extra help, it was still hard for us to sleep soundly, but it was nice to have the extra hands.

It was almost dark when two sets of headlights pulled up to the house. We weren't expecting anyone, and it was late for visitors. I was in the laundry room when Rhonda announced the cars' arrival; she told Patricia to take Grandmother to her room. I started the washing machine and headed to the front door, arriving just as Rhonda said, "You've gone way too far this time!"

Standing at the door was a sheriff's deputy named Michael, Tanya, and Adam. Anger bubbled up again. "What can I do for you?" I asked the deputy. Michael was so tall that I had to look up to him to ask that question. I knew Michael well. Years ago, he and Momma had dated, and his daughter and I graduated from high school in the same year.

"Lizzy, I'm sorry." His voice was kind, and his big blue eyes were full of concern. "Tanya says you have something of hers, and you're keeping her from it."

I didn't acknowledge Tanya or Adam as I looked at Michael. I could see why my mother had been attracted to him. "Michael, what exactly does she think I'm keeping her from?"

"She's made a list of items," he said, passing me a paper.

Rhonda started reading over my shoulder, but Tanya barked, "This doesn't involve you, Rhonda."

Rhonda shot her a look that would have killed had her eyes been full of bullets. I eased her down by calmly saying, "No, I don't believe I have anything on this list." How good was Michael's memory? Surely he'd seen some of these things in our home.

Adam lost his cool. Without thinking, he spat, "We know that stuff is in there, we just had it—"

Tanya grabbed his arm, stopping him from revealing the ugly truth about the previous night. "We know Pam has some of these things," she began calmly, "because we've discussed them over the years. As for the silver, Pam was the last one to borrow it from Mother. As the oldest daughter, it belongs to me."

"Have you checked Grandmother's house for the items on your list?" I asked, returning the paper to Tanya. Adam snatched it from my hand.

"Lizzy, Tanya's reason for calling us was mainly the silver. Do you know anything about it?" Michael was uncomfortable; he knew Momma sometimes did borrow the silver for dinner parties.

"No, I sure don't. Rhonda, have you seen the silver? It's in a beautiful mahogany box lined with velvet. I think you'd know if you'd seen it, right?" I was very composed, as I looked her in the eyes, even though I was trembling inside.

"Michael, the only time I've ever seen that silver is at Pam's last dinner party, I believe last Christmas," Rhonda said. "It's magnificent! It was an anniversary gift from Lizzy's grandfather to her grandmother. I believe Grace was going to give it to Pam. Isn't that just sweet?" Rhonda concluded sarcastically as she turned to face Tanya and Adam.

"So you have seen it!" Tanya exploded. "I want you to go in there right now and get it!" she screamed at Rhonda.

Rhonda continued calmly, "First of all, I said I'd seen it at that party, but that was a year ago. Second, you said this didn't involve me! So don't bark orders at me. Lizzy, do you want me to look for it?"

I shook my head. "I'll do it. Do you want to come with me, Michael? I want you all to know that it's not here. But if for some reason we find it"—now I was speaking directly to Tanya—"you just heard that Grandmother planned on giving it to Momma, so I don't see where you have any right to it."

"She does have a point," Michael said to Tanya and Adam, trying to be diplomatic.

"I still want to look," Tanya said, taking a step forward.

"Maybe I didn't make myself clear last night," I said, blocking the door and holding my hands up to stop her. "You are not welcome in this house, for this reason. And in case I need to make myself any clearer, that includes you, too, Adam. Bring that list, Michael."

We began the search. Tanya and Adam watched through the front windows while Rhonda waited by the front door. Once we were out of everyone's earshot, Michael said, "Lizzy, none of us wanted to come here, but Sheriff Brown said somebody had to. I'm sorry. I thought it might be better if I was the one who came."

"I don't blame you. You're only doing your job, but please know it's not here." As he stopped to look at me, an unspoken truth was spoken. I prepared for the worst, even though I hadn't actually admitted to removing anything from the house.

"We'll just look around for appearance's sake, okay?" He was being so sweet.

After several minutes, Michael returned to Tanya and Adam and said, "There's nothing on this list here."

"She's hidden it! I bet it's in Pam's room. Go look in there!" Tanya demanded.

"I am not going into Pam's room! Don't you have any respect at all?" he replied, losing his composure.

"Tanya, the stuff on your list is just not here," I said.

"What have you done with it, Lizzy? I want you to tell me right now!"

"I've been way too busy to do anything but take care of the people in this house. When would I have had time?" I spoke softly and innocently.

"Then one of the people who were here last night took it," she said.

"You've known most of those people your whole life. Who exactly are you accusing?" Damn! If she gave me a name, I'd have to call them. I hadn't considered that. I knew Tanya would stop at nothing to get what she wanted.

"I want to file a theft report," Tanya said to Michael.

"Tanya, the only person who can do that is the owner of the house, and at the moment she's busy being in a coma." Michael was clearly tired of Tanya. "The next person would be Lizzy." Turning to me, he asked, "Do you want to file a report?"

"As far as I know, nothing has been stolen, so no."

Tanya was angrier than I'd ever seen her; I could have sworn I heard her growl. It was all I could do not to laugh!

"Little girl, I will have these things," Tanya said. "You mark my words." She looked at Adam the same way she had the night before. Why did it mean? What did they know that I didn't?

"Tanya, I really don't care what you do, but right now I want you to leave. I have work to do."

Adam stepped in. "Lizzy—"

"I told you people I have stuff to do, so both of you need to shut up and get out of here! If you don't, I'll make sure Michael's trip is worthwhile. Can you do a restraining order here?" I knew he couldn't, but I hoped my comment would be enough to get them to leave.

With that, Tanya and Adam stormed to their cars, groaning and grumbling. Michael apologized to me again. After assuring him I held nothing against him, I asked if he wanted to see Momma. His eyes teared up, and he said he just couldn't. I didn't push. Before he left, he hugged me and gave me his cell number in case Tanya came back.

Even though there were extra hands in the house and Momma was comfortable, I couldn't settle my uneasiness. I couldn't stop wondering what Tanya and Adam knew that I didn't. How could she be so sure that she'd get everything she wanted?

I retrieved Momma's important documents from the closet where she kept them. Then I sat at the dining room table, sorting them all out. There were funeral arrangements, life insurance policies, and a list of people she'd known over the years who she wanted me to contact after she passed away. From a long envelope I withdrew her will. Another good friend of hers, Bill Simmons, had drawn it up at his law firm. Everything was nice and neat. There was no mention of Tanya or

Adam. As Momma's only child, I received the bulk of everything, but there were specific people to whom she'd assigned specific things. It was nothing major, just tokens of her love for them or things that held sentimental value for the people they were designated for. It was mostly stuff I would have given to them anyway. But when I got to the last page, I saw it.

Chapter 8

In familiar handwriting, a note read, "Amendment, see insert." The handwriting was Adam's, but the date and initials were Momma's. The amendment had been made the night before we sat down with Dr. Elliot as a family. Had Tanya been thinking about the silver and everything else even before she knew Momma wasn't going to go through treatment? I flipped the pages again and again, trying to find an insert. Then I picked up a big orange envelope, and it fell out—a yellow legal-sized paper, folded in half.

"In executing this will, I assign Adam Pitzer as chief administrator to oversee that it is carried out as he sees fit." All handwritten by Adam, then signed and dated by Momma with two copies, but only one was in this envelope. What was I looking at? What did "administrator to oversee that it is carried out as he sees fit" mean? I must have looked over the paper for hours, trying to make sense of it all. Then I felt a hand on my shoulder and heard my grandmother's voice. "Lizzy? Baby? Have you been here all night?"

My head shot up. Trying to get my bearings, I looked out the window and saw that it was still dark outside. Grandmother was night-walking again. I felt immediate relief to know she hadn't gotten out of the house.

"Grandmother, what are you doing up?" I asked, rubbing my neck.

"Well, it's time to get up. I needed some coffee. Would you like some?" she asked sweetly.

She had a cup in her hand, containing something resembling coffee. I couldn't recall the last time my grandmother had made coffee; with her mind the way it was, she wasn't allowed to do anything in the kitchen but make sandwiches. Even so, we were apt to find the mayo in the oven. I eased into the kitchen, wondering what I'd find. To my amazement, I found only the electric coffee pot on, with coffee in the carafe and a cup on the counter. Before filling the cup, I opened the coffee maker to make sure Grandmother had put in a coffee filter and grounds. She had. *What the hell?* I thought. If she'd made it strong enough to move mountains, I didn't care. I needed to be awake for what was happening. As I poured the coffee, I saw the clock on the stove—it was 4:30 AM. This was the time my grandmother had gotten up every morning when she worked in order to have some "her" time before going to her job.

After tasting the coffee, I told my grandmother how good it was. It really was.

A sweet word of thanks came out of her mouth, but then she asked, "Baby, why are you sleeping at the table? You know it's not good for you. Right now you need to be rested to do what you're doing."

Did she know what was happening? "Grandmother, what is it that I'm doing?"

"The way you've been caring for Pam has got to be taking it out of you. We can't afford for you to get sick because then she'd be sent to the hospital for sure," she said. I hadn't heard her calm, steady voice for a very long time.

"What am I doing?" I asked again. I was amazed at the lucid conversation my grandmother was carrying on.

"Taking care of Pam and caring for me. It's got to be hard for you, Lizzy. Don't think I haven't noticed." I was shocked, but I wasn't getting my hopes up. Grandmother sounded almost normal, and I knew she hadn't been "normal" for quite some time.

"Grandmother, do you know what's wrong with Momma?"

"She has cancer, and it's not going to end well." A tear slid down her cheek. She really did know what was going on. All of this was getting to be too much. "Now, baby, I want you to tell me what's there on the table."

"Grandmother, yes, Momma is really sick, but other things are taking a toll—things I can't stop."

"You tell me what's wrong, and I'll try to help you. You know I've always been here for you."

"Do you know what's happened with Tanya?" I asked.

"Is she here?"

So she knew about Momma but not about Tanya. I wondered if she even remembered what we were talking about. I couldn't dump this on her, especially if this clarity was fleeting. I just wanted to enjoy her being here like her old self.

"No, Grandmother, she's not here, but it's not important."

Irritated, she said, "It is very important!"

"Honey, don't get upset."

She continued, "It's just like when Buddy died." I knew she was talking about my grandfather. "She didn't help when he was sick or even when he died."

"I know she didn't, but that was a long time ago." I was shocked to hear her talk like this. She'd always defended Aunt Tanya and her actions.

"Not long enough for me to forget how she came to me after the funeral and tried to make me give her the silver."

"You're telling me she asked you for the silver?"

"Oh, yes. But I told her Buddy would have wanted Pam to have it, or even you."

"Why would she ask you for it then?" Grandmother seemed lost in thought. "Grandmother?"

She replied softly, "It's my fault."

"What is?"

"Pam and Tanya may be sisters, but it's my fault for not seeing how Buddy's favoritism toward Pam affected Tanya. Does that make me a bad mother?"

It had never been a secret that my mother was Grandfather's favorite. When I was born, I was his favorite over Adam. I said, "No, Grandmother, I don't think it makes you a bad mother."

"I really should have gotten her some help when she cut up Pam's clothes."

My mouth fell open.

She didn't seem to be talking to me anymore; she gazed vacantly into the room. "I believe she'll grow out of it. I think it's just sibling rivalry." She was now talking as though the past were the present. The Alzheimer's had taken her back.

"Grandmother?"

A tear slid down her cheek. "I know Buddy loves her. He just has more in common with Pam. Where have we gone so wrong?"

This had to stop! Even though I wanted to know more, seeing her so stressed broke my heart. I lightly touched her arm. "Grandmother, it's me, Lizzy."

She sat very still for a beat, staring out the window. Then, in a lighthearted voice, she said, "Let's just have some breakfast and talk for a while, okay?"

I didn't know where we were in her mind. I asked, "Why don't you let me cook for you?"

"Lizzy, that would be really nice, but I don't want you overdoing it."

"I won't. You know I learned from the best, and I know all the shortcuts." We both laughed. She'd never formally taught me how to cook, but I'd learned by watching and asking questions. "Let's get you another cup of coffee."

As I cooked, Grandmother sat quietly at the table, picking at her bathrobe. By the time I brought breakfast to the table, the door into the

Grandmother I knew and loved had been slammed shut. "What's this?" she asked absently. "I'll get something when I get home, but thanks."

I knew we were back in the present. I sighed so hard that I almost dropped the plate I held. I persuaded her to eat a little here and told her she could make a better breakfast when she got home. She began picking at the food on the plate.

A few minutes later, Rhonda came in, and I told her about our conversation, hoping she'd share more insight. But she asked, "Lizzy, why were you sleeping at the table? This is getting too stressful for you. It's been two nights now that you haven't truly rested."

If she was trying to change the subject, she succeeded. I said, "I completely forgot. Go look at that paperwork on the table."

When she returned moments later, her face was filled with concern. "We need to get in touch with Bill first thing this morning," she said brusquely. "He wrote the original will, and we need to find out if he knows about this. I'm not good with all this legal jargon, but if this came from that bunch of vultures, it can't be good. Don't worry, Lizzy. We'll get this all figured out. Let me take over for you here, and you go relax for a little while." She started coaxing Grandmother to eat some more. I was too tired to argue about it. Rhonda was on my side, and she'd help me.

I went straight to Momma's room so the others could go home. She was still holding her own. I sat down and took her warm hand in mine. *Was Grandmother's revelation this morning what you were trying to warn me about?* I thought. *Have you tried to give her one more chance? Now that I have more information into your relationship with Tanya, so many questions are answered.* "Don't you worry," I said out loud to her. "I'll get this worked out. Everything will work out the way it's supposed to." I lifted her hand and kissed it. I thought I felt a small squeeze, so I squeezed back and waited. I tried to will her to do it again, but it didn't happen.

Chapter 9

Rhonda was able to catch Bill Simmons on his way to work. Once she told him about the will, he sent word to me to sit tight—he was on his way. This calmed my nerves; he'd understand the amendment and how it affected the original will.

Mr. Simmons, an older southern gentleman, inspired immediate trust. His round belly and stocky frame gave way to a face that was always warm and attentive. Though he looked nothing like my grandfather, their mannerisms were so similar that if I closed my eyes and deepened Mr. Simmons's voice in my mind, I could believe I was listening to my grandfather. Mr. Simmons spoke authoritatively but kindly. He knew what to say and when to say it. His choice of career always struck me as ironic; a legal career is among the most cutthroat. I could more easily see him playing Santa in a local department store, surrounded by children waiting to tell him their Christmas wish list. Whatever it was about him, I trusted him—and so did Momma—when it came time to put her worldly affairs in order.

When Mr. Simmons arrived, Patricia and Grandmother came to Momma's room. Patricia told me they'd read to Momma and that I should join Rhonda and Bill in the dining room.

Mr. Simmons stood when I entered the room, and then he took my hand. "Lizzy, various people have kept me up to date on the situation here, and I promise we'll get this figured out. First, though, I need to hear from you what you've been going through. How are you holding up?"

"This is all making me a little crazy," I admitted softly. "It's hard enough caring for Momma and Grandmother, but Tanya is making it even harder." I knew I was an emotional train wreck.

"Let's see if we can ease your mind some. Show me what you've found, and tell me firsthand what's happened." He pulled out a chair and motioned for me to take a seat.

Rhonda made coffee while I relayed the incidents with Tanya up to that point, including putting her out and Michael's visit. Mr. Simmons listened diligently and took notes. When I completed my explanation, he asked, "Do you have a dollar?"

"I don't know. I think I have some change. Why?" I hadn't thought about money since arriving home to be with Momma, so I didn't know what I had.

"Anything you can give me is fine," he said. "I'm going to consider it a retainer so you and I can talk freely. I need to ask you some questions, and we wouldn't want it to backfire if Tanya got word."

I understood and was able to find some loose change for him. I was so eager to get started that I forgot about Rhonda. Only when she took my hand for reassurance did I remember she was there.

"Wait, what about Rhonda? Will she be held accountable for anything we say?" I could guess what he was going to ask me, and I didn't want to put Rhonda or Patricia in the middle of the battle between Tanya and me. It was one thing for them to help with Momma, but it was different to ask them to get involved with legal issues.

"Rhonda, she's right," Mr. Simmons said. "You might want to wait in the other room until I've had a chance to talk with Lizzy." Rhonda nodded.

After she left the room, Mr. Simmons said, "Lizzy, I need to be brutally honest with you, but I also need you to be honest with me. Will you do that?"

I looked at him. "Yes. If you can help me, then I can take whatever you have to say, and I'll tell you what you want to know."

Mr. Simmons leaned forward. "First, this 'amendment' in the will gives Adam control over everything in this house. If he feels Tanya deserves the TV, he can give it to her. There are a couple of things we can do that may or may not help."

"Just like that? He can come in and give everything away?" I was horrified, and I closed my eyes to steady myself. I could feel anger brewing, and I didn't want to lash out at Mr. Simmons.

"I hate to say it, but yes," Mr. Simmons said. "Right now, this will cannot be executed because Pam is still with us. We don't know when that will change, so we have limited time. At the appropriate time, we can contest this amendment due to duress. Was Pam on morphine when this was done?"

"No, we started the drip the next day. Does that matter?"

"If she'd been on morphine, we could have done away with the amendment by claiming she didn't know what she was signing. Since she wasn't, that won't work. The other thing you can do is have me oversee Adam. He'd then have to let me know before making any move against the estate, and we could contest. How serious do you think he is about being the administrator?"

"Will this be time-consuming?" I asked.

"Yes, very, especially with us fighting anything he does," he said.

"Then he may not be that serious. As you know, he lives and works four hours from here. Being just like his mother, he may not want to put time into anything that isn't just handed to him." I felt a flicker of hope.

"I'll have to get in touch with him. Do you know how?"

"He hasn't been here enough for me to find out where he's staying, but I'm sure Tanya knows. I'm not sure she'll be willing to give me that information, though, considering all that's happened between us."

"Give me her number, and I'll give it a shot. You don't need to talk with her right now. If you do, I need to know, okay?"

"I promise!" At this point, I didn't care if he needed to move in to oversee every conversation that took place. I was too thankful for the help.

"Lizzy, when you left the other day with the items in question and the silver, where did you go?" He sounded so official.

"To the bank. I rented a safe deposit box and put everything inside. I planned on getting it all out and giving the silver back to Grandmother once this was all over."

"Speaking of, what's going to happen with her when everything is said and done?" Neither of us would say anything about death. We both danced gracefully around the topic.

"I know that Momma has legal guardianship of Grandmother. She's had it for almost six months now. Grandmother can't live by herself anymore."

"Why hasn't Tanya taken your grandmother, especially now?" His face showed genuine concern.

"Because Tanya is Tanya. The sun rises and sets because she takes a breath. She'd have to lower herself too much to take care of the woman who gave birth to her and gave her all to her children." I couldn't control the sarcasm. "We couldn't have that, now, could we?"

He nodded, understanding what I said about Tanya. "Will you take over guardianship?" he asked.

"I have no choice. She needs care, and it's too soon for a nursing home, even though that will eventually be in her future."

"What a bitch!" Mr. Simmons burst out. "You, Pam, and your grandmother have your hands full, while they have all the time in the world to plot against you." He lowered his voice, becoming stern but calm. "I'm sure we could fill the rest of the day talking about that, but I need to start trying to reach Adam. I want something to ease your mind. Let's both hope he doesn't want to go through the hassle." Mr. Simmons rubbed my shoulder in an attempt to calm my nerves. I guess my face was giving away my stress.

"Mr. Simmons, can I ask you something?"

"Anything!"

"Why would Momma do this? I mean, why would she sit down

with you, go through all the trouble with the will, and then turn around and sign something for the band of vultures?"

"I believe your mother has always wanted to heal her relationship with Tanya. Maybe she felt it was a way of telling Tanya she loves and trusts her. It's the only reason I can think of. If anyone else treated her the way Tanya has, she would have put them out of your lives long ago."

"Do you think this is what Momma meant by 'don't trust the people you think you can trust the most'?"

"Yes, I do. I think she saw how Tanya dealt with her final diagnosis and noted her absence during the last week she was able to be with friends and family."

His words hit me hard. Momma was trying to mend things, but Aunt Tanya was still harboring feelings she'd had since childhood. Mr. Simmons excused himself to start contacting Adam. I returned to Momma's room, where I found Patricia and Rhonda looking through photo albums with Grandmother. After a while, Grandmother grew restless and wanted to lie down. As Patricia helped her out, I asked Rhonda, "Could I be alone with Momma for a while?"

"Of course. Do you need anything?"

"Will you please close the door on your way out? I just need some time alone with her."

I saw the concern on Rhonda's face. "Lizzy, I wish I could do something for you."

I knew she meant it, and I loved her for it. As she closed the door, I took Momma's hand and held it close to my heart. I sat in the quiet, watching her breathing. Every once in a while she took in a deeper breath and released it slowly. There was no crinkle in her forehead. She looked peaceful.

"I love you, Momma." I squeezed her hand and waited, hoping she'd squeeze it back, but there was no response. Then I heard the doorbell. If it was a visitor for Momma, I knew Patricia or Rhonda would explain that it wasn't a good time, so I didn't move.

I heard faint voices coming from the living room, and then Patricia opened Momma's door. "Lizzy, I'm sorry."

Before she could say anything else, I said, "I don't care who it is. Just please close the door and leave us alone." I regretted sounding so rude. She and Rhonda had been wonderful to me; I should have chosen my words better.

Patricia didn't seem fazed. "If it were anyone else, I would. But it's Adam."

I was stunned. "What?"

"Bill is on his way back here, and Adam is waiting for you in the living room."

"Where's Grandmother?" I asked automatically. "She doesn't need to be exposed to any of this." I tried to say this as calmly as possible; I didn't want to affect Momma.

"She's fine. She doesn't know who Adam is, but she's talking with him. I think you'll really want to hear what he has to say." Her urging was irritating, but if Mr. Simmons was on his way, then something was up. How could it have happened so fast?

"Can Rhonda come sit with Momma? And will you please take Grandmother into the dining room? Is it lunchtime yet?"

"Honey, lunchtime passed hours ago. We didn't want to disturb you. We'll handle it. You just take care of your business."

"I'm sorry I haven't helped you two more. I'll be right there."

She nodded and closed the door. I stood up, kissed Momma's forehead, and whispered, "I love you so very, very much." Rhonda came in and hugged me. I had to fight back tears; I was so tired. Tired of the disrespect my mother was getting from her so-called family, tired of this never-ending fight, and emphatically tired of being pulled away from Momma. Reluctantly, I let go of Rhonda and left the room without a word.

Adam was standing up with his hands in his pockets when I walked into the room. After initially making eye contact, he lowered his head, and I saw tears on his cheeks. What was going on? I wanted to be with Momma, not standing there with Adam.

My words were heartless when I finally broke the silence. "Are you just going to stand there crying, or will you tell me what the hell is going on?"

He took a deep breath. "I got a call from Bill Simmons."

Really irritated now, I snapped, "I know. Are you pissed off that he contacted you?"

"I understand your anger."

"How can you? Do you even know what I'm angry about?"

"I do now. Bill said something…" His voice trailed off, and he began to sob.

I wish Mr. Simmons had called to tell me what was going on, I thought. *At the rate we're going, I'll never find out what this is really about.*

"Adam, look, I really don't know what's going on here, but I need to get back to Momma, and you know I'm not going to leave you here by yourself." If this was a ploy to get back into the house, he'd succeeded. I wondered what he'd said to Patricia and Rhonda to get in.

Between his sobs, he said, "I'm sorry. Please, just give me a minute."

I couldn't control my anger. "You want me to give you about as much time as you've given to Momma. In that case, you've overstayed your welcome. Will you please leave now?"

He pulled himself together. "I can't do that until I make some of this right. I'm supposed to meet Bill here."

"Why?"

"Because I'm signing over the role of administrator on that amendment to you."

What in the world could Bill have said to him? "I'm sorry if I don't believe you. This all seems too easy. What's the catch?"

"Lizzy, there's no catch. I promise! I just hope one day you'll be able to find a way to forgive me." He sounded sincere, but I wasn't about to let my guard down. He continued, "I'll be honest—Bill and I had an argument. I was more than ready to fight you so my mother could have what's hers."

"Hers! Nothing in this house is hers."

"I know. I know. Wrong choice of words."

"You both have the same problem. You're too worried about material things and not what's really important."

Tears filled his eyes again. "You're right. When Bill was talking to me, he asked if I knew how long death lasted. His words hit me hard; I've been listening to my mother and haven't been my own man. Aunt Pam was never anything less than good to me."

"Because she loves you. She loves her family, even with their faults." Momma would have been proud to know I'd listened the day she said that to me.

He said softly, "And we do have our faults."

I was still suspicious. "Does Tanya know you're here?"

"Yes, and she's not happy."

Before I could say anything, Mr. Simmons rang the doorbell. When I let him in, I noticed he had a fistful of documents. He asked, "Is Adam here?"

"In the living room." I followed him.

He got started immediately. "Adam, I'm Bill Simmons—we spoke on the phone. Thank you for meeting with us here so we don't have to take Lizzy away from Pam. I explained everything to you this morning, and I've drawn up the appropriate documentation."

"Yes, sir. Just tell me where to sign so Lizzy can get back to Aunt Pam."

As we signed the paperwork, a wave of relief flooded over me. When we were done, Adam asked, "Can I please see her?"

"Of course. But I do want to say something to you first." I took a deep breath. I wanted to be sure my words were precise, not just angry. "I know you're trying to make this right, but I still don't trust you."

Adam's hands went back into his pockets. "I don't blame you. After what we've done, I wouldn't trust me, either."

"Are there any other surprises we need to know about?" My question got Mr. Simmons's attention.

"None that I know of."

"Then enough of this. Mr. Simmons, would you like to see Momma, too?"

Holding up the paperwork, he said, "Lizzy, thank you, but I'm going to head on to the office and wrap up our business here." I walked him to the door, and then Adam followed me to Momma's room.

Adam hadn't seen her since our meeting with Dr. Elliot. Taking her hand, he began to apologize. "Aunt Pam, I've been so wrong. I hope you can forgive me." Tears streamed down his cheeks. "I'm so sorry. You trusted me, and I let you down. But I've tried to change all that now."

As he talked, a change came over Momma's face. She'd had only one seizure, but I feared she was about to have another one. Patricia saw it, too, and we both moved closer to the bed. Seeing the alarm on our faces, Adam moved back.

"Momma?" I said softly. My heart was pounding. Her eyes were rapidly rolling under her lids.

Patricia whispered, "Get Rhonda." Adam ran from the room.

"What's wrong?" Rhonda demanded when she came in. Patricia quickly lifted her finger to her lips. I just kept talking.

"Momma, it's Lizzy. Are you okay?" Just like that, she began to blink; then her eyes opened. There were those beautiful eyes I'd hoped to look into again! My own eyes welled up with tears.

"Hey, you," I said in a drawn-out way. She looked toward me but not directly at me.

In the sweetest voice I'd ever heard, she said, "Lizzy, it's so beautiful." Her speech was slow and slurred.

"What's so beautiful?" I watched her eyes land on a spot in the corner of the room, close to the ceiling. "Momma, have we been keeping you too medicated?" I felt Adam's hand on my shoulder.

A tiny smile came over her face. "Yeah. Can you see it, too?"

"Momma, I can't see it, but I'm sure whatever you see is beautiful." Tears rolled down my cheeks. I knew what she was seeing. Then she said something to confirm my thoughts.

"Daddy." When this simple word left her lips, I knew she was seeing the end of her life with us. I looked around and saw that Patricia and Rhonda had their arms around each other. Both of them were crying. Adam, too, was crying. Everyone in the room knew our time with Momma was very short.

I began sobbing as I stroked her hair. "I love you," I whispered.

"I love you, Lizzy," she said. Then she closed her eyes and fell back into the coma. No one spoke. We all just put our hands on her, standing silently in support of what was coming next.

Adam left after a time, but Rhonda, Patricia, and I spent almost every moment in her room until the sun went down. Grandmother was the only reason we left the room, but even she came in and sat quietly, holding Momma's hand. We all felt it could end at any time.

When Sandy returned at dusk to help out on the nightshift, I told her what had happened. "I know this is going to be hard, but if she needs to go on your watch, you'll have to let her go."

Sadly, she replied, "I know."

As Sandy settled into Momma's room, Patricia helped Grandmother to bed. Rhonda started the laundry, and I went in search of some hidden pictures. Momma had never liked having her picture taken; whenever she got her hands on one, she hid it. Now I needed to find her hiding place. Some time ago, as I was helping Momma to bed, she said, "If I have all this fluid when I die, please don't have an open casket. Maybe just a picture of me." Her words had rattled me so much I hadn't thought to ask where the pictures were.

I was so involved in my search that Rhonda startled me when she asked, "Baby, what are you doing?" I jumped as though I was guilty of something, and she laughed.

Jokingly, I said, "Shut up." Then I couldn't resist laughing myself.

Before I could explain what I was doing, Patricia joined us— now I could ask them both at the same time. "Where are Momma's pictures?"

"I believe we have all the photo albums in Pam's room, right, Pat?"

"Not pictures of Momma and someone else," I said. "Pictures just of her."

Patricia giggled. "Oh, you want the hidden treasure. I have no idea."

Rhonda agreed. "Me, either."

"You mean to tell me neither of you know?"

They looked at each other and shook their heads. Rhonda asked, "Why?"

I shared my conversation with Momma. After what we'd witnessed today, they agreed to help me look. Rhonda found a shoebox full of pictures, and we all headed to the dining room to look through them and find one that would be appropriate.

Looking through the pictures was very emotional. The snapshots told the story of her life, covering every milestone and happy occasion.

Patricia asked, "How can we pick just one?"

"Jesus, you're right. There's no way," Rhonda replied.

"Then let's don't," I said. "I saw a collage frame in one of the closets. Do you think it would be okay to do that?"

They both smiled. Patricia said, "I think that's a wonderful idea."

We worked on it for hours. When it was finished, there were ten pictures arranged in a story line from high school graduation to last Christmas. As we looked at our work, sadness overcame me. This would be my final tribute to my mother. I sobbed uncontrollably.

Rhonda tried to console me. "It's okay. Just let it out." She rocked me slowly, and Patricia wrapped her arms around both of us. We shared a long cry.

I hadn't meant to cause such a breakdown. I'd been able to control my feelings as we worked on the collage, but seeing the final product reminded me that time was ticking away on Momma's life.

Afterward, I was drained. Even though only three hours remained before the sun came up, I just wanted to sleep. Pulling away from them, I wiped my face. "I think I need to lie down." Neither spoke, but I knew they understood.

I reclined on the couch, believing sleep would swallow me up, but it didn't. Instead I found myself talking with God.

Why? If only you could tell me why. When all of this began, you could have healed her or seen fit that she not go through this at all. She spent so much of her time helping as many of your children as possible. Why? Grandmother would whoop my butt for questioning you, but isn't it okay to ask why? She always said I should fear you, but now I only fear what I feel for you. Why!

My pain was overwhelming; I knew deep inside that Momma would soon be gone. I walked quietly down the hall and stood just outside the doorway of Momma's room. Sandy was flipping through a photo album by lamplight, and she didn't notice me. I could see Momma's face. She looked peaceful. There was no crinkle in her forehead, and her breathing was slow and steady.

Returning to the couch, I gave in to my exhaustion and fell into a deep sleep. Eventually, Rhonda woke me and shared the devastating news that we were closer to the end than I could have ever imagined.

Chapter 10

As we gathered around Momma, I couldn't get my conversation with Tanya out of my head. I had given her every opportunity and the benefit of the doubt. Still, I wished I would look up and see her standing there. I took Momma's hand, regretting that this was the one thing I couldn't do for her before she died.

I felt a hand on my back; when I turned around, I was shaken to see Grandmother. None of us had seen her come in. "Grandmother…"

Keeping her hand on my back, she placed her other hand on Momma. "Pam, it's time you were at peace. Daddy's waiting for you," she said. A tear slid down her cheek, and I wrapped my arm around her shoulder. Before calling Tanya, I had been grateful that Alzheimer's had kept Grandmother away. But now I was relieved to have her here.

We stood vigilantly for almost an hour, watching Momma's breathing slow. As the sun rose and beamed on her face, she drew in one deep breath and then let out a sigh. Another breath would not follow. She was gone. For several moments, no one moved. We stood there like statues. Grandmother broke our trance. She placed Momma's hand under the sheet and then pulled it tight to her chin as if she were tucking her in. I was stunned as I watched her leave the room. Patricia followed her out.

I picked up the bedside phone and called Dr. Elliot. When he answered, I began, "Dr. Elliot, it's Lizzy." The rest of the words got caught in my throat.

"Lizzy, I'm on my way!" It seemed like only minutes before he was standing there with us in Momma's room. He listened to her chest and checked for a pulse. Once he announced the time of death, he said, "Lizzy, why don't you wait in the living room while we remove all this stuff. We have to take the catheter out, along with the IV line."

"No, sir, I'm going to help," I said.

"You really don't have to be here for this."

"I'm afraid I do," I replied. I had to see this all the way through. I wanted her to have the dignity she deserved. I knew everyone there would be respectful; but it was just part of my way of dealing with what had happened.

After Dr. Elliot removed the equipment, I retrieved the bath basin from the bathroom. Dr. Elliot asked if he could step out, and I understood his reason. After we finished bathing her, we dressed Momma in a gown. Dr. Elliot had called the mortuary to arrange her transport, and now we just had to wait. I didn't expect them to arrive so fast. This was a hard moment. They didn't want me to be in the room when they moved her to the gurney, but I didn't want to leave. My mistake! Big mistake!

As I tried to convince them that I was okay with it, Grandmother came into the room. She began talking to Momma. "Pam, I need to go to the store. Will you take me?" We all turned to look at her. She had forgotten.

"Sweetie, let's go make a list of the things you need," Patricia said, trying to coax Grandmother out of the room.

"No, thank you. I'll get Pam to help me."

I walked across the room to her and put my arm around her shoulder. "Grandmother, Momma can't help you right now, but I can."

"Lizzy, you're so sweet, but I really need Pam to help me," she said. She pulled away from me and moved closer to Momma's bed.

"Pam? Pam? Can you hear me, Pam?" she asked. When I saw her hand reach toward Momma, I tried to stop it, but my brain was moving too slowly. As she touched Momma, it hit her. Her eyes shot up from Momma and landed on me. Her face was filled with terror, and her eyes filled with tears. She started to scream, "Lizzy! Something's wrong with Pam! Help her!" I grabbed her hands and pulled her close to me, but she still screamed. "Pam! Wake up, Pam!"

I couldn't help but cry. It was heartbreaking to see Grandmother like this. "Grandmother, Momma is where she needs to be. Remember being with her a little while ago?" I tried to stay calm, but this was extremely difficult. Rhonda and Patricia helped me hold her up; it felt like her knees had buckled. Then she lashed out at everyone.

"I want you people to do something! Don't just stand there! Do something!" She was striking me on the arms.

Everyone froze. When no one moved, she started screaming for my grandfather. "Buddy, I need you! Buddy, no one will help Pam, and she's real sick. Buddy, come in here!"

From the corner of my eye, I saw Dr. Elliot rush out of the room. In a moment he was back with a syringe. Over my grandmother's screams he asked, "Lizzy, is she allergic to anything?" I shook my head. In a split second he'd exposed Grandmother's skin and injected her with the clear liquid, then slipped his arm around her waist. The screaming stopped, and she slid into Dr. Elliot's chest.

The men from the funeral home rushed over to help. Grandmother was petite, so they had no trouble lifting her up and taking her into her bedroom. Rhonda went with them to help get her into bed. I watched in horror.

"Are you okay?" Dr. Elliot asked. I just nodded. He took my shaking hand and led me into the living room. "I gave her a sedative. She'll sleep for a while. I'm going to call for a prescription in pill form for her, okay?"

"Do you think she'll need it again?" I asked softly.

"I can't answer that. Alzheimer's is unpredictable. She may or may not remember what's happened, but with Pam not in the room, she may not even think about it."

"Thank you." It came out in a whisper.

"Do you need me to get something for you, too?"

"No, I'm fine. It's just overwhelming," I said as I began to sob.

Patricia came into the room and said, "Lizzy, your grandmother is resting, and the guys need to know if it's okay for them to go ahead."

"Do I need to do anything?"

"No, Rhonda and I will handle it if you're okay with that."

"That's fine."

She kissed the top of my head and then headed back to Momma's room. As they worked, I called the funeral director to begin the process. When I hung up, I leaned back on the couch and tried to breathe. I knew I was breathing, but I didn't feel like I was getting enough air. Dr. Elliot held my hand and said, "Lizzy, just let it out. Don't try to be strong right now. You need to grieve and not hold back. I'm very impressed with your strength and your dedication to giving Pam what she desired the most. You're as incredible as your mother is—" He stopped when he realized his mistake. He took my hand, and we sat in silence. Soon Patricia and Rhonda joined us.

Patricia said, "I checked on your grandmother, and she's still sleeping."

Dr. Elliot replied, "She probably will for a while. Lizzy, this will give you time to do some things you need to do."

"I guess I need to call and let people know the wake will be tonight," I said.

"Tonight?" Rhonda was shocked.

"Momma wanted it that way. When we made her arrangements last week, she said, 'Please don't drag things out. Get my funeral over with as quickly as possible.' If it's what she wants, then it's what she gets." I was on autopilot now; there was quite a bit of work to be done.

Patricia said, "I'll start making some calls. Do you have a list or anyone you want me to call first?"

I remembered how I'd been with Dr. Elliot on the phone when

I'd called to get him here. I choked up and couldn't say anything, so I knew it would be way too hard to try and tell the news repeatedly. The outpouring of sympathy would only make it worse. I went over to the table and found a napkin and a pen. I wrote down four names and four numbers for Patricia.

"Thank you," I said. "The first name on that list is the pastor. He needs to know about the arrangements for tomorrow. He'll know who all to contact, pallbearers and so forth, and is prepared to do so. The next three names are some of Grandmother's old friends. I want you to tell them what happened, the time of the wake, the funeral arrangements for tomorrow, and that you're trying to let everyone know. Oh, yes, and please tell them that after the funeral the family has requested that no one come back to the house."

Looking down at the list, Rhonda asked, "Lizzy, you only want us to call four people?"

"For now. There are others out of town that we'll have to contact, but I don't think they could make the funeral on such short notice," I replied.

"What I meant was, what about everyone else?"

"I figured you'd contact the hospital. But the women on that list are people I've known my whole life. If you let them know what happened, I promise you everyone in town and the three neighboring counties will know before I can get Momma's funeral outfit out of the closet." I wasn't trying to be curt, but it was the truth. Today I appreciated how fast things got around in a small town.

When the women finished their calls, they came back to sit with me in the living room. The house was extremely quiet until Patricia broke the silence. "Do you want me to call Tanya?"

Coldly, I replied, "No." It had been over two hours since Momma had left us, and I felt that she'd had ample time to get here or call to check on the progress. It had been her choice not to come when I called, so there would be no more calls.

I got up and checked on Grandmother. She was still sleeping. I went into Momma's room to get her funeral outfit. The hospital bed was gone, and the regular bed was back in its normal spot, all made up. The room seemed so empty. My heart felt just as empty, and I realized that from that day forward my life would always have a hole in it.

When I returned to the kitchen, I asked Rhonda and Patricia if they'd mind if I went to the funeral home alone. I explained that I needed to make a stop, and I just needed some time to breathe. They didn't put up too much of an argument and agreed to stay with Grandmother. I promised not to be long; I knew they wanted to get home themselves to deal with their loss as well.

On the way to the funeral home, I stopped by the cemetery. After sitting in the car for a moment, I got out and walked over to my grandfather's grave. Softly I spoke to him.

"Hey, Grandfather. It's been a while, and I'm sorry for that. I know you've been blessed today, and I hope you were there to meet her. You know she saw you the day before"—I started to cry—"the day before she died. She spoke to you. I love you both, and I'll miss you always. There's so much to be done now, and I hope you'll watch out for me. This is going to be as hard as having to say good-bye to you. I love you."

Once I was back in the car, I leaned over the steering wheel and cried some more. When I started the car, I couldn't take the silence, so I turned on the radio. I smiled as Willie Nelson sang out "Blue Eyes Crying in the Rain." That was Grandfather's favorite song. As I drove out of the cemetery, I sang along. When the song was over, I said, "Thanks, Grandfather. I needed that!"

It didn't take long to drop the clothes off and get back to the house. I joined the women in the living room. As I was about to sit down for a breather, a loud slam came from the kitchen. We all ran toward the noise and ran right into Tanya.

Chapter 11

Tanya didn't seem to notice that we nearly collided. "My sister dies, and you don't call me," she spat. "I found out from my CEO in a mass company email! This is the lowest thing you could ever do, Lizzy!"

I sighed and said, "You've got to be kidding me! It is a small town. They graduated together and you both went to school with almost everyone that works there. I'm sure he thought you'd already have known."

Rhonda lit into Tanya. "Tanya, she called you this morning to let you know the severity of the situation, and it was your choice not to come. How can you blame Lizzy for your not knowing? I suggest you change your tone or get out. She doesn't need this right now."

"I don't care if she needs it or not. It's my sister's death, and she didn't respect me enough to call and let me know. Why are you even here, anyway? This is a family matter."

She'd lashed out at the wrong person; the girls had been there for me twenty-four hours a day from beginning to end. I flew into a rage. "That's enough! I want you to shut up, just shut up, please!" Tanya blinked in astonishment. Lowering my voice, I continued, "First, let me say they have every right to be here, so you won't speak to either of them like that. Now I'm sorry you had to find out the way you did,

but you have only yourself to blame for that. So please, just be quiet."
My own grief left me no room to think about Tanya and her feelings.
She was clearly more upset that I hadn't let her know than she was that
Momma had died.

"You embarrassed me in front of everyone at the office!"

"No, you embarrassed yourself," Patricia said.

Tanya snapped, "I really wish you two would stay out of this. This
is not your concern."

I couldn't take listening to her snap at them. "Stop it! I mean it
now. You are not the martyr here. If you can't address them nicely, then
don't address them at all. Better yet, why don't you just stop talking
altogether!"

Tanya opened her mouth to speak, but I threw my hand up to
stop her. "I'm not kidding, Tanya. Not one more word." I was angry
that my mom was dead, and I was sad that Grandmother had had to
go through what she had that morning. Tanya had no right to speak
to any of us the way she was, so I had to diffuse the situation before it
got out of hand.

I began instructing her without pausing to let her speak. "The wake
is tonight at six, and the funeral is tomorrow at eleven. I want you to go
home and put on the saddest face you can muster. Grandmother will
need us, so I expect you to pretend you care that my mother has died.
Family visitation will be for us at five. I'll take Grandmother to that,
but I'm going to make arrangements for her after. She won't sit through
all of this. If you must bring that husband of yours, be prepared to keep
him on a short leash. Better yet, your whole clan better be on their best
behavior, or I'll have you all removed. Am I making myself clear?"

She just nodded. I had only one question left. "Do I need to show
you the door, or do you think you can find your way?" I thought she
was going to leave without incident, but I wouldn't be so lucky.

Tanya stopped just before getting to the door. She took the stance
I knew all too well: back arched, shoulders back, jaw firm. "I may be
leaving, but you and I have unfinished business."

I thought she was talking about the damn silver again. I was sick of hearing about it, and she'd found a way to push my buttons. "Can you at least wait until we get her in the ground before you start circling? Jesus!"

"Oh, yes, I'll wait." She smiled slyly. Without saying another word, she left, slamming the door just as hard as she did when she entered.

Rhonda said, "Does she ever stop?"

"You've known her as long as you've known Momma. Honestly, some of this is new to me. Has she ever stopped?"

"What a bitch!" Patricia said.

Rhonda and I nodded in agreement. Regretfully, I told them both, "I just don't know how Momma did it. I would have had to just walk away." I ran my hands through my hair in frustration.

"I agree with you. Pam and I used to argue about that growing up." Rhonda was remembering their childhood. "But her family was important to her, and she wouldn't give up."

"After everything I've seen in the last couple of weeks, it's not going to take much for me to give up on her," I said. I meant it, too. Momma and Grandmother were the seams holding this family together. I feared I wouldn't be as accepting of Tanya and her self-serving ways now that I was seeing her true colors.

Patricia seemed to hold out hope. "Maybe actually seeing your mother this evening will help soften this assault."

"I don't even want to think about tonight. How do you think Grandmother is going to do?"

Rhonda reassured me. "We'll be there to help, and I'm picking up her medicine in a little bit."

"One of us will be with you for anything you need," Patricia confirmed.

"I know you've been busy and have a lot on your mind, but have you called any of your friends to let them know what's happened?" Rhonda asked.

I'd thought about it earlier but wasn't ready to talk about it. "No, but I guess there's no time better than the present to take care of that." I was dreading having to actually tell anyone she'd died.

The girls told me to take my time; they'd listen for Grandmother. I grabbed the phone and headed for the rocker on the porch. I realized it had been a week since I'd talked to Spencer. *I should have called him sooner,* I thought. Not wanting to deal with a lot of questions from anyone at work, I tried him at home first.

"Hello?" he said. The lump in my throat made speaking impossible. "Hello?" he said again.

I managed to say "Spencer" and then began to sob.

"Aw, Lizzy. Oh, man." I heard him sigh. "Just take your time. Oh, man."

The sobs seemed to be never-ending, but he waited for me to be able to speak. Finally I was able to say, "I'm sorry."

"Don't apologize. I completely understand. Are you okay?"

"I thought I was." Again I sobbed, and again he patiently waited. "It happened this morning."

"I knew it had to be today. I've called every day and talked with Patricia or Rhonda."

I'd had no idea. "Really?"

"They told me what happened yesterday while Adam was there."

"A telltale sign." I was able to say only short sentences without completely falling apart.

Rhonda came onto the porch and put a glass of tea beside the chair. She whispered, "Is that Spencer?" Wiping my eyes, I nodded. She held out her hand, and I gave her the phone. I picked up the glass of tea and held it to my face. The coolness felt good on my hot skin.

"Hey, Spencer, it's Rhonda." I could hear only her side of the conversation, but I could guess what he was saying. She ran her fingers through my hair with her free hand. "She's going to be okay...Tonight at six and tomorrow at eleven...Pam asked for it to be fast...Lizzy called her, but she didn't come...Let me ask her."

She turned to me. "Honey, Spencer wants to know if you need anything from your apartment." I shook my head. "Do you want him to call Kay and your boss?" I nodded. She conveyed both my responses and then asked, "Do you need the address?" For a moment she was silent. "Okay, I'll tell her. I know she'll be happy. Bye." She disconnected and then told me that he was on his way. I smiled but started crying. I was on a nonstop emotional roller coaster.

I heard tapping behind me—Grandmother was at the dining room window. I wasn't ready to face her but knew I couldn't put it off. When we walked inside, she immediately asked, "Baby, did you eat? I've got a sandwich for you."

Patricia called to Grandmother from the kitchen, "Ms. Grace, that's your sandwich. I've got Lizzy's right here." She walked through the door with a plate in each hand. "I have one for Rhonda, too."

"Well, then you need one," she replied.

"No, ma'am, mine is fixed, too. I guess you'll have to eat that one."

Their exchange lightened the moment. We enjoyed our lunch, and Grandmother seemed to have forgotten about the morning.

As we finished, Rhonda said, "I'm going to the pharmacy and then home to get some clothes." I suddenly realized we had to be at the funeral home in a couple of hours.

"Patricia, if you'll stay with Grandmother while I shower, I'll get us ready, and then you can go home too and meet us at six. Ya'll need a break."

She replied, "Sounds like a plan."

After Patricia left, Grandmother and I were alone in the house for the first time. I helped her dress, fixed her hair, and applied a little lipstick. She never asked where we were going. She was unusually quiet, which gave me time to think. What would happen when it was just us in Montgomery? I didn't even want her to be alone while I took a shower, and I expected to take her to live with me even though I worked. Momma had been able to do it because people in the community checked on her during the day; I didn't have that kind of support system. I'd have to think about that later. If we didn't leave soon, we'd be late for the viewing.

From the living room, where I put on my shoes, I called down the hallway to Grandmother, "Are you ready?"

"Yes, Lizzy. Where are we going?"

I didn't know how to tell her. My mind was blank. Finally I said, "Honey, we're going to the funeral home." She didn't question me; she just headed to the door. I helped her into the car and put her cane in the trunk.

As I pulled away from the house, I remembered the time she'd used her cane as a weapon against Momma because she'd wanted to go home to her house. Alzheimer's left Grandmother a little unpredictable; she'd do and say things now that she never would have before. On that day, she told Momma she wanted to go home. Momma was polite, trying to explain for the hundredth time that she couldn't. "Mother, why don't you just stay here? Remember how we moved all your stuff here, and you said you wanted to stay with me?"

At first Grandmother was sweet. "Thank you, but I want to go home."

Momma had told me about their tiffs, but this was the first time I'd actually witnessed one. "Mother, why don't we go later?"

Just like that, Grandmother snapped, "I'm going home, dammit!" and out the door she went.

Momma stopped me as I headed to the door. "Don't move." I froze in my tracks. I could see Grandmother from the window. After a few minutes, my mother asked, "Where is she now?"

"Almost to the curve." We lived on a dirt road a mile from the main highway. If she continued walking, I'd have a clear view of her until she reached the highway. Momma joined me by the window. "How far are you going to let her go?"

"I don't know; she's never gone this far before. Normally she gets mad, walks out, gets to the end of the driveway, and comes back." The phone rang, and Momma told me to watch her. When she returned, she had her keys. "That was the neighbor. Let's go see if we can get her."

Momma stopped the car close to Grandmother, and we got out. "Grandmother?"

She just kept walking.

Momma tried. "Mother, let's get in the car."

Grandmother asked, "Are you going to take me home?"

Momma and I looked at each other. I shrugged. I knew it would be a trick, but at least she'd be safe.

"Yes, Mother, I'll take you home."

We all got in the car. When Momma turned the car around to head back to our house, however, Grandmother went ballistic. "You said you were taking me home! This is kidnapping!" She grabbed at the door handle; I reached over from the back seat to hold the door shut. Grandmother started hitting the windshield with her cane. Momma sped up and got us back in the carport. They were both mad.

Momma came around to Grandmother's door and opened it. "Mother, you stop that right now!" When she swung at Momma's leg, Momma grabbed the cane. Grandmother let go. Without another word, Momma went in the house and left us in the carport.

Within seconds, Grandmother forgot what had happened. She sat quietly for a moment and then turned to me in the backseat. "Lizzy, baby, when did you get here?"

This and many other moments made me wonder what I'd do with her in Montgomery. She'd been so quiet since we left the house. Right now, we both just needed to get through tonight.

Chapter 12

When we pulled into the funeral home parking lot, I went around to help Grandmother out of the car. Rhonda's car pulled in behind us. Patricia was with her. "What are you two doing here? I thought you were coming at six," I said.

"We were, but you know us. We just can't stay away," Rhonda said with a smile. Patricia took Grandmother's hand. Whispering in my ear, Rhonda said, "Plus, I have Grace's medicine if she needs it."

"Thanks," I said. "I don't know what she's feeling or thinking. She's been so quiet."

When I opened the funeral home's front door, a soft, sweet chime alerted the staff. Then I was hit by the smell of flowers and saw that both sides of the hallway were lined with arrangements. Mr. O'Reilly, the funeral director, appeared at the other end of the hall and gestured at the flowers as he approached us. "These are all for Pam," he said. He was such a nice man and had been so respectful the day we came in to plan the funeral. And he'd been very accommodating this morning when I told him I wanted the wake tonight.

"There are so many!" I was amazed.

"You should see what's in the chapel." He guided me through the door. The front of the room was filled with double rows of flowers; more flowers lined the outer walls. I stood speechless.

"They're from all over the Southern states," he continued. "The florists have had their work cut out for them today. But if anyone was worth it, Pam was." I walked around slowly, glancing at the cards attached to each arrangement. There was no way I could see them all at that moment, and I knew in my heart I'd never be able to thank all these people properly.

"Lizzy, Pam is in Parlor B. It's the biggest room we have, and if the flowers are any indication, we're going to need all that space and then some. Would you like to see her? I think you're going to be relieved." Mr. O'Reilly knew my concern about the fluid. He escorted us out of the sanctuary and down the hall. My breath quickened and my chest tightened as we approached Parlor B. Inside the room, he lifted the casket lid, and there she was. She was beautiful. With the exception of the wig, she was back to her old self, the Momma I had known before we knew about the cancer.

I looked back at Grandmother, Rhonda, and Patricia. "She's beautiful. Don't you think so?" The three of them stepped forward and couldn't believe what they were seeing. As we stood there holding hands, we weren't aware that Mr. O'Reilly had left the room. I realized then that this room, too, was filled with flowers. I focused on them so I wouldn't fall apart. I was numb from head to toe; I felt I could float away. But I had a long night ahead; so falling apart would have to wait.

I reached inside my shoulder bag and pulled out the photo collage. "What do you ladies think? I know we said we'd use these if she wasn't presentable, but I think these would just add to her memory. These pictures will remind people who she was—a mother, daughter, and nurse."

"She was a savior to some, Lizzy, and I think it's a wonderful idea," Patricia said.

Rhonda agreed. "I think people will appreciate it. I know I do." She wiped a tear from her eye.

"Grandmother?" I showed her the frame. "What do you think? How would you feel if we put this inside the lid?"

"I remember that," she said, pointing to one of the pictures. She smiled. "That's the day she brought you home from the hospital. We were all so happy!" Her response was what I had looked for—she remembered my mother during a happier time. It was settled. I placed the frame in the casket lid.

I moved some chairs around so Grandmother and I would be accessible to anyone who came in. We'd just gotten seated when I heard the small chime again. "What time is it?" I asked. I didn't know if I was ready for the crowd yet.

"It's only five-thirty. I'll go see who it is," Patricia said. Before she could get to the door, it opened, and there were Tanya, Brad, and Adam. We all looked in their direction, but only my Grandmother spoke.

"Isn't she beautiful?" Wordlessly they moved to the side of the casket and stood quietly for a moment. Then Tanya said coldly, "Mother, please! Death is not beautiful." Tanya turned and looked at me. "Where did these pictures come from?"

"Momma had them hidden. We worked on it last night."

"This is just tacky, Lizzy! You need to put this away." She reached for the collage.

I moved closer to her to stay out of Grandmother's earshot. Rhonda was on her feet. "Tanya, I'm going to ask you politely to put that back, and then I want you to speak to your mother." Adam was already trying to put the frame back in place. Brad was heading for the door.

"Now look what you've done. I think you've upset him," Tanya said. Then she exited the room as well.

I looked at Adam. "Go speak to your grandmother," I said. Then I adjusted the frame. He sat beside Grandmother and held her hand. I motioned for Rhonda and Patricia to stay where they were, and I went out the door myself. I found Tanya and Brad in a heated conversation but was unable to make out what they were saying. I didn't care.

"Tanya, Brad, this isn't about either of you or even about me; it's about my mother, and I'm not going to battle either or both of you tonight. Whatever issues the two of you are having, I suggest you suck it up and act like adults. People will be arriving soon, and if you don't feel like you can be supportive, then you can leave. Now, if you feel like you can, then I welcome you both to stay. But"—I shifted my gaze to Tanya—"you'll go in there and speak to your mother regardless of your decision. She lost a child today." With that I turned and went back into the parlor.

In a matter of moments, Tanya returned alone and started gushing about how pretty Grandmother looked, and Grandmother started chattering to her as well. The first visitor to arrive was Spencer.

He hugged me. I struggled to fight tears. "Do you need anything?" he asked. I just shook my head. "There were a ton of people behind me when I pulled up, but Kay wanted you to know she'll be here tomorrow. We'll have time to talk later. I'm here if you need anything."

"Thank you."

"Which of these ladies is Patricia or Rhonda?"

I pointed them out to him. As he moved in their direction, people began pouring into the room. Tanya disappeared. Hundreds of people came through that night. People who saw the pictures were moved to discuss their memories, smiling, laughing, and crying as they did so. Not long after the wake started, I moved Grandmother to the back of the room with some of her friends. She was overwhelmed by all the strangers talking to her, and besides, only close friends and family would know who she was. They'd be sure to see her if they wanted to. Rhonda and Patricia checked on her periodically and reported back to me.

About an hour into the wake, I began to overhear snippets of conversations: "disrespectful," "she's always been that way," and things of that nature. At first I thought the comments were about the pictures—but then I figured out they were about Tanya. The next time Patricia came over to speak to me, I asked her to find out whether Tanya was still there. I hadn't seen her since the beginning of the wake.

Her face told me Tanya was still there. When there was a break in the stream of people, Patricia said, "Down the hall is a smoking room. Tanya and Brad are there. That's where they've been all night."

"That doesn't sound too bad." I was holding out hope.

"It wouldn't be bad if they weren't acting like we were throwing a party here." I gave her a confused look but paused to speak with some more people. Once they'd moved away, I asked Patricia, "What are you talking about?"

"Lizzy, I'm not kidding. She's making an ass of herself."

"Can you ask Adam to come over here?" He was sitting in the back of the room with Grandmother. Patricia bent down and whispered in his ear. He immediately made his way over.

"Go find out what your mother is doing," I instructed him. "I haven't left this room, but people are talking about her, and I need you to find out what she's doing and make her stop." He nodded and left.

When he returned, he told me she was out of control; and she refused to listen when he asked her to tone it down. I asked him to greet people for a few minutes and then made my way out of the room. It took a while; many people stopped me to offer their condolences. Finally, I neared the laughter I heard farther up the hallway. Mr. O'Reilly looked mortified as he peered in the door. I looked in and then turned to him. "I'm sorry. I'll deal with this." He just nodded.

As I entered the room, several people moved toward the door, looking disgusted. I smiled and nodded to them. No one spoke; they just left silently and began talking only when they were back out in the hallway. I reached for Tanya's purse with one hand and firmly grabbed her elbow with the other. "Don't speak; just walk," I whispered in her ear. Brad followed, just as I thought he would. As I escorted Tanya to the parking lot, she snatched her arm out of my hand and then grabbed the purse I held out for her.

"Where's your car?" I asked calmly.

"Down there," she said, pointing. "What's your problem, Lizzy?"

"Are you on drugs? Drunk? What is it? Never mind! I don't even care, to tell you the truth; I just want you to go home."

"We didn't do anything! You wanted us here, so here we are. You haven't so much as thanked us for coming!" Brad screamed. I saw Spencer coming across the parking lot.

Thank them? I was appalled. This was a wake! Before I could respond, Spencer said, "You must be Tanya."

"Who are you?"

"I'm your escort to your car."

Tanya screamed, "That's my sister in there!"

Brad tilted his head back in an attempt to look down his nose at Spencer, but he actually had to look up.

Spencer said, "That's what makes it worse. I've watched you two make spectacles of yourselves all night." I hadn't seen him since the wake began, but it seemed he'd been watching them. He continued, "Now Lizzy was in the process of politely asking you to leave."

Brad's face reddened, and he stepped up to Spencer. "Who do you think you are?"

"I'm the one who's going to make sure Lizzy gets what she wants. I'd appreciate it if you'd step back." Spencer wasn't letting Brad get to him. "Lizzy, why don't you go back inside?" I left them in the parking lot. There must not have been too much of an argument; within minutes, Spencer reappeared in the parlor. He nodded at me and then made his way to Patricia.

The wake was supposed to last for two hours, but due to the number of people, it lasted four. Grandmother's friends took her home early; and I didn't even realize when Adam left. Spencer and the girls were still with me. By the time the last person left, I was exhausted.

Rhonda put an arm around me. "You okay?"

"Just tired."

Spencer said, "You need to go home and rest."

"I think you're right. You're not going back to Montgomery tonight, are you?"

"No, Patricia and her husband have offered me their guest room."

I was surprised. "You aren't staying at the house? I have a guest room."

"Lizzy, I don't want to upset your Grandmother with everything that's already going on. She doesn't need another strange face around."

"I hadn't thought of that."

Patricia said, "He'd booked a hotel room, but I wasn't having that."

I thanked her.

No one mentioned Tanya or what had happened, and I didn't put up a fight about going home. When I walked into the house, Grandmother's friend Mrs. Culpepper let me know that she'd taken her medicine and was sound asleep. I thanked her profusely for helping me, and then we said goodnight.

Once Mrs. Culpepper left, I peeked into Grandmother's room. I heard a soft snore. I gently closed the door. Once I'd changed into comfortable clothes, I sat on my bed, wondering what to do next. I'd spent so much of the last ten months going to radiation, going to chemo treatments, and, finally, providing continuous care for the past two weeks. I felt lost. At that moment, no one needed me. There were no schedules to keep, no people arriving for the night shift. The house was quiet and still. At first, I was uneasy; then sadness set in. I'd been numb at the funeral home, and angry with Tanya for being such a bitch, but now not even she mattered to me. My thoughts raced. What would tomorrow be like without Momma? What would I do about Grandmother's care? I'd have to get guardianship of her so she could move home with me once the funeral was over and done with. I'd have to remember to talk with Mr. Simmons about the legalities. Soon, exhaustion took over, and I drifted off to sleep.

Chapter 13

The next morning, through half-open eyes, I saw sunlight streaming through the window. Memories flooded back. Today was Momma's funeral. I caught sight of the clock—it was almost eight. Grandmother! In a panic, I ran from the room and looked into hers. The door was open, and she was no longer in bed. She wasn't in the bathroom, either. "Grandmother! Where are you?" I screamed. Then Rhonda appeared at the end of the hallway.

"Lizzy, Lizzy, it's okay. I got here early this morning. She wasn't even up yet. We're having some coffee in the dining room. Take a deep breath." She took my hands.

I was almost hyperventilating. "I was so scared. I thought she'd wandered off. Thank God you were here."

"It was her idea to let you sleep. She said we shouldn't wake the baby." Rhonda and I both smiled. Wiping my face, I followed Rhonda into the dining room and saw Grandmother drinking coffee. The plate in front of her was empty.

"Did you have breakfast?" I asked.

"I sure did. Rhonda is a fine cook. We had eggs, toast, and bacon. Would you like some?" She started to get up.

"No, I'm good. I'll get a cup of coffee and sit with you. How about that?" I was trying to sound chipper but was still a little panicked.

"That sounds like a fine idea." She smiled sweetly.

After I got the coffee and returned to the table, Grandmother started chattering. She was really talking this morning. The chatter soothed my soul, and I was grateful for it. I'd been worried about how quiet she'd been last night before the wake. I wondered how she'd adjust when she moved to my apartment in the city. She'd been born and raised in this small town. How would I move her from here, where everyone knew everyone, to the city where I didn't even know my neighbors? It didn't matter. I loved her, she needed care, and I knew Tanya wouldn't provide for her. I'd do what needed to be done.

I refocused on the present. Rhonda was telling Grandmother it was time to start getting ready. "Already?" I asked. I wanted time to stand still.

"I want to get her bathed so all you have to do is help her get dressed. Enjoy your coffee and take a moment."

I kissed Grandmother on the cheek and told her to behave her silly self, like Momma used to tell me. She laughed, and away they went. She was still talking as they walked down the hallway.

Hearing the doorbell made my stomach sink. I prayed it wasn't Tanya and hoped it was Spencer. We hadn't gotten our chance to talk after the wake, and it would be nice to talk with him before the funeral. I saw a male figure standing on the porch, but it wasn't Spencer—it was Daddy. I'd seen him at the wake but only for a moment. I was glad there'd been so many people there; I hadn't had to deal with the awkwardness of seeing him. Now there was no way to avoid it.

I opened the door. "What are you doing here?"

"I'm here for you. Can I come in?"

So much had happened between us in the past, and I had so much awaiting me today, that I wasn't sure letting him in was a good idea. I saw so much of myself in his face: the ocean-blue eyes, the distinct cheekbones, and the thin nose. But the wrinkles told me exactly how much time had lapsed. "Listen, I don't know if right now is the time for all this. I know there are things I probably need to work out with you, but right now I can't," I said.

Very patiently, he said, "Pam sent me."

"Momma? How?" I was very confused.

"Lizzy, she called me a couple of weeks ago. She told me about her prognosis, and we had a long talk. Will you let me in to discuss it with you? She said you might not be willing, but I made a promise to her, and I'm not leaving, so please, let me in."

I didn't have any fight in me, so I motioned him in. We sat across from each other at the dining room table. "I really don't have a lot of time. Why are you here?" I asked.

"Lizzy, as I said, Pam called me. We had a long talk about you and about her. She reminded me that even in my absence you've never been without family." He paused.

"I'm still not without family. I have Grandmother, Tanya, and Adam."

"Really? I've heard about Grace's condition, and Tanya—let's just say I know about that, too. Pam had hoped she'd change, but from what I've heard, she's worse than ever."

I didn't know what to say. I'd been caught in my own lie.

He continued, "I know I haven't always been who I'm supposed to be, but I promised Pam I'd be here for you. It was my promise to her, and now it's my promise to you."

"And how exactly did she expect you to do this if I told you to go to hell, that I don't need or want you?" I asked.

"Pam warned me it wouldn't be easy," he replied.

"She was right. Where I'm concerned, you've had it easy your whole life." Hatred filled my voice. I felt like I was talking to a total stranger. This man was my father, but wasn't he really just a sperm donor? To hurt my mother during the years after their divorce, he found it easier to hurt me. Momma hurt when I hurt, and God knew he'd hurt me so much that I'd finally given up all contact with him.

Momma and I had fought about this over the years. She'd tell me he'd called or wanted to see me, and when I'd roll my eyes, the lecture would start. "He's still your father," she would say.

"I don't care. I don't want to hear it," I'd reply.

This exchange was like a bell at the start of a boxing match. Our conversation was always the same: I needed to forgive him, I needed to overlook his faults, he sounded regretful, and he knew I was avoiding him. Over the years, when I debated her, Momma said many times that she regretted raising me to be an independent young person. "Isn't he the parent and I the child? Why do I have to do anything where he's concerned? Life seems pretty good with him out of the equation. He only brings emotional drama that I don't have time for. Am I important at this moment, or does he mean it for a lifetime?" The older I got, the harder it was for her to fight my arguments, and the less I heard about his calls. I didn't know whether he'd just given up and didn't call, or whether she just didn't tell me about it. But now here he was. She had called him.

"Here's the deal," I said to him. "I'll make this easy for you, again. I release you from whatever promise you made to her. You can walk away. I have to get ready. You do whatever you want to do." As I stood up, I said, "This isn't something I can deal with right now. We owe each other nothing."

Without letting him respond, I walked down the hallway and closed the door to Momma's room. Tears welled up in my eyes. *Why would you do this?* I thought. I stood behind the closed door until I knew he would have left. When I opened the door, I could hear Grandmother laughing with Patricia.

When I opened the closet, the black outfit I'd chosen for the funeral was all I could see. I laid it on the bed beside my shoes. As I gazed at my funeral wear, I felt like someone had placed a boulder on my shoulders. As I showered, my entire body was so heavy that it was an effort to lift my arms to shampoo my hair and wash my face. I leaned against the wall of the shower and cried.

Once I was out of the shower, I dried my hair and applied makeup as though it were any other day. When I got to the eyes, I applied, reapplied, and reapplied again. I heard Momma's voice clear and sweet: "You can't put makeup on a waterfall." She'd said this when I was a teenager and had broken up with a boyfriend. That night, before taking me out to dinner, she found me in the bathroom crying while trying to put on my eye makeup. "You can't put makeup on a waterfall," she said. I laughed, but when she took me in her arms I cried like it was the end of the world. I wished she were there now to take me in her arms; this, too, felt like the end of my world.

There was a soft knock at the door. "Lizzy, are you okay?" It was Patricia.

I opened the door slightly. "No," I whispered, the mascara wand still in my hand. Without another word Patricia came in and held me for a moment. Then she helped me finish getting ready. I was on autopilot again. I wasn't aware of leaving the bedroom or riding to the funeral home.

There was a final visitation for the family right before the funeral. As I entered the parlor with Grandmother and Rhonda, I saw him standing there—Daddy. Grandmother remembered him. "Oh, Doyle, thank you for coming."

Alzheimer's was becoming a real thorn in my side. It would have been so much easier if she hadn't remembered him. I could have said he was a stranger and asked him to leave; but no, Alzheimer's was going to make sure that didn't happen. Lucid as could be, Grandmother was already asking him to sit with us in the family section. This had to be some kind of cosmic joke that I'd surely find hilarious at a later date.

"It's up to Lizzy," he said.

"If it makes her happy," was all I could say.

As Grandmother chatted with him, Patricia and Spencer came in. I grabbed Rhonda's hand and walked over to them.

"He says Momma called him," I said.

Spencer asked, "Who is that?"

"Her father," Patricia replied.

As Spencer took another look at him, the girls exchanged glances.

Rhonda said, "She told us she was going to call."

"You both knew about it? Why didn't you warn me?" I asked, hurt.

"We didn't know if she really had or what he would do. We didn't want to give you something else to worry about," Patricia said. Our conversation was cut short by Tanya's arrival.

"What are you doing here?" she asked Daddy.

Grandmother said, "Doyle came to pay his respects, and I've asked him to sit with us."

"You did what?" she said angrily, spinning around to face Daddy. "You aren't seriously going to do this, are you?" Then she turned to me. "There's no way you're going to allow this to happen."

"He's Lizzy's father and was married to Pam. I think he should be here for Lizzy," Grandmother said innocently.

"No one cares what you think, Mother," Tanya said, not even looking at Grandmother.

"Enough!" I said in a harsh whisper. I was tired of seeing Tanya plow over my grandmother every time she opened her mouth. "If she wants him there, then so be it. I want you to be quiet. Like I've said before, this is not about us." We looked at each other for a moment before Tanya stormed out.

"Patricia, will you and Rhonda take Grandmother to the family section in the chapel?" Turning to Daddy, I said, "Please go with them." Grandmother touched my face gently. As I kissed her hand, I said, "I just need a minute. I'll be right there."

Placing a hand on my shoulder, Spencer asked, "Do you want me to stay with you?"

"Do you mind?"

Once everyone left the room, I pulled a chair up to Momma's casket. "You've put me in a very precarious situation, but I'm sure you know that," I said to her. "I didn't know the fine line we were all walking."

Spencer softly said, "I only met her the one time. But from what

Patricia has told me, she would have moved heaven and earth for you. I think she was only trying to help."

"I know. That's what makes this even harder."

Silence fell over us as I gazed at her. She looked as though she might open her eyes at any moment, but I knew that would never happen.

"Lizzy? I hate to disturb you, but it's time," said Mr. O'Reilly as he entered the parlor.

I rose and stumbled over my words. "Okay. What do I need to do?" This had become my standard response when it came to doing things for my mother.

"We're going to close the casket and move Pam to the chapel now."

I didn't say anything as he and his assistant carefully draped a floral blanket over the casket. The picture collage had been removed from the casket but would be placed on a stand next to it in the chapel. The men were closing the lid when it hit me. I wouldn't be able to see her anymore. I'd never see her again.

"Wait, wait, please wait!" I said, rushing toward them. I was shaking, driven by fear. The men stopped. "Please don't do that," I pleaded in a soft but firm voice. "Please, please." The assistant held the lid halfway closed. I pushed it open. "Please don't close it." The two men looked at me as I stared down at Momma.

"Lizzy, are you okay?" Spencer asked. He touched my shoulder, but I pushed his hand away. "Will one of you go get Patricia or Rhonda?" he asked Mr. O'Reilly and his assistant.

I studied Momma's face as I'd done for so many months. I could hear Spencer explaining to someone that I'd been fine until they came to take her.

Soft hands touched my back. "Lizzy, sweetie, what's going on?" It was Patricia. I couldn't speak. I didn't even know if I was breathing.

I heard Rhonda's voice. "Give us a minute, please." Doors closed. My knuckles were white from grasping the side of the casket so tightly. I felt an arm around my shoulder and another around my waist, but I wasn't releasing my grip.

"If they close it, I'll never see her again. I'll never see her face again. I can't live without her. I just can't do it. The funeral, Tanya, Grandmother, Daddy, the people out there, I just can't do it!" I didn't recognize my own voice. "I know it doesn't make sense. I know she's gone." I drew a deep breath, hoping to clear my head, but it didn't help.

Rhonda said, "Baby, it's okay. It's all part of grieving."

"That doesn't make it easier."

Patricia said, "Honey, if she were here right now, you know she'd have something smartass to say, like 'Well, I can't just lie here forever.'"

As tears fell down my cheeks, I laughed; that was exactly what she'd say. "I'm being stupid."

"No, you're scared. Pam's always been here for you, but she's prepared you for this," Patricia said.

"She built the foundation for you to stand on, and that's a solid foundation. She'll always be with you. She's in that foundation, in your heart, and in your memories," Rhonda added.

I reached up, and Rhonda and Patricia raised their hands, too. We all closed the lid. I gave the casket one last glance over my shoulder as we walked out of the room.

"She's okay," Rhonda said to Spencer, who'd been waiting outside the door.

I didn't hear much during the funeral. We stood, and we bowed our heads for prayer. As "Amazing Grace" was sung, I looked to my left and saw my dad, his mother, and his sister, strangers to me. Then I looked to my right and saw Grandmother, Tanya, Brad, and Adam, people who were becoming strangers to me. My family would never be the same. I had no idea how much it was about to change.

At the graveside service, an announcement was made requesting that no one return to the house. But when I walked through the door with Grandmother, there was Daddy.

Chapter 14

"Why are you here?" I asked, half expecting Grandmother to say she'd invited him. But now she walked past him like she'd never met him. I was drained, but he didn't seem to be giving up.

His eyes followed Grandmother into the living room, where she sat on the couch. Patricia and Spencer stayed in the kitchen with me. Rhonda came back in to make some tea for Grandmother, who was exhausted—as we all were.

"I meant what I said before the funeral. I promised Pam I'd be here for you, and now I promise you that, too," he replied softly.

Spencer started to speak, but I didn't let him. "Can you mean it another time? I don't have the energy for this, and I've got to make even more decisions on what to do about Grandmother coming to live with me. My mind is racing, and this isn't helping right now," I said as calmly as I could.

"Hear him out," Rhonda said matter-of-factly before joining Grandmother on the couch.

I was stunned, but then I decided that since he wasn't going away, I'd have to deal with it.

"I don't want to involve Grandmother in this discussion or even let her hear us talking. Follow me," I commanded. "You, too," I said to

Patricia and Spencer. We moved to the dining room. Maybe I'd have an ally in Spencer. He knew about my father, and I hoped he'd be on my side.

Once we'd taken seats, I looked into Patricia and Daddy's faces. I wanted Rhonda to hear it all, too, so I got up and looked into the living room. Grandmother had fallen asleep, so I whispered to Rhonda to join us.

The four of them sat at the table, but I was too fidgety to sit, so I stood. After taking a deep breath and gathering my thoughts, I said, "This is a fine fix we're all in. The two of you knew Momma wanted to call him, and I understand you didn't say anything because of his unpredictability. There's something that I'm having a hard time with, though. If she called you two weeks ago, why did you wait until now to show? Did she die thinking you'd be here or not?"

Patricia jumped in. "What did she tell you?" she asked Daddy.

"Pam said Lizzy was a grown woman with thoughts and ideas of her own," he said. Turning to me, he continued, "She said you'd inherited the stubborn gene from the both of us and that she'd raised you to be independent, but she was worried about you. Growing up as an only child had its benefits, but it would also leave you very alone." Daddy's tone suggested that he knew more than he was saying. "You've only known your mother's side of the family, and this upset Pam."

"Okay, stop sugarcoating this, please. What in the world could bother her so badly that she had to call you in?" Before I could stop myself, I added, "You of all people?"

His face changed, and I knew we were about to get down to business. "Your grandmother has Alzheimer's and half the time doesn't know herself. That's a huge responsibility to take on. Then there's Tanya. She's been waiting for your mother to die so she and her pack of wolves can move in to pick the bones clean. Is that what you wanted to hear?"

"No, but at least we're getting somewhere now." I wasn't angry; I was ready for whatever he'd prepared himself to say. I didn't know how much he knew, and I wasn't sure I wanted him to know everything about our altercations over the silver, but I was sure he knew something. It was a small town, after all.

Indeed, he revealed that nothing is secret when you live in a small town. "I haven't asked about the silver yet, but I know Tanya wants to get her hands on it as soon as possible. She's telling everyone you've stolen it."

"Stolen it?" I laughed out loud. "Priceless! She's always had a flair for drama." I continued to laugh—it was all absurd, and I was too tired to do anything else. At that moment, a car in the driveway caught my eye. Tanya. As she climbed out of the car, she reminded me of the Wicked Witch from *The Wizard of Oz*.

I didn't want her to wake Grandmother, so I rushed to the door. As I opened it, I asked, "Are you here to get me and my little dog, too?"

She looked at me very strangely. I heard snickering from the dining room. "Just come in," I said to her, irritated. She was always so serious. I pointed her toward the dining room.

"We were just talking about you. I'm so glad you're here," I said sarcastically. I could feel myself entering attack mode. "It seems you've been a busy little bee, and we need to get some things straight."

She was walking in front of me, so when she stopped I almost ran into her. "What are you talking about?" she asked. The shock and fear on her face caught me off guard.

"Have a seat, and I'll bring you up to speed," I said, pointing to a chair. We stood eye to eye for a moment; then she slowly sat down.

When she saw Daddy, she huffed under her breath. "What are you stirring up now?" she asked belligerently.

"Please sit, and all will be revealed," I said. Before, I'd wanted to stand, but now I wanted to be eye to eye with Tanya. *Poor Spencer—he didn't know he was in for all this,* I thought. "There are rules in this house. Rule number one is that you'll keep your voice down so as not to wake or upset Grandmother. Understand?" I waited for her to nod. "Rule number two: you will listen to what is being said and wait your turn. I won't have you coming in here and trying to overpower me. I promise you, today is really not the day for that. Understand?" Again, I waited for her to nod. The look on her face was one of bewilderment.

"Okay, then I guess we'll jump right into it," I said, clasping my hands and placing them on the table. "Are you telling people that I stole the silver from you?"

"You did steal it!" she said loudly.

I squeezed my hands, trying to stay calm. "Refer to rule number one, and keep your voice down. I'm not playing with you, Tanya."

Her voice came back so soft and innocent that everyone at the table looked at her. "Lizzy, it's been a trying day for all of us. I'm really not here to fight with you over material things. I'm here to help you."

"What in the world could you help me with?"

"Mother, of course. I know you're probably exhausted. I didn't know you were going to have a house full of people. I wanted to take Mother home with me tonight so you could get some rest." Who was this person sitting in my house, talking about helping me?

"Do you think that's a good idea?" Rhonda asked.

Without hiding her distaste, Tanya snapped, "This doesn't concern you."

"Hold up," I said to them both. Rhonda was getting ready to throttle Tanya. Everyone was uneasy, shifting in their chairs. "Tanya, I'm afraid I have to agree with Rhonda. I don't think your house is suited for Grandmother. She could fall on your stairs."

Trying to regain her composure, Tanya said, "I set up a room for her downstairs. She wouldn't even need to go to the second floor."

"She may not need to, but that doesn't mean she won't. And doesn't that room have doors leading to the outside? She could wander off. This really isn't a good idea at all," I said.

Tanya, still speaking sweetly said, "I wouldn't let her. I promise I'll keep a good eye on her."

"How can you do that, Tanya? Brad didn't even want you to visit your dying sister, but now he's agreeing to having your mother, who has Alzheimer's, come and stay overnight? I find all this hard to believe." I was getting the same feeling I'd had the day she mentioned the silver. Something just wasn't right. "What is it you really want?"

"Nothing! I know I've misbehaved, and I just want to give you a night of peace. There she is!" I hadn't heard Grandmother come into the room, and now Tanya was rushing over to her. We all watched in amazement as Tanya hugged her and helped her over to the table.

Spencer leaned over and asked me, "What's going on?"

"I don't know yet," I said. "Don't take anything the way you're seeing it. She's always up to something."

Tanya gushed, "We were just talking about your coming and staying the night at my house, Mother. Would you like that?"

"Is Lizzy coming, too?" she asked, her face still looking sleepy. She looked like she'd aged a hundred years since all this started.

"No, you'd come home with me, and Lizzy would stay here." Tanya spoke in a very sappy voice.

"Tanya, I don't think I can come tonight. Who would stay with Lizzy?" Grandmother was looking past Tanya at me now, her face full of concern.

"Nothing has been decided, Grandmother. It was just an idea Tanya had. You don't have to go," I said, reaching out to touch her hand.

For some reason, she turned to Daddy. "Do you think I should go and leave Lizzy alone?"

"No, ma'am," he replied. "I think you're just fine here."

"Mother, it's only for the night. It's already after lunch, so you wouldn't even be gone a whole day," Tanya pleaded.

"Do you want me to go?" Grandmother asked me. She was getting upset.

The look on her face broke my heart. "I want you here with me, but if you want to go, I'll look forward to your coming back, and I'll miss you." I knew Grandmother couldn't make this decision, but I wanted Tanya to see that she didn't want to go—that way she couldn't claim I was keeping her hostage. There was no way she was going to stay overnight with Tanya and Brad. The knot in my stomach grew bigger with every breath. I'd have to get guardianship of Grandmother first thing Monday morning. I'd call Mr. Simmons when everyone was gone. "Do you want to go?"

"No. Can I stay with you?"

"Of course!" I said. Then I turned to Tanya. "She's staying here. End of discussion." Tanya's face hardened; once again she was the Tanya we all knew and loved to hate.

"You can't hold her here!" she said loudly.

Ignoring Tanya's outburst, I asked Grandmother, "Would you like something to drink?" I wanted to get her out of the room as quickly as possible. Tanya was about to blow a gasket.

"No. I need to go to the bathroom."

Rhonda jumped up. "Let me help you, Ms. Grace." We all waited quietly for Grandmother to leave the room.

Tanya spoke first. "Like I said, you can't hold her here."

"She's not 'holding' her; we were all here to witness that!" Patricia said, then added, "And don't say this isn't my concern. I'm a witness now."

"Tanya, I don't think you're ready to take her with you because I didn't see you offering to help her," I said calmly.

She replied snidely, "I believe she can get to the bathroom by herself."

"Actually, she can't, unless you want to clean her up when she doesn't make it."

She raised her voice. "It's only because you and Pam made her so needy!"

"These walls aren't soundproof, so please don't yell. I'm sorry she didn't want to go with you." What I was thinking was, *I'm glad she doesn't want to go with you.*

"Well, I want you to remember that she's my mother!" She was so angry she was shaking.

"I'm not doing this with you. She's a human being, and you'd be a lot better off if you'd stop viewing everything as a possession—yours or mine." I wanted this to stop; I wanted to rest for a while. Getting out of my funeral clothes, lying on the couch, falling asleep with Grandmother—it was now a distant dream.

"Tanya, I think we should give Lizzy a few days to take everything in," Daddy said.

She spun around wordlessly and slammed her way out the door. I heard her car engine revving; then we heard spinning tires and spitting gravel. Again I envisioned the Wicked Witch of the West flying off on her broom with flying monkeys following behind her.

I knew Patricia wouldn't be able to hold her tongue for long. "Who does she think she is?" she spat.

Daddy answered, "Somebody special, I promise you." We all laughed.

I said, "Honestly, though, my anger toward her has really kept me going."

Spencer looked concerned. "What do you think she's up to, asking your Grandmother to come and stay with her?"

"That's a good question. I need to get in touch with Mr. Simmons so we can transfer guardianship on Monday."

"I wish you could do that today—this is leading to something. I can feel it," Patricia said. I was glad I wasn't the only one feeling this.

Daddy pushed his chair away from the table. "Is there anything you need?"

"No." My answer was directed more toward Daddy himself than his immediate question. He didn't linger long after telling me he'd be in touch.

Patricia and Spencer headed back to Patricia's; Spencer wanted to get his truck. "I'll come back after you've had some time to rest."

"That sounds good. I feel like I haven't had time to talk to you," I said.

Rhonda fixed plates for Grandmother and me and left them on the stove before going home herself. After Grandmother ate, we sat on the couch and watched TV until she drifted off to sleep. I closed my eyes, too, forgetting everything else.

Chapter 15

Grandmother's movement woke me up, and I had a few moments of confusion. The sun had set, and I didn't know how long we'd been sleeping. Grandmother was used to sleeping on the couch or in a chair in front of the television and then getting up and going to bed. She'd put a blanket over me. When I woke up, she said she was going to bed. I got up to help her, despite her protests.

I helped her find her pajamas and then went into the bathroom to get her pillbox out of my secret hiding place. If left on her own, she'd either take too many or forget to take them at all, so I kept them separated and gave them to her at the appropriate times. Doing this made me think about the care she was going to need. When I returned to her room, I saw that her pajama pants were on backward, and her shirt was buttoned wrong. After handing her the pills and the cup of water, I began working on the buttons.

"I'm glad I didn't have to go to Tanya's. She's such a damn pain in the ass!" Grandmother said. She spoke with such conviction that I laughed out loud. I was still caught off guard when she cursed. She would have gotten my behind for saying such a thing, but she said it without compunction.

"Well, you don't worry about that; you're here." I really needed to get in touch with Mr. Simmons; I'd call him once she was in bed. "Let's just get you tucked in. Don't worry about anything tonight, okay?" She nodded, set the water down, and headed for bed.

I turned the light off but stood at the doorway for a while, listening. When I heard her usual small snore, I knew she was asleep. I closed the door but then stood outside for a moment, wondering how I'd know if she got up. I found a box of Christmas decorations in the closet and took out several things with bells. I attached one to her bedroom door and one each on the front and back doors. I decided I'd sleep on the couch just in case.

I wasn't much of a drinker, but after today, I felt I could use a stiff drink. I rummaged through Momma's cabinets until I found some vodka. After mixing it with some orange juice, I sat on the couch and listened to the eleven voice messages that had been left since I'd turned the phone ringers off. Most people had voicemail on their phones, but Momma still had an old answering machine. There were calls from Patricia and Rhonda, from several community members checking to be sure we had food, and from Mr. Simmons, letting me know he'd be up until eleven if I needed anything. "Was he psychic?" I said out loud. It was right at nine, so I decided to give him a call.

After a couple of rings, he picked up. "Mr. Simmons, it's Lizzy. Am I disturbing you?"

"Not at all, Lizzy. I half expected you to call. How's Grace?"

"I've just gotten her to bed, and she's holding up pretty well. The Alzheimer's keeps her from remembering a lot of what's happened. In a way, I wish I had it, too. She's actually why I'm calling you. I need to know what I can do about Momma's guardianship."

"Have you spoken with Tanya? I know things are strained, but in the eyes of the law, you and she are now equals. You've taken your mother's place, with her rights."

"She was here earlier, and it was kind of strange. She wanted Grandmother to spend the night with her, saying she wanted to help me out." It still sounded strange when I said it.

"That is very strange. Why do you think she'd do that? It can't be that simple," he said.

"I didn't think so, either, but I left it up to Grandmother. She got upset and told Tanya she didn't want to go, so she's here with me."

"Well, I think until we get everything figured out, she shouldn't go with Tanya. I don't like the sound of this, so hold her off until I can go to the courthouse on Monday and work on the paperwork. We also need to get together on Monday to discuss the estate and the will. Even though you know everything in it, your mother left some instructions with me to pass on to you. But let's not get into that tonight. I think you need some rest. You've been a trooper through all this, Lizzy, and the funeral was beautiful. Pam would have been proud."

I laughed. "She should be: she planned all of it the week before she went into the coma."

He laughed, too. "Are you kidding me? That woman, I swear!"

"Tell me about it. While we were picking out the casket, she wanted to know if I liked this one or that one, and of course I had to be a butt and tell her I didn't like any of them." She'd laughed at me and told me to behave my silly self, but I didn't tell him that.

"She knew it was hard on you. It was hard on her, too, having to let go of you, so let's not worry about anything else right now. There's time for all that next week. You just get some rest tonight and tomorrow, and I'll be in touch on Monday." His voice was sad now. We said our good-byes and hung up.

After checking in with Patricia and Rhonda, I got another drink and then wandered around the house. I looked at all my mother's "worldly possessions," as the will called them, remembering when she'd bought this or who had given her that. During one of our talks, she'd made me promise to buy a house. "I want you to have a place that's yours, that no one can take away from you. You'll have enough in life insurance for a sizable down payment, but don't use it all. I want you to have a little money in the bank, too." Since I was going to get all her belongings, then yes, I would need a house. Her lifetime of memories would never fit into my apartment, and now there was Grandmother to consider, too.

"Oh, Momma, how am I ever going to do this without you?" I said out loud. "It's not supposed to be this way." Then I glimpsed someone in the window—I startled so violently that I dropped my glass.

"Lizzy! Lizzy! It's just us!" The man's voice was muffled behind the window; as he spoke, another face appeared out of the darkness. Spencer had returned, and Kay was with him. I ran to greet them.

On the porch, I hugged Kay. "I totally forgot you were coming tonight."

"I'm sorry I couldn't get here earlier, but I've been covering the ER," she said.

"You?" I laughed.

"Yes, me! I won't even tell you what you owe me for this."

Every time she said I owed her, my debt was always repaid with a drink. Beating her to the punch, I said, "Well, come inside, and I'll fix you a drink."

"Now you're talking."

I told them that Grandmother was sleeping and said we couldn't be too loud. After we went inside, I cleaned up the drink I'd spilled on the floor and joined them in the dining room. I set the vodka and orange juice on the table. Kay poked fun at me when she saw the three glasses of ice. "Why, Ms. Lizzy, you sharing a drink tonight, too?"

Spencer said, "After what's been happening here, hell—she deserves to drink the whole bottle."

I laughed. "Or have it piped in through an IV!"

"I don't want to darken the mood, Liz, but be serious for a minute. You holding up okay?" Kay asked.

"Honestly, it depends on the moment. But it will get better."

"Spence told me about this chick Tanya. As if you didn't have enough to worry about with your Grandmother! I take it she'll be coming to live with you?"

"Well, I can't let Tanya take her, but the attorney is working on that."

She smiled. "Guess I'll find me another designated driver."

We all laughed again.

She lifted her glass and said, "To Lizzy's momma."

Spencer lifted his and repeated, "To Lizzy's momma."

I'd always thought Spencer and Kay should be together, but neither would have it. Tonight I was just glad they were together for me. We shared a lot of laughs about what had been going on at work while I was gone. Kay could make me laugh in the middle of a tornado.

Because I was such a lightweight when it came to alcohol, I felt the effects early. I invited them both to stay before crashing on the couch.

Bright and early the next day, the doorbell rang. I jumped up, thinking it was the Christmas bells I'd put on the doors, but then I heard it again. When I got up, I saw Spencer on the floor and Kay on the loveseat.

"Don't people around here sleep in?" Kay grumbled, rubbing her eyes and looking at her watch. "It's not even seven in the morning."

"I have no idea who that is, but before they ring the bell again, please answer it," I said, bolting out of the room to check on Grandmother. She was still sleeping. I pulled her door closed and headed back to the living room.

"I'm not a 'you people.' I'm a friend of Lizzy's. Who exactly are you?" I heard Kay asking.

"I'm Lizzy's aunt," Tanya said sternly, pushing her way in. "Lizzy, what in the world is going on around here? What did you do, have a party last night?" she demanded.

Ignoring her accusation, I said, "What are you doing here so early? And please keep your voice down. Grandmother is still sleeping."

"Well, she needs to get up, because I'm moving her out of here today," Tanya said. She headed toward the hall.

I put my hands up and stopped her in her tracks. "What do you mean, you're moving her out of here today? Where do you think she's going?"

"Home!"

"I'm sorry, I must have still been sleeping. Did you say 'home'? Home as in her house, or home with you?" I positioned myself in front of her. Kay and Spencer stood together behind her. From the window I could see a truck backed up to the front door; Brad was standing beside it.

"To her house, her home," she said, putting her hand on my shoulder to move me out of her way.

"Get your hands off her!" Kay said, grabbing at Tanya's arm.

Spinning around, Tanya said angrily, "I recommend you take your hands off me."

Spencer's face was red with anger. "Haven't you caused enough trouble?"

I nodded to Kay, who let go of Tanya's arm.

"Do I—" Tanya peered at Spencer. "I remember you from the funeral home. We're not related, so I don't owe you any explanation."

Before she could push too many of Spencer's buttons, I said, "Tanya, what are you doing? Grandmother cannot be by herself. She needs looking after all the time."

"That's just something you and Pam came up with. She'll be fine." Again Tanya reached up to move me out of the way, but this time I grabbed her arm.

Holding her firmly, I said, "We did not make it up. Your mother suffers from Alzheimer's; that's a medical fact. You are not taking her home to dump her off because you're mad at me. Isn't that what this is about?"

"Lizzy, you're hurting me!" Tanya said in a high-pitched voice. I knew she was in pain.

"And I'm going to keep hurting you if you continue with this. Do we understand each other?" I was so angry that I didn't see a high road. There was no diffusing this, because today she'd gone too far. I heard the bells on the front door chiming, and soon Brad appeared. "Get out of my house!" I shouted. He saw the pain in Tanya's face and backed up.

"Lizzy, you're out of control. Let go of her!" he pleaded.

"She's not out of control, you two are. She told you to get out," Spencer said, stepping between Brad and me. Everything was happening so fast; I didn't want anything to happen that I would regret later for myself or for Spencer.

"Kay, there's a number beside the phone. Please go call it and ask Michael to come here right now." I was glad I'd left it there the night he came with Tanya to look for the silver. I needed him here, and five minutes ago wasn't fast enough. My anger was boiling, and I truly wanted to hurt Tanya.

"I'm not leaving her in here with you, Lizzy," Brad said defiantly.

I grabbed Tanya's arm so hard that she yelped. "Last chance, Tanya. Get him out of here. His voice is grating on my last nerve."

"Brad, just go outside," Tanya whimpered, and with that, he left. Spencer shut the door behind him. I eased up on Tanya's arm a little.

"He cares so much for you that he sees me physically hurting you and he walks out. Leaves you in here alone. That's true love right there. You two are some sick bastards." I was still in her face, saying anything that might hurt her.

Kay came back to say that Michael was on his way. "He told me to tell you not to hurt her, that he'd be right here with backup." I heard faint sirens in the background. Michael didn't live very far away, so I knew it wouldn't be long. I just had to hold on till he got there. I eased my grip on Tanya a little more, half expecting her to slap me. But she stood stiffly and watched me. I saw fear in her eyes.

"Did you think you'd walk in here this morning and just remove my grandmother without a fight, Tanya? Where have you been the last ten months, while her mind and my mother's health deteriorated? I don't know who you think you're dealing with here. What did you think was going to happen?" The questions flew out of my mouth, but Tanya said nothing. "I know you're mad at me over the silver. Honestly, if you'd just backed off, I would have given it to you, but you came in here this morning and—just forget it! You'll never get it, will you?" I let go of her now, and she ran out the front door.

"Are you alright?" Kay asked.

"No, I'm losing control," I said softly. *I'm angry,* I thought, *and it's been one thing right after another, but I'm supposed to remain calm. What a joke.*

"Michael's in the driveway," Kay announced.

Without moving, I said, "Let Tanya tell him what I did, and y'all will be bailing me out for attempted murder."

"But Lizzy, she came in here—"

"Doesn't matter," I told her. "Just let Tanya do her thing. I'm going to check on Grandmother again." Someone was watching over me that day, because she was still sleeping, which meant she was going to have a good day.

When I came back into the living room, Kay and Spencer looked at me in horror. Michael was there, and he had the same look. "Am I going to jail?" I asked.

Michael stepped forward. "Lizzy," he said so softly I almost didn't hear him.

"Michael, do what you have to do. Just please let me make arrangements for Grandmother first, okay?"

"She has papers."

"What papers?" I asked.

"She got guardianship of your grandmother." He was still speaking softly.

"I know I heard you wrong. Who got guardianship?"

"Tanya went Friday morning and got guardianship of her mother," he said.

I stood there for a moment, looking at each of their faces. Then a calendar started rolling in reverse in my head. Last night, Spencer and Kay showed up. Yesterday, Daddy came here after the funeral. Before that, we were at the graveside and funeral. Friday night, we were at the wake. Friday at lunchtime, we were calling people about Momma's death. And Friday morning, Momma was dying. That meant that when I called Tanya, she wasn't going to work like she said—instead, she went to the courthouse. She didn't want to be here for her sister's final breaths. She wanted to take control of Grandmother.

"Did you say Friday morning?"

"Yes," he replied. Michael knew what had been happening Friday morning.

I heard the bells on the door again, but it wasn't Tanya; it was Patricia and Rhonda. They stopped dead in their tracks and looked at me from the doorway.

Without looking at them, I said, "While Momma was dying, Tanya was getting guardianship of Grandmother—I'd told her that when Momma died the silver would go back to Grandmother."

"Michael, can she do that?" Patricia demanded.

"I'm afraid she did," he answered. "Lizzy, she has every right to take your grandmother."

"I'm calling Bill Simmons," Rhonda said, running to the phone.

We all stood in silence. Our silence was broken by the sound of bells in the hallway. "It's Grandmother," I said.

"Baby, are you okay?" she asked. She must have seen the distress on my face.

"Yes, ma'am." I tried to pull myself together. "We have some company this morning. Why don't we get you dressed?"

"Lizzy, you stay here. I'll get her dressed and try to keep her out of this for as long as I can," Patricia said.

"Thank you. Turn on her TV so she can't hear this, okay?"

Once they were out of sight, I sprinted outside and confronted Tanya and Brad in the front yard.

"You are an evil person!" I screamed at Tanya.

"*You* assault *me* and *I'm* evil?" Her confidence had returned. Brad stepped in front of her.

"How about we make a trade?" I asked. "You go with me in the morning to the courthouse and sign over guardianship of Grandmother to me, and we'll stop at the bank for the silver. Sound good?" I hadn't meant to reveal where the silver was, but I couldn't stop myself.

She stopped and considered this for a moment. By this time, everyone had made their way onto the porch. "She's considering an offer," I explained to them.

"One more thing. Once you get the silver, you never get to contact either Grandmother or me again," I continued.

Tanya and Brad started whispering to each other. Then Tanya said, "No, there are things of mother's that are rightfully mine as her only living daughter."

"Oh my God. You've got to be kidding me! Now you're looking forward to Grandmother's death, too!" I was shocked and infuriated. "You may not know this, but in the eyes of the law, you and I are equal now, fifty-fifty partners, so I'll sweeten the pot for you. The silver and whatever of Grandmother's you want from her house for guardianship of Grandmother."

Again, she and Brad put their heads together and discussed my offer. I continued, "Just think, no doctors' visits, no medication refills, no meals. I'll take full responsibility."

"No," Tanya said. "Brad thinks there's something you're holding out for that you and Pam may have known about."

"Like what?"

"We don't know, but there's a reason you want guardianship," she replied.

"Yeah, actually there is—it's called her well-being. Love and care that she won't get from the two of you. It has nothing to do with monetary gain."

"Where is her money, anyway?" Brad asked.

"What money?" I asked.

"She gets money every month. Where is it?"

"You mean the little Medicare and retirement checks she gets? Those go into her account to pay for medication and doctors. Momma took care of all her other needs, such as food and clothing, because those little checks don't cover everything."

"She has to make more than that!" Tanya said, astonished to find out that her mother wouldn't be able to make it on her own.

"I bet she does, and they've been taking it from her," Brad said.

I snapped. I lunged forward, and Michael grabbed me around the waist while I fought tooth and nail to get my hands on either Tanya or Brad.

Tanya started screaming, "No more dealing! I'm done with this! Get her out of the way and let me get my mother and her things."

"You can't take her back to her house. She can't stay by herself, you stupid bitch!" I was still fighting to get free, but we were on the move. Before I knew it, I was in the back of Michael's patrol car.

"Take a breather, Lizzy. She could still file charges against you. I'll call Chief Brown," he said through the glass, pulling his radio from his belt.

Rhonda, Spencer, and Kay pestered Michael to open the door; I sat watching helplessly as things were removed from the house. Then Patricia yelled from the door, "Michael, they're removing things that belong to Pam!"

Immediately Michael opened the door, and we all ran to the truck. We found numerous things that belonged to Momma. Tanya said she thought they belonged to Grandmother. About that time, the chief of police, Irwin Brown, drove up. Tanya and I were going at each other verbally.

"Stop, you two! Stop, I said!" He stepped between us. He looked around and surveyed the stuff lying on the ground that I'd gotten from the truck. Michael explained why I was out of the car.

"Tanya, your sister has not been dead forty-eight hours. Did you really need to start this today?" he asked her.

"I'm due what's rightfully mine," she said, shoving the court papers in his face.

"I suggest you take a better tone with me, ma'am," he replied, looking past the papers. She withdrew her hand a bit, and he took the papers. After looking them over, he looked at me.

"Lizzy, we have to make sure these orders are carried out, as tacky as I think it is," he said, glaring at Tanya. "But with that said, we won't stand by and let you steal Pam's things from Lizzy, either. I've been in this house enough to know that several of these items you've removed from the home are Pam's. You were her sister and should know this yourself. Michael, go in the house with Lizzy and let her tell you what goes and what stays. Where's your grandmother?" he asked, looking at me now.

"Patricia has her in the house. I've been out here," I snapped. I then realized he wasn't happy with my tone, so I lowered my voice and added, "Sir."

"I want you to go and check on her, and if you can, please bring her out here with a chair."

"Yes, sir." When I went inside, I found Grandmother at the table with Patricia. She was crying.

"Grandmother, what's wrong?" I said softly, rubbing her shoulders.

"Tanya says I can't stay here. I don't want to go with her, Lizzy. I don't want to go." She was crying harder now and grabbing my shirt. I didn't say anything to soothe her; I wanted Chief Brown to see her distress.

"Come with me." I helped her up and asked Patricia to bring a chair. When we got outside, Grandmother immediately began saying she didn't want to go. The chief looked pained as he tried explaining it to her. I couldn't watch. I went back in the house to point out what they could take. I took the medicine from my hiding place and set it next to her toothbrush in the bathroom, and then I went out the back door.

Michael sent Kay and Spencer to console me while he went into the house to oversee the move. I didn't know what was going on with Grandmother and the chief, but I could hear her sobbing. I sent Kay to get her one of the pills she'd been prescribed for the funeral. By the time everything was loaded into the truck, Grandmother was sleeping in the cab.

I was told when they were ready to go, and I asked to see Grandmother again. Of course, Tanya and Brad just wanted to leave, but the chief made them back off and give me a moment.

I crawled in next to her, putting my arm around her and letting her head slide onto my shoulder. I was trying very hard to hold it together in case she woke up. I rested my head on top of hers.

"I'm so sorry. I thought I could prevent this from happening, but I couldn't. I'll check on you once they've gone home. I'm just hoping you won't remember any of this ugliness. I love you so much!" I felt her sigh. I carefully eased my arm from around her shoulder and got out of the truck.

Tanya, Brad, and I said nothing to one another, and everyone was silent as we watched them get into the truck. Watching them pull away, I was overcome with grief. This was my fault. I ran into the house and down the hall to Grandmother's room. Nothing was left but indentations in the carpet where her furniture had been: her recliner, television, dresser, bed, and my grandfather's rocking chair, all gone. Looking in her bathroom, I saw her pillbox. The toothbrush was gone, but they'd left her pills. As I touched the pillbox, a tear rolled down my cheek. "Oh, Grandmother, this is all because of me," I said.

Chapter 16

I walked slowly to the living room, trying not to faint. Holding the pillbox, I looked up slowly and saw horror in everyone's eyes. Only Rhonda and Patricia knew what I was holding. They ran to my side.

"Lizzy, baby, you don't look good. You're pale as a ghost," Patricia said, grasping my elbow. "Let's sit you down on the couch."

I felt myself moving, but it was like I was floating. I didn't feel my legs or my feet; then I was sitting. Softly I said, "They didn't even take her pills. They think she's worth something to them. They didn't even take her pills." I was holding the box like an egg.

Rhonda took it from my hands. "We'll get them to her. Don't you worry."

"But why?" I pleaded. "Why would they do this? They asked about her checks and talked about wanting things from her house." I was shaking. Patricia's arms closed in tighter around me. "What do I do? Are they really going to take her to her house and just leave her?"

"Michael, will you please go see if they are at the house?" Patricia asked.

"Chief is following them. I'll find out what location they're going to," Michael replied, heading for the door.

"Let's see what Michael finds out first, okay? Tanya may have just wanted to hurt you by saying she was taking Grace home," said Rhonda.

"Do you really think she wants that responsibility?" My voice was cold. No one responded.

My mind was racing so much that my head hurt. The silence in the room was too loud. "I know they won't stay with her. I'll just go up there once they're gone," I said.

The bells on the front door chimed as Michael entered. "They've taken her to her house on Second Street."

"Lizzy, is there anything we can do for you?" Spencer asked. I'd forgotten he and Kay were here.

"No, but thank you. This is just something else I have to deal with. I appreciate you both coming, and I'm sorry you've gotten involved in this mess."

"We don't want to hear that noise!" Kay said. "We wouldn't have believed you if we hadn't witnessed the Wicked Witch of the West with our own eyes." She was attempting to cheer me up, and she did make me smile.

"I don't know what's going to happen, but I do know I have to go to Grandmother's. Are you going to stay here, or do you need to get back?" I was praying they'd go; I needed to focus on Grandmother, and I was truly embarrassed by what they'd witnessed.

"We have to get back to work, but we'll stay if you need us to," Spencer replied.

"No, I understand. Maybe it's for the best, with all that's going on."

"Lizzy, don't you let this get the better of you," Kay said, giving me a hug. "Would it be okay for us to let our boss know what's going on? I don't want to say anything that you don't want known."

"Yes, please, tell her I'll be in touch soon. I just don't know what's going to happen now."

Spencer joined our hug. It was hard to hold it together. They made it easier on me by not saying anything else and just leaving. Michael left with them to guide them to the interstate. For a few minutes, everyone was silent, wrapping our heads around what Tanya had done.

Finally I said, "Alright, some decisions need to be made quickly. I need to get in touch with Mr. Simmons to find out what I can do." I felt like a failure. *I should have taken care of this*, I thought.

Patricia said, "Lizzy, he's been called and is waiting to find out what he can do about the court papers. I'll call back and see if he has an update."

Rhonda took my hands. She must have seen the terror in my eyes. I wanted to jump in the car and go straight to Grandmother's, but I knew as long as Tanya was there, it would be useless. I'd have to wait until they were gone.

Patricia quickly returned. "Bill said he'll call Judge Culpepper and try to get an emergency hearing."

"Culpepper?" The name was familiar to me; Grandmother's neighbor and best friend's last name was Culpepper. *Could I be that lucky?*

"Yes, that's who you're thinking of." I was relieved to hear that Judge Culpepper was Mrs. Culpepper's son.

Time seemed to move at a snail's pace as we waited to go to Grandmother's. When I couldn't stand it anymore, I said, "Let's go!"

Pulling up to the house, I was flooded with emotion. I remembered growing up in this house, playing in this yard—it had always been a safe haven. After my parents' divorce, Momma and my grandparents had shared the parenting. My grandparents were always supportive of Momma and never once turned me away. After the divorce, Momma made the difficult decision to return to school to get a degree that would support both of us. I stayed with my grandparents for two years and visited Momma on weekends. Once she graduated from nursing school, Momma's career took off. She quickly worked her way up the ladder to a nurse supervisor position, taking on more responsibility but still doing a wonderful job juggling motherhood and her job. As a little girl, I never noticed her absence; no one ever missed any important events in my life. If I had a recital or a play, Momma and my grandparents were there.

My grandfather stepped in for my father, serving as a male role model for me until his death. His death hit me hard. I gave Momma and Grandmother a hard time after that, becoming very rebellious and trying their patience, but I never heard either of them complain. I regretted the time I wasted being such a shit; I knew now that after Grandfather's death, Grandmother needed me as much as I needed her. Grandfather had been her one true love, and having me around helped ease her loneliness. On the days that I wasn't plotting how to defy her discipline, Grandmother would talk to me about missing him. He was the person she'd called out for when Momma died.

Now that Momma was gone, was I trying to lean on my grandmother? I'd been her distraction when Grandfather died, and now I was looking for that distraction as well. We were traveling full circle.

"Are you okay?" Rhonda tapped on the car window.

"Yes, sorry," I said, getting out of the car. "Just taking a moment."

As the three of us approached the front door, my heart pounded in my chest. Pulling the screen door open, I saw a deadbolt that hadn't been there before. I could see inside the kitchen, but I didn't see Grandmother. I tried the door—it was locked. We all headed for the back door, and again we found a new deadbolt—also locked. I could see into the back of the house, and I could see Grandmother pulling boxes out of a closet. I started to knock and stopped.

"What if she can't open the door?" I whispered, as if we were trying to break in. I strained to get a better look at the deadbolt. It was a double-sided lock. She'd have to have the key to open it. Running down the porch steps, I went back to the front door and found a window I could see in. The same kind of lock was on that door, too. Then I caught sight of the stove—and panicked.

"That stove has to be moved to be unplugged—and it hasn't been," I said. "Tanya hasn't taken Grandmother's condition seriously. She could set the house on fire and not even know it!" I tried the door again, as if my words could magically open it. Then Grandmother appeared in the kitchen. She tried the door from the inside and talked to me, but I couldn't understand her through the glass. My one-time safe haven had now become my grandmother's cage.

Tapping on the glass, I got Grandmother's attention. "Grandmother, Grandmother, I need you to feel on top of the refrigerator for the key." As she turned to do that, I barked at Patricia and Rhonda, "Get Tanya here!" Both scrambled for their cell phones. She must have been home because I could hear them arguing with her, but my focus was on Grandmother. When she didn't find a key at the edge of the refrigerator's top, she went to get a chair. "Grandmother, don't get on that chair! Stop!" I was screaming uncontrollably. Again, she was talking, but I couldn't understand her, and she left the kitchen with the chair.

When Rhonda returned to the porch, I shouted, "Start trying the windows!" I didn't know where Grandmother was going with that chair, but I suspected she was going to try to use it to remove the boxes from the hall closet. Why had I put this thought in her head?

Patricia joined us in the search for an unlocked window. "She's mad as hell, but she's on her way!"

"Let her be mad!" was all I said. We worked furiously to find a window we could get in. Tanya wouldn't arrive for ten or fifteen minutes, and I was hoping to be inside well before that. After checking all the windows we could reach, we were still stuck outside. I went to the back door to see if I could see Grandmother. Just as I'd feared, she was standing on the chair in front of the closet.

"Damn!" I said, trying the door again.

"She seems to be just looking in the boxes, so let's wait," Rhonda said. "I'm afraid if we distract her, she'll fall." Rhonda said. The three of us watched as she continued to pull papers out, read them, and then throw them on the floor. We all held our breath, praying she wouldn't step off the chair.

My mind raced back in time. Years ago, this was the behavior that had given her away. During my frequent visits home, almost every other weekend, Grandmother repeatedly asked me about her mortgage papers. I told Momma about it, and at first she blamed it on age; since Momma visited with her almost every day, Grandmother's condition was less apparent to her. Tanya visited less than I did, and she got angry with Grandmother for asking the same questions over and over again. This gave Tanya an excuse to visit even less; she said she just wished Grandmother would snap out of it.

Finally, on one of my visits, I left Grandmother's house and went to Momma's work. "There's something wrong with Grandmother," I announced.

This freaked Momma out. She jumped up from her desk. "What's wrong?!"

"No, not physically, mentally! Calm down!"

"Lizzy," she said, easing herself back into her chair and sighing with relief, "she's getting older, and she may have the beginnings of dementia."

"That's fine, but there's something more to this. She's not herself."

"Well, who is she?" she asked with a laugh.

"I don't know, but she's just not herself, and I need you to be serious with me."

She saw my concern. "Tell me what you see."

"Papers everywhere. She's looking for a mortgage payment on a house that's been paid off for years. I looked in her checkbook—did you know she's paid the gas bill three times this month?" Momma was listening now, and I wanted to tell her everything as quickly as possible before we were interrupted. Momma's office was always busy. "The dishes in the clean dish drainer are dirty, and several of the handles are melted. Something is very wrong." Grandmother had always been a very meticulous woman, and now her house and life were a mess.

After that conversation, Momma took Grandmother to the doctor, and she was diagnosed with Alzheimer's. Momma felt guilty about not recognizing it herself, and Tanya never came to terms with it—even now. If she had, Tanya would never have locked Grandmother inside her house like this.

I saw movement at the front of the house—Tanya and Brad. I could hear Tanya's voice as she started yelling at Grandmother. The three of us bolted to the front door.

Chapter 17

Inside the house was chaos. Patricia and Rhonda shouted at Tanya to stop yelling; I shoved Brad out of the way to get to Grandmother. She was trying to get off the chair as Tanya was yelling at her, and, just as I reached her, she started to fall. I was able to grab her just in time, and Patricia and Rhonda rushed in to help steady me.

"Look at this mess! What are you doing?" Tanya yelled. It never occurred to her that Grandmother might break a hip if she fell.

Once I had Grandmother on both feet, I looked at Brad. "Make yourself useful. Please help Grandmother to her recliner." For once he didn't argue. "You and I need to talk outside," I said to Tanya.

Without waiting for a response, I started for the front door. Patricia and Rhonda stood behind Tanya when she stepped onto the porch. I somehow managed to speak to Tanya in a calm voice. "Is this your plan?"

"You're just here to make trouble!" she snapped.

"No, actually, I'm here to help you. We need to work this out."

"I have guardianship, and there's nothing to work out. She was excited about being back in her house."

"I'm sure she was, but you locked her in—which means you've accepted that something is wrong with her, right?"

"I just didn't want someone to break in," Tanya replied.

"Then why double-sided locks? Did you leave her a key?"

"There's no need for that."

"Alright. Then can you and I work together on making this a safe place for her?" I asked, remaining calm even though I wanted to scream. I had to do this for Grandmother, and screaming at Tanya for being such a bitch was not going to help.

"What are you up to, Lizzy?"

"Nothing. I just want what's best for her. If you want guardianship of Grandmother, then let me help make that easier for you."

Tanya pondered my statement for a moment. "What do you suggest?"

Though I didn't yet know what Judge Culpepper would say, I had to do something while Tanya was here. If nothing else, maybe I could show Tanya how much work this was going to be for her and she'd agree to let me take Grandmother with me.

For several hours, we all worked together to make Grandmother's house a safe haven and not a prison. I let Tanya know that she wouldn't be able to plan or cook her own meals, and I made sure to unplug the stove. We'd have to replace the coffee pot with one that had an automatic shutoff and an unbreakable carafe. We put everything from the top of the closets at the bottom; if she wanted to search boxes, she wouldn't have to climb on furniture to get to them. Mrs. Culpepper, Grandmother's neighbor and friend, agreed to take a key so she could get in. She expressed distaste to Tanya for what she was doing, but out of respect for Momma, she agreed. She also agreed to bring Grandmother meals, which reminded me of the medication. Mrs. Culpepper wrote down the instructions for the pills and again scolded Tanya for what she was doing.

Whether out of fear or respect, Tanya refrained from responding to Mrs. Culpepper. Mrs. Culpepper had kept Momma and Tanya when they were children; when I was a child, she kept me when I got out of school before Momma and my grandparents got off work. She was very stern, and age had not affected her in the least!

We boxed up all the knives and scissors. Patricia made a few calls, and people came immediately to install grab bars in the bathroom. Mats were put in the tub to keep Grandmother from falling—if she even remembered to bathe. This could be an issue, but I knew Mrs. Culpepper would stay on top of it.

I was exhausted. I thought Tanya would have given in by now, but then again, the girls and I were doing most of the work.

I whispered to Patricia and Rhonda, "How far should we go with this?"

They both agreed that we should go all the way since we had no way at this point to reverse the guardianship. We continued working feverishly.

We replaced the old rotary phones with big push-button ones, and we taped our numbers on the walls. We called Life Call and made an appointment for Monday to install the necessary equipment for push-button help and monitoring. All of this was adding up to be a very large bill. I still didn't know what Tanya was up to and why she so desperately wanted to have this responsibility—other than her desire for the silver service and whatever else she thought Grandmother may or may not have.

I instructed everyone to take a break; we'd been working for hours. I looked for Tanya and found her where she'd been most of the time, outside with Brad.

Looking at Tanya, I said, "I need to talk to you."

Brad snapped, "Are you done yet?"

It took all the restraint I had not to get into another verbal altercation. I took a deep breath, calming the rush of anger I felt boiling up. "No, Brad. There's still a lot to be done."

"Well, we've wasted almost all day here. When are you going to be done?"

I had to ignore him; otherwise, he'd get to me. "Tanya, we need to talk."

She said, "There's nothing to say. You need to finish up here so Brad can get home."

"He may intimidate you, but the way I see it, he's a grown man. If he wants to go, let him." I wasn't going to let up. "We need to talk."

Brad's face reddened. Tanya grew uneasy and began to fidget. She said, "Why don't I just go and talk with her? It may help speed things up."

He replied, "Whatever. Just make this quick. I'm tired of being here."

I didn't really care what was going on between them. The fact that Tanya would bring my Grandmother into the middle of it made me want to shake her until she saw how wrong it was. Since I knew I couldn't do that, I thought I'd try to reason with her. "I know you and I have had some bad moments over the last couple of weeks. All of this has been hard for everyone."

"Shouldn't you apologize for the way you've treated me and my family?" Tanya asked.

I held my tongue and replied calmly, "I'm sorry for how badly we've both handled things."

"I'm not to blame for any of this!"

"Screaming gets us nowhere. Please just talk with me. It's me, the same girl you taught to put on makeup, wear heels, and love music. I'm still here." I waited to see if we could have a civil conversation.

Her face softened, and I knew I'd cracked the wall she'd built between us. "Something terrible has happened to us, both of us. You lost a sister, I lost a mother, but we can work together to help your mother. Whatever you want, I'll give to you, but please don't take your anger at Momma or me out on her. She doesn't deserve that."

Her head snapped up so quickly that it startled me. Her voice was full of venom. "There's nothing you could give me that would make up for what's been taken from me.'

Thinking about Grandmother's memory of Tanya shredding Momma's clothes, I knew I was fighting an invisible beast. I couldn't see it because I didn't know the complete history. Tanya wanted to get back at Momma, but, since she died, Grandmother and I were going to have to pay. I didn't know what to say.

Neither of us heard Brad approaching. "Okay, you got what you wanted, Lizzy. We're leaving now."

"Brad, I needed to talk with my aunt, but she's no longer in this woman. So, ultimately, I didn't get what I wanted. I'm going home to get some clothes; someone has to stay with Grandmother tonight."

With a smirk on his face, he said, "And you think that's going to be you?"

"Tanya has guardianship, so she could stay." My statement wiped the smirk off his face. He stormed off.

I turned to Tanya. "I'm going to ask Patricia and Rhonda to stay just in case you can't be here until I get back." Before she could answer, I walked away. My attempt to get through to her had failed. I wouldn't try again.

I ran home and grabbed some clothes and food—as well as a tumbler of vodka and orange juice. I started pulling out of the driveway and then stopped. I didn't trust Tanya, and if she knew no one was at Momma's, she might view it as an opportunity to rob me blind. It was very uncommon for anyone in such a small town to lock their doors, and I'd never been in the habit of locking Momma's. I had to search, but I finally found the ring of keys that had the door key on it. I locked the doors and windows and then headed back to Grandmother's.

On the way back, I took a small detour. Soon I was at the cemetery. Following the path through the headstones and markers, I pulled the car over when I reached the site where the graveside service had taken place. My breath caught in my throat. Fresh dirt peeked out from the arrangement of flowers over the grave. Shutting off the engine, I grabbed the tumbler and sat down at the foot of Momma's grave. I began to sob.

"Momma, I need you. You told me you'd be with me forever. If this is forever, then I don't want it." Looking a little to the right of Momma's grave, I saw my grandfather's headstone. "Granddaddy? I'm so sorry! I've given your heart to the devil herself. I'm so sorry for the both of you!" I was sobbing so hard that I couldn't speak or breathe. I felt like I was being dragged down in the undertow at the beach. A light breeze hit my face, and even though it was the dead of winter, it was warm. My chest relaxed. My breath came easier now. Looking down, I saw the tumbler. I downed the whole thing. Now I felt just like that glass—empty. I crawled between my mother's new grave and my grandfather's older one and lay on my back like they were in their caskets, looking at the sky. Few clouds were in the sky; the ones I saw looked like huge pillows.

I had mixed more vodka than orange juice in my cup, and now my head was swimming a little. I knew I needed to get back to Grandmother's house, but I couldn't make myself move. Tears rolled out of my eyes and landed in my ears, muffling the sounds around me. I didn't care.

After Grandfather died, I often rode my bike to the cemetery to sit and talk with him. For a long time I didn't tell my mother. She'd ask if I wanted to go, and I always said no. Then one day I was late getting home. Momma scolded me because it was almost dark; she'd called around, trying to find me, and she couldn't. Fighting the structure of my life with her, I screamed, "I went to the cemetery!" and ran to my room. After a few minutes she came into my room and lay on the bed next to me.

"Lizzy, I'm sorry. I was worried about you. I didn't know where you were, and even though you're a teenager now, you're still my little one, my only one," she said softly. "I'd never get onto you for going to Daddy's grave."

Her words were soft and sincere, and I opened up. I told her about visiting his grave several times a week. "I just want him to come back," I said tearfully. I'd been so distant since his death. I saw her reach out to touch me, but then she withdrew.

"Can I share something with you?" she asked. "I know Daddy was not only your Grandfather, but also your best friend. He was my best friend, too, and I've hurt for him, you, and me so badly. I loved the idea that you and he were so close, and I felt guilty that I got so much time with him, when yours was cut so short. There's nothing he wouldn't have done for Mother or his family. I was having a really bad day about a month after he died. I felt like I wasn't giving you everything you needed to help heal your heart, and it was killing me. Instead of coming straight home to you after work one day, I stopped at the cemetery. I told Daddy that I felt I was letting you down. I didn't know if I was doing anything right. You were so withdrawn, and there was no light in your eyes anymore, no matter what I tried to say or do." She paused for a deep breath. I could tell it upset her to talk to me like this.

After a moment, she continued. "I don't want you to think I'm crazy, but I asked Daddy for a sign; anything to let me know I was doing right by you and we were going to be okay. I don't know what I expected, so I sat there for awhile. When nothing happened, I came home, and you and I shared one of the deafening silences we'd had since his death. I don't remember us saying two full sentences to each other the whole night. I cried myself to sleep. The next morning, when I dropped you off at school, I told you I loved you and that, believe it or not, I understood what you were going through."

"I remember that," I said to her. I also remembered thinking there was no way she could possibly know, and I hadn't told her I loved her, too.

"Well, on my way to work that morning, the car started sputtering, and all the dashboard lights came on. The first thing I did was look at the gas gauge. I had more than a quarter of a tank left. I managed to get it to the side of the road before it died. Someone came by, and, after looking under the hood and finding nothing wrong, he asked if I was out of gas. I told him how much the gauge read, but he went up the road to the gas station and brought back a couple of gallons. I knew that wasn't it, and I didn't have any cash in my purse to give him for it, but he told me not to worry about it—he said he recognized me and knew I was Buddy's daughter. The car started right up."

"But there was gas in it, right?"

"Yes," she replied. "I viewed it as my sign."

Lying there now, between their two graves, I told them what had been happening with Tanya.

"Momma, if I'm doing the right thing, will you send me a sign?" I closed my eyes. I felt relaxed, and my head was no longer swimming.

Faintly I heard a man's voice. "Lizzy?"

My eyes shot open, and, without moving, I looked around. Seeing no one, I thought, *I'm losing it.*

"Lizzy, are you okay?"

Sitting straight up, I turned to look behind me. Daddy was standing about five feet away. I remembered what he'd said the first time he showed up at the house after Momma died: "Pam sent me."

Chapter 18

"I was riding by and saw your car. Are you okay?" he asked. "I didn't want to scare you. I've been here about thirty minutes, and you were so still."

Thirty minutes? I hadn't even heard him pull up behind my car. I must have dozed off. "I'm fine."

Kneeling down in front of me, he said, "I understand how hard this must be on you."

I ignored him. "When you came to the house, did you say Momma sent you?"

"Yes." He looked confused.

"Why are you here?"

"I don't know. I was just driving around, and I saw your car. Do you want me to leave?"

"No. Actually, I want to tell you something. Do you have a minute?"

"Of course." He listened as I described what had happened that morning with Grandmother. I told him how I was headed back to her house when I decided to stop here.

I could tell by the redness in his face that a solution—or what he thought was the solution—was about to come out of his mouth. Before

I could stop him, he spun around and stormed to his truck. "Get in your car, and let's get this over with," he demanded.

"Stop! I mean it, stop!" I said.

Looking over his shoulder, he saw I hadn't moved. "Lizzy, I'm going to Grace's with or without you," he said.

"No, you're not. I want you to stop and finish listening to me, please."

"What is it?"

"If Momma sent you, then you need to know how this goes, and I want your full attention when I tell you because I'm not going to repeat myself." He started walking back.

"Your way of doing things and what I need you to do are totally different," I said. "You need to get all hotheaded and run off and 'teach people a lesson.' I need to talk to you and hear myself talk, and then count on you to tell me if I'm being irrational or not. Can you do that?"

"But Lizzy, you know Tanya has it coming to her, and she's taken your grandmother," he insisted.

"And?" I asked.

"And what?"

"And what is your jumping in your truck and going up there and getting her all stirred up going to get me? A big fat headache and pain in the ass is what!" I told him.

"Well, what am I supposed to do?" he asked in irritation.

"I need you to do it the way Momma would have. You let me tell you the issues, and I figure out the solution. If, and only if, you have something productive to say, then you tell me your ideas. Beating the snot out of Tanya is not a productive idea," I said. "A really good idea, but not productive."

"Do you want Grace to come back home with you?" He was calmer now.

"I never wanted her to leave. I won't say I haven't worried how the two of us would do in Montgomery, but, considering the alternative, there's really no choice. Now I have to figure out how to get her back."

"From what I've seen—and that hasn't been much—I do know that living in her own house is not going to be good. That has to be terrifying for you. What can I do to help?" He was so sincere.

"For now, there's nothing we can do. Mr. Simmons has arranged an emergency meeting with Judge Culpepper tomorrow afternoon. I just have to get through tonight."

"Do you want me to stay with you two?"

For a moment he caught me off guard. "No, you don't have to do that."

"I do have to do this. There's no choice. You're so much your mother's daughter," he replied, looking down at Momma's grave.

I snapped back defensively, "And this is a bad thing how? You divorced Momma, but you can't divorce blood, and now is your chance to make up for years and years of bad judgment. Prove you want to be part of my life, or leave now and don't come back."

"Whoa! I only meant you're just as headstrong as she was. It was a compliment," he said.

My face flushed. "I have to get going," I said. Part of me wanted to believe him, but bad memories kept me from being relieved.

"I'm sorry it was her and not me," he said emotionally. "I haven't done a whole of lot of good things in my life, and she did so much to help others, not to mention how well she did with you."

I wanted to say, "I hate that it wasn't you, too," but instead I said, "You're being given a second chance. Only you can choose how you handle it." I didn't look back when I said it. I just got in the car and drove off.

Grandmother's house wasn't too far from the cemetery, so I had to get my head clear before I got there. I hadn't meant to be away so long. When I returned, Patricia and Rhonda jumped up from the swing and ran over to the car. I saw that Brad and Tanya had decided to wait.

"Lizzy, is everything okay?" Rhonda asked.

"Yeah, there was just something I had to do." I left it at that, and neither of them pushed. Getting my stuff out of the car, I said to Tanya, "You really need to stay here tonight, too." I waited for her to respond, but she just looked at Brad. "I only say that because there are things you need to know about Grandmother's care and to protect your own interests. I wouldn't want you accusing me of taking something." I was trying to be honest, not malicious. Without waiting for her to answer, I walked into the house, where I saw Grandmother lying on the bed. I gently set my stuff down and walked into her room. She was snoring softly. Pulling her door shut, I turned and saw everyone watching me.

"I have to work tomorrow. I don't know how I can stay tonight," Tanya said.

"I can stay," Patricia said.

"Me, too," said Rhonda.

"As much as I appreciate the offer, this is really between me and Tanya now." Everyone was looking at me like I was about to do some kind of trick, but I was just drained. Looking at Tanya, I added, "It doesn't matter to me what you do. I know this is something I can take care of, but you do whatever makes you happy and what you can live with." My words were flat; I no longer cared about fighting with her. The decision had been made, and Grandmother was back in her home. I couldn't worry about what tomorrow held. I went into the kitchen and started putting the food away in the refrigerator.

"I have a meeting in the morning that I can't miss," Tanya said.

"I don't care about that. You either are or you aren't staying. Completely up to you," I replied. I knew now that Tanya hadn't given her actions any thought at all. She'd gotten guardianship of Grandmother without considering the consequences. *Typical Tanya,* I thought.

"Could you write down what it is I need to know?" she asked.

"Tanya, you can't expect—" Rhonda started, but I interrupted her.

"Sure," I said. "Rhonda, Patricia, I appreciate everything, I really do, but Grandmother's care is now up to Tanya. If I can help, I will, and I know Grandmother can count on more than a handful of people to help out, too. I'll work it all out tomorrow and start on that list tonight for Tanya." I went out the front door. Everyone followed. "It's been an exhausting few days, and I just need some quiet for a while."

Jumping on the invitation to leave, Tanya said, "I'll call you in a little while to check on Mother."

"Please don't," I replied. "I'll call you." With that, she and Brad got in their car and left.

"What's going on?" Patricia asked.

"For now it has to appear that I've given up. I knew she wouldn't stay here tonight, and I hope that will play against her tomorrow."

Rhonda added, "You do have a good point. But is something else going on?"

I didn't want to talk about my conversation with Daddy. "I'm just tired, and there's still so much to be done. As much as I hope this is just for tonight, we still have to be ready for anything."

Patricia said, "We'll help you with anything you need."

We went back in the house and worked through every room, moving things that Grandmother might get hurt on or by. We used old pillowcases to pad the corners of the tables and picked up the loose rugs she had on the floors. When Grandmother was up, we checked the smoke detectors and kept a close eye on what she was doing to identify other dangers. Once Grandmother was asleep for the night, I said good-bye to Patricia and Rhonda and then sat down to start on the list Tanya would need. I knew it was going to be a book, but if it was what she wanted, then I'd hit her with everything.

Because Tanya hadn't left me with a key, I had no way of locking the doors. I put a chair in front of the doors to the outside, and I slept on the couch. However, I failed to hear when Grandmother woke up; she was moving the chair by the front door before I heard her. I glanced into her room and saw she wasn't there. I found her heading out the door.

"Grandmother, where are you going, hon?" I asked her.

"I need to go home," she said.

"You are home." She was thinking of the home she'd grown up in as a little girl. This had happened before. "Why don't you come back in, and let's get you some clothes on. You can't go out in your pajamas." She stopped and looked down at her attire.

"I need to get some clothes to take with me anyway." We walked down the hall and into the bathroom. I handed her some clothes from the closet.

"Why don't we get a bath first?" I asked, yawning.

"I've already had one. Whose clothes are these?"

"They're yours, and I don't think you've had a bath today. Let's at least wash up some in the sink."

"Don't tell me what I've done! I had my bath today, and I don't know whose clothes those are, but I'm not wearing them!" she shouted.

Great! I thought. *It's going to be one of those days. Where's Tanya when you need her?*

Calmly I ran through the questions, hoping to jar her into the present. "Where did you put your bath cloth?" As she looked around, I waited patiently for the answer.

"You must have moved it."

Grabbing the dry soap bar and placing it in her hand, I persisted. "Did you use soap?" Again waiting for the answer. This was a series of questions Momma and I had come up with; they either confused the hell out of her or made her realize that she hadn't done what she'd claimed she'd done. We had her name written in the tags of her clothes to prove that they really were hers, so when we finished with the bath scenario, we could move on to getting dressed.

She looked at me, confused. "I don't know why the soap isn't wet. I know I used it."

There was no rushing this process. "Why is the tub dry, too?"

She looked in and then ran her hand across the bottom. "I don't know. I—" Then she started looking around the bathroom. It was registering.

"If you bathed, then why would you still be in your pajamas?"

"Because I don't have anything to put on."

"Whose name is on the tags in those clothes?" I asked her as I started running water in the tub.

"Grace Jenkins," she replied.

"Aren't you Grace Jenkins?" I asked with a smile.

"Oh, you think you're so smart." She was a little annoyed now, but everything was going to be okay. After I had her in the tub and she was bathing herself, I looked for a clock. It was six-thirty in the morning. I decided to call Tanya since I hadn't even thought of it the night before. Thankfully, she'd followed my instruction and hadn't called.

When she answered, I could tell I'd woken her up. "I thought you had an important meeting this morning."

Still half asleep, she said, "What meeting?"

"Well, either you're going to miss your meeting, or you outright lied to avoid staying with your mother. I don't care either way, but rise and shine; your mother's up," I said.

"What's wrong? Is Mother okay?"

"Yes, everything is fine. She's taking a bath. I didn't call you last night, and I thought you'd be getting ready for work. I'm just checking in with you. The Life Call people should be here at eight. What's your address?"

"My address?"

My assault on her had to continue as much as possible before the hearing. My dream was that she'd walk in and concede. "Yeah, your address. They have to know where to send the bill—Grandmother can't receive bills. Didn't you know that?" I was almost amused at how little she knew. "You'll need to put in for a change of address today so her mail will stop going to Momma's house."

"I hadn't thought of that."

"Chop, chop! It seems you haven't thought about a lot of things, but that's okay. I'm going to be here for the next week, and I've made you a ton of notes that we'll review before I leave. If you can find the time." My sarcasm was uncontrollable this morning.

"Will you please change your tone with me?" Tanya asked.

"There's no tone. I'm just being matter-of-fact with you. You really don't know what you've gotten yourself into, but you better figure it out quickly. You can't rely on me to hold your hand through the rest of

Grandmother's life. Hold on a minute." I put the phone down and went to check on Grandmother, who was getting out of the tub. Without letting her see me, I watched as she used the grab bars, got her towel, and stepped out of the tub. As usual, she forgot to let the water out of the tub. I smiled as I saw her look at the tags in the clothes again.

"Yep, still Grace Jenkins," I said to her.

"Oh, shut up," she bantered back and laughed.

"I've got Tanya on the phone. Are you okay?"

"I'm fine."

"Don't forget to brush your teeth." I pulled the toothbrush from the medicine cabinet and placed it beside the toothpaste on the vanity.

As I walked back to the phone, I could hear Tanya shouting, "Lizzy! Lizzy, are you there? I'm going to hang up this phone!"

"Keep your panties on!" I said when I picked up. "I had to be sure Grandmother got out of the tub okay."

"Oh, well, if you need to go…"

"Like I said, I have that list you wanted. Would you like to get together before the hearing this afternoon?" I waited for a response. I wasn't sure if she knew about the hearing but assumed her attorney would have contacted her. After a long silence, I said, "Hello?"

"Um, I'm here. I don't know. Is there somewhere you can leave it?" She was stumbling over her words.

"I'm sure there is, but don't you want to go over it?"

"Of course, but today is just not a good day." Again she was stumbling over her words. I should have known something was wrong, but I really didn't care.

"I can't leave Grandmother here alone. Do you want me to take her with me?"

"No, I'll come by as soon as I'm ready for work, and you can just go," she snapped.

"What's going on with you? You're acting like you can't be in my presence. And did you forget about the Life Call people already?"

"Damn it!" she whispered.

"Just tell me what seems to be the problem."

135

"Nothing, it's nothing! I'll throw on some clothes and come now so you can go and get your stuff done. I'll wait for the Life Call people." Tanya was talking really fast.

"What about your meeting?" I asked. I couldn't resist.

"It was canceled."

"Riiight," I said skeptically. "Whatever. See you when you get here." When I hung up, I looked at the phone for a second. "She's so strange!" I said out loud.

When I returned to Grandmother in the bathroom, I said, "Honey, you've got pants today, you don't need that slip." As I finished helping her get ready, there was a knock at the door—Mrs. Culpepper with some coffee. We all sat at the dining room table. Between Grandmother's chatter, I tried to fill Mrs. Culpepper in as much as possible about Grandmother's needs and care. She took notes; there was a lot to absorb.

"Mrs. Culpepper, I hope your son can help me today and that all these precautions are for nothing."

"This is one area I have no control over. He has a job to do, but I talked with him last night."

She wasn't offering a lot of information, and I didn't want to push. "I understand."

About forty-five minutes later, Tanya blew in, and Mrs. Culpepper quickly reprimanded her again for bringing Grandmother back to her house. Tanya once again took the tongue-lashing without comment. It dawned on me that I'd handled Tanya all wrong this whole time. I should have just gotten Mrs. Culpepper to the house when Momma was sick and dying. I almost laughed out loud at the thought.

"Don't you have a lot to do?" Tanya asked.

"Yes," I said. I turned to Grandmother. "I've got to go out for a little while, okay?"

"Where are you going?" Grandmother asked.

"I've got some stuff to do at my house, and then I'm coming back."

"Can I go with you?"

"You need to stay here," Tanya told her.

"I want to go with Lizzy," Grandmother said, rising from the table.

"No, Mother, you need to stay here with me and Mrs. Culpepper."

Ignoring Tanya, Grandmother said, "Where's my purse?"

This interaction would be a learning experience for Tanya. She didn't know how to handle Grandmother.

"Mother, you're not going with Lizzy. Now sit back down," Tanya demanded.

Mrs. Culpepper was about to step in, but we locked eyes, and I shook my head at her. This needed to play itself all the way out. Mrs. Culpepper leaned back in her chair.

Grandmother looked at Tanya. "I'm going," she said like a defiant child.

"No, you're not, and I'm not going to continue arguing with you," Tanya spat. "You need to sit down."

Grandmother lifted her cane. I'd learned to watch for that after she'd taken a swing at Momma when we tricked her into coming back to the house. The stern approach was a bad idea when trying to negotiate with Grandmother.

Tanya hadn't noticed that Grandmother was no longer balancing with the cane. "You don't tell me what to do, damn it!" Grandmother shouted.

Tanya was shocked. "You stop this right now!" she yelled. Before she could even get out the words, the cane caught her left leg with a whack.

"You will respect your elders, young lady, and not talk to me that way!" Grandmother yelled in return. Tanya stumbled back to keep from getting hit again. I stepped in front of Grandmother and pushed the cane back to the floor. Both Mrs. Culpepper and I were fighting laughter.

When I was growing up, Grandmother had been very serious about punishment. You picked your own switches to get a whipping with, and she didn't tolerate being talked back to. The Alzheimer's had exacerbated this intolerance. You had to be careful when you reasoned with her, but Tanya didn't know this.

"Grandmother!" I said, acting shocked. "You stop that!" I kept my hand on her cane.

"I can't stand a smartass child!" she said back to me.

"I know, but look, I need you to stay here and do something for me."

She was calm now. "What do you need me to do, baby?"

"I saw some pictures over here that I need you to put in that album for me. Will you do that?"

"Anything to help out," she said as she walked past Tanya, who stepped aside to give her a wide berth. I'm sure she was expecting Grandmother to swat at her leg again, but as far as Grandmother was concerned, the moment was over.

I looked at Tanya. "Lesson number one: don't argue with her. She has violent tendencies now, and yeah, she cusses, too. These are the things I needed you to know, but maybe you'll figure it out as y'all go. Lord knows Momma and I had to. Can we cancel the hearing now?"

Tanya was still rubbing her leg and watching Grandmother with wide, shocked eyes. After waiting a beat for a response, none came. "I'll be gone for a few hours, but I'll be back as soon as I'm done," I said to Mrs. Culpepper. Looking at Tanya now, I added, "She's busy, and she'll be fine for a while. She'll probably go to sleep there on the couch. Tanya? Tanya, are you listening?"

Jerking her gaze away from Grandmother, she said, "What?"

"I'm leaving." I knew Mrs. Culpepper had heard me, and that was what mattered.

"But wait—"

Gathering my things, I asked, "For what? You'll be fine."

"What do I do with her?" Tanya was close on my heels now.

"She's your mother. She's grown at times, childlike at other times. You have to find what works for the two of you."

"How do I reach you if she needs something?"

"You don't. You handle it, and if you can't, you'll figure something out," I said. Tanya shadowed me as I walked out the front door. "The Life Call people will be here shortly. That will give both of you something to do. She's had her meds, and you have to make her lunch around eleven thirty. Be sure she eats and doesn't just push her food around."

"What if she doesn't eat?" Tanya sounded pitiful.

I spun around and almost collided with her because she was following so closely. "Then you figure it out. You act like you're terrified of her. She's your mother, for Christ's sake! Be a grownup! Her grownup!" I got in the car and drove away without another word. In the rearview mirror I could see her still standing in the driveway. "I need to make this fast, or there's no telling what will happen," I said to Tanya in the mirror.

Chapter 19

It was a little before eight when I pulled the car into the garage at Momma's house. Forgetting I'd locked the outside doors, I had to fish around in the car for the keys. The house seemed eerily quiet. I looked around as if it were the first time I'd been there. I walked slowly through each room, taking it all in. The sadness in my heart was about to explode. I thought about all the things I'd miss about Momma, and I suddenly realized all the firsts I'd go through without her in my life.

I'd been planning my wedding when we found out Momma had cancer, but she insisted the wedding go on anyway. I regretted that decision from the time I said, "I do." Before the wedding, I explained to my fiancé that I didn't know what kind of wife I could be since I had to be there for Momma. He said he understood—but within six months, it was over. His insecurities overwhelmed him; he couldn't handle the fact that I was always gone, working or taking Momma to treatments. My so-called home life was hell on earth. To relieve both of us of that pain, I divorced him. Although she'd been there for my first wedding and divorce, there were still so many other things in my life that she'd never be there to witness.

Then I thought of the special days I'd experience without her: Mother's Day, her birthday, my birthday, Thanksgiving, Christmas.

I had no children, never thought I wanted to be a mother myself, but what if I changed my mind? I'd have to do it without her. One of the conversations we had when she was sick was about me having a baby. She told me she wanted me to and that I'd make a good mother. I told her it wasn't something I could even conceive of—especially without her there. I believe that made her sad.

The memories in this house, both painful and happy, flooded my mind. Walking through the breakfast area, I remembered the peeping Tom we used to see. Seeing him was creepy, and we never knew when he'd be there. I also remembered a particular Christmas meal. A year after I moved out, I came home for Christmas when Momma was at work. My mother wasn't much of a cook, and, since I was, I did all the holiday meals. I walked into the house and saw a ham sitting on the breakfast table. It was cooked and looked wonderful. I called Momma at work and asked if she'd changed the menu. We were supposed to be grilling steaks—that year, it was eighty degrees at Christmas. It was one of the joys of living in the South: you just never knew.

She was confused by my question, and I told her about the ham. "You're kidding, right?" she asked.

"No. Did you do this? It looks wonderful!" I replied, proud that she'd cooked this beautiful ham herself.

"Don't touch it! I'll be right there." She hung up the phone and was home in twenty minutes. In the kitchen we stared at the ham for moment, and then we both burst out laughing. There we stood over that piece of meat like it was a bomb. I picked up the platter and saw Mrs. Holiday's name written on a piece of tape. Any good Southern woman puts tape on the bottom of their best serving platters and bowls so they get their dishes back when the event is over.

Mrs. Holiday's son was Momma's peeping Tom. He was slow and lived with his mother. He hadn't actually been peeping on Momma— he was attracted by the ambulances in our yard. Momma managed the ambulance service in addition to her hospital duties, and whichever ambulance wasn't in use stayed at our house.

"Oh, damn! Do you think I should call her?" she asked me.

"And say what? 'Mrs. Holiday, is your ham at home'?" We both laughed again.

I hadn't been able to cook another meal in that kitchen without thinking of the ham and smiling. Running my hand over the table, I could hear her laughter. Every inch of every room held some kind of memory. I decided the memories would still be there at a better time and headed for the shower.

Just as I stepped in, I heard the phone ringing; I decided to let the answering machine get it, even if it was Tanya. I stood in the shower for a long time, letting the water run over my shoulders and back. The hot water on my tense muscles was very welcome. Once my fingers were pale and pruney, I decided I probably needed to get out and get in touch with Mr. Simmons about the hearing.

When I stepped out of the shower, the phone rang again. *Jesus, wait your turn,* I thought. The ringing stopped, and I got dressed. With wet hair I finally listened to the messages on the answering machine—there were fourteen. The first three were from some of Momma's friends, just checking on me. Message four was Mr. Simmons. Message five was Rhonda saying she'd tried me at Grandmother's and Mrs. Culpepper had told her I'd gone home. Message six was the same but from Patricia. Seven through fourteen were from a Mr. Warren Beasley saying it was imperative that he speak with me as soon as possible.

"Warren Beasley, Warren Beasley, why does that name sound so familiar?" I muttered. "Well, Mr. Beasley, you'll just have to wait a damn minute." I was pouring myself a glass of tea when the phone rang again.

"Oh, my God!" I screamed and stormed toward the phone. "What is it!" Picking it up, I was irritated when I said, "Hello?"

"Could I please speak with Elizabeth Wallace?" a woman asked.

"Speaking."

"I have Mr. Warren Beasley needing to speak with you. Can you hold please while I get him on the line?"

"Who or what is Warren Beasley? I got seven messages from him this morning, and it's not even ten o'clock yet," I said.

"Mr. Beasley is an attorney. Please hold." Before I could say anything else, she had me on hold.

Attorney? Was Tanya ready to give up? I sipped my tea while I waited for Warren Beasley to pick up.

I heard a click, then a man's voice. "Mrs. Wallace?"

"Yes, Mr. Beasley, this is Lizzy Wallace. You're a persistent person," I said.

"Yes, ma'am, I've been needing to speak with you."

"Well, if you've had time to call me seven times in under two hours, you must not have too many other clients." Then it hit me. Warren Beasley, a slimy little underhanded attorney with the greasiest hair I'd ever seen on a human being. I'd met him a few times in the hospital where Momma had worked. He was a glorified ambulance chaser, and Momma despised him.

"No, ma'am, on the contrary, I'm quite busy. But as I understand it, I'm on a time limit with you," he said.

"A time limit for what? What can I do for you?"

"I represent Mrs. Tanya Dumas, and she has informed me that you're in possession of her belongings."

"Then, Mr. Beasley, I suggest you get your facts straight!" I was getting angry.

"Well, Mrs. Wallace, I'm calling to give you an opportunity to forfeit the items before we pursue this in the courts."

"Really, now? Then tell me exactly what it is that I'm supposed to be in possession of, and I'll see what I can do to help you out. I'm sure there are ambulances out there for you to get to chasing."

"There's no need for you to be rude."

"My mother, do you remember her?"

"Yes, ma'am, I do."

"Well, she died on Friday, and I buried her on Saturday, and today you're blowing up my phone to tell me you have a client, my mother's sister, who wants to sue me already. How exactly would you like for me to be toward you, sir? Were you the one who helped Tanya get guardianship of my grandmother?"

"Yes, ma'am, I helped Mrs. Dumas with that."

"Is nothing sacred to you, Mr. Beasley? Couldn't you have advised your client to wait before pursuing this?" I was furious now, trying my best not to scream at the man.

"It's not my place to determine the appropriate time for my clients to pursue a case."

"Let me tell you, there's a place in hell for people like you! Now again, let me ask you: what is it that I'm in possession of?"

He ran through all the items Tanya had pulled out the night of the card game, the same ones that were in the bank vault at that moment. "I believe these are all the items due to my client," he concluded.

"Mr. Beasley, I've taken note of these items, and I will get in touch with my attorney, Mr. Bill Simmons. I'm sure he'd be more than happy to discuss this matter with you. If you thought you were going to call this morning get an immediate okay from me, then I hate to disappoint you. Unless you want to make a deal."

"Now, Mrs. Wallace, there must be a way we can work this out."

"Sure there is! Are you representing Tanya this afternoon in the hearing about my grandmother?"

"Yes, I am."

"Then do you want to make a trade? The items on your list for guardianship?"

"I'm not at liberty to make that decision without discussing it with my client."

"Well, you can find her at my grandmother's. Why don't you discuss it with her and call me back? I'm sure you know the number by heart!" I hung up on him. My first instinct was to get in the car and drive to grandmother's to confront Tanya, but my gut told me this wasn't a good idea. Instead, I called Mr. Simmons.

His assistant answered and told me he was in a meeting. I explained that it was urgent that I speak with him soon, and, ten minutes later, Mr. Simmons called back.

"Lizzy, what's wrong?" he asked.

"Are you my attorney or just the estate attorney?" I asked quickly.

"I'm whatever you need me to be. Are you okay? You sound upset."

As I ran through my call with Mr. Beasley, there were a lot of "uh-huhs" and "I sees" on the other end of the phone. When I finished, Mr. Simmons calmly told me that he was my attorney and that I was to not to speak with "Mr. Weasley" again. When I corrected him, he said, "No, Warren is a weasel, and I've always wanted to go toe to toe with him."

"Mitch, I need you to get Warren Beasley on the phone for me," I heard him say. "Is Tanya bringing your grandmother today?"

"I don't know. I don't see where that would be in her favor, since Grandmother wants to be with me."

"Well, you can't bring her without Tanya's permission, since she has guardianship."

"I'll have to make some arrangements with Mrs. Culpepper—I'm sure Tanya won't."

"If you see her, I don't want you to mention this. And Lizzy, I need you to stay away from her as much as possible."

I told him how she'd sounded when I called her and that it seemed she was trying to avoid me at all costs.

"That's a guilty conscience! She knew what was going to happen when you got home today, and she didn't have the nerve to tell you or to try to work this out with you." His voice was angry. "Can Michael go back up there with you? If you two have a confrontation, I want someone there to witness it, someone who will remember what was said."

"I'm sure he won't mind. I'll call him. He can say he's just visiting or looking things over since Grandmother will be there by herself."

"That's good. Give him a call and let me get on the phone with this little weasel Beasley. I'll let you know what happens. We still need to get together about the estate and the will. You want to do that tomorrow since all this is going on today?"

"That would be great. Thanks so much!" I was relieved that Mr.

Simmons would be handling things now. I knew I didn't have to worry about it anymore. I trusted him.

"I'll meet you at the courthouse at three."

After we hung up, I called Michael and explained what was going on. I told him I needed him to be present in case Tanya was still there. I knew once I got there she'd go home; she was a coward and wouldn't be able to stay in the same room with me.

"Unbelievable! Of course, Lizzy, you can count on me. When do you want to go?" he asked.

"Is one okay with you?"

"That's fine. I'll meet you at Pam's."

"Thanks so much for your help, Michael."

I began to think of the reasons I'd come home this morning. I had so much to do, and this battle with Tanya was adding to my stress. I called my boss, Monica, to let her know when I'd be back. I kept it short and didn't mention any of the drama surrounding Tanya and Grandmother. I just explained that I had to handle a few unresolved issues. Monica assured me that I should take all the time I needed.

As I began sorting through Momma's papers and organizing what Mr. Simmons would need to help me with, the phone rang. Thinking it was an answer to my deal, I ran to the phone.

"Hello!"

Daddy asked, "Expecting someone?"

My voice had given away my anticipation. "Oh, hey."

"Don't sound so disappointed."

"I'm sorry. I really was expecting a call."

"Something to do with Beasley?"

I was stunned. "How do you know about that?"

"Small town; people talk—especially him. He was running his mouth at the diner."

"Wonderful!" I sighed.

"Listen, I'm still here at the diner. Would you like me to bring you something?"

"No, but I appreciate it."

There was a pause. Then he said, "Are you really not hungry, or are you trying to keep me away?"

I had to give him some credit for making an honest effort. "I'm not hungry, and I'll be heading back to Grandmother's soon, and then to the hearing. How about I call you to let you know what I find out this afternoon?"

"I'll be expecting your call."

This was the longest he'd ever stuck anything out with me, and I hadn't been the easiest person to get along with the last few days. Was losing the only family I'd ever known opening the door for family I should have known? There wasn't time to think about that now.

When Michael showed up to escort me back to Grandmother's, it dawned on me that no one else had called. I assumed there was no deal and that we'd still be going to the hearing. I threw some clothes in a bag and grabbed a shoebox of information just in case Grandmother wouldn't be coming back with me. *There's no way she won't be given back to me. There just can't be any way!* I thought.

Chapter 20

Once I was in Grandmother's driveway, my stomach dropped when I realized Tanya was still there. I'd truly hoped she would have given up and gone home. I had to remember to keep my mouth shut unless she mentioned something—and then limit any conversation to the matter at hand. I hadn't even turned off the car before Tanya came onto the porch. She looked very disheveled.

Walking toward her, I remarked, "You look like shit!"

"I didn't think you'd ever get back." She was being so dramatic that she hadn't even noticed Michael getting out of the car. "She's been into everything, and nothing satisfies her!"

"And to think it's only been five hours." I couldn't help snickering. As she moved closer, I saw a clump of something in her hair, and if I was not mistaken, it was mashed potatoes. *Lunch must not have gone well,* I thought.

"This isn't funny, Lizzy! This is very serious!"

"You act like I don't know that. I wasn't laughing at Grandmother. I'm laughing at no one other than you because your perfectly controlled world has just come to a screeching halt. Can we call off the hearing now?"

"I don't think this is going to work." Now noticing Michael, she added, "What's he doing here?"

Michael must have planned on facing this question; before I could answer, he jumped right in. "I'm here to be sure Ms. Grace is safe. Be sure no one will be able to break in, check the tool shed, make sure it's all secure. If I find anything, I'll give you my recommendations."

Tanya bought it, even though I couldn't recall the last time there'd been a break-in in this little town. Michael moved away but stayed within earshot. I'd invite him in when the time came, but it looked like Tanya wasn't yet through feeling sorry for herself.

"I think we need to hire a daytime sitter," she said.

"Where is she now?" I asked before hitting Tanya with more of the cold, hard truth that awaited her in my car.

"She's sleeping, finally."

"If you feel you need a sitter, then by all means hire one," I said, correcting her pronoun.

"We need to have one in place before you go back home. When is that, anyway?"

"First, let me clarify something for you. There is no 'we' in this equation. There is you, and there is me. It is still yet to be seen if she'll be staying here, so I might as well share with you something I have in the car." Reaching in, I grabbed the shoebox that contained Grandmother's financial records. Momma had kept good notes in a journal with all the debits and credits, including the money she put into Grandmother's account to cover her bills. I handed it to Tanya. "Let me know if there's anything you don't understand."

Looking it over, she began whining. "There's nothing here. How much money was Pam putting in this account every month?"

"Those amounts are in the pink highlighted areas."

"Some of this stuff could be eliminated, couldn't it?"

"What exactly are you going to eliminate? Her food? Meds? As you see, this is all essential to her life now, even down to the cost of that cane she hit you with this morning. Everything costs money, and that is the one thing Grandmother doesn't have a lot of. With age come ailments, and Medicare—well, let's just say it won't cover it." As the words rolled out of my mouth, Tanya's face began to droop. "If you thought you found your cash cow, you are sadly mistaken."

Almost in a whisper, she said, "No, I just didn't know..." She trailed off into a mumble. I couldn't understand the rest of what she said.

"So, as you can see, if you want to hire a day sitter, then that money will have to come straight out of your bank account. Grandmother's just won't cover it. But there's another option."

She looked at me pleadingly. "What?"

"You could stop this campaign to hurt your family and let me take guardianship of Grandmother."

"I couldn't do that. He wouldn't allow it," she whispered.

"Who? Brad?" *How much of this is really Tanya's doing?* I suddenly wondered.

Without warning, Tanya stormed into the house, and I looked over at Michael. Before we could speak, Tanya ran back out of the house and headed for her car. Grabbing the box from where she'd thrown it on the passenger seat, I stepped in front of her. "You wouldn't want to be forgetting this. Let me know what Brad has to say."

She snatched the box from my hand, threw it into the car, slammed the door, and started the engine. She almost lost control before the tires caught on the asphalt. She seemed to have forgotten about the police officer standing there watching her.

"You want me to go after her?" Michael asked.

"No, but maybe radio ahead and let someone know she'll be blowing through." We both laughed, and he did just that.

"I do have to tell you, that was quite impressive!" Michael said.

"What? Her acting like a child?" I saw skid marks on the street.

"No, I was talking about you. I love how you avoid the elephant in the room by bringing your own rhino to play with the gang. I don't think you even gave her an opportunity to think about Mr. Beasley or the silver."

"Correction, Michael: Grandmother hasn't given her a chance to think about much of anything. Let's go check on my girl. I bet all that tantrum bullshit woke her up." I didn't know why I avoided Michael's compliment, but I knew there was going to be a loser in this situation, and I feared it would be Grandmother.

The house looked like a tornado had hit it. The lunch dishes were still on the table, and, as I'd suspected, mashed potatoes were stuck to the chair where I assumed Tanya had been sitting. The water glass was still full, but particles of food were floating in it. All the kitchen cabinets were open. As I looked around, I saw that almost every other drawer and cabinet door throughout the house was open as well, with things half pulled out.

"Whoa!" Michael said in a shocked tone. "What happened in here?"

"I guess we aren't having a good day. All the changes must be wrecking havoc on her. She's out of her routine," I said.

"You want me to stick around and help clean this up?"

"I appreciate it, but no, thank you. I can work faster alone. But will you please go across the street and ask Mrs. Culpepper if she'll stay with Grandmother while I go to the hearing?" I wished I had a camera. The scene in the house would show that Tanya had no clue how to take care of Grandmother.

We both heard a sound coming from the bathroom. We rushed in and saw Grandmother sitting on the floor, pulling everything out from under the sink. I glanced at Michael; he read my mind and eased away, pulling the door closed behind him.

She'd had bad days before, but this was the worst I'd ever seen. Kneeling down beside her, I said, "Grandmother, what are you doing, hon?"

"Lizzy!" she said excitedly. "Lizzy, listen, when is Pam getting off work? The mortgage is due, and I can't find my booklet. Pam had it last, and she really needs to bring it to me so we can go pay it."

The words stung, but I knew she didn't know what she was saying. What was I supposed to say? Should I make her relive what had happened? I decided it wouldn't matter what I said.

"Momma's got to work late, and I'm going to stay here with you. Is that okay?" I asked softly.

"That would be lovely, but what about the mortgage?"

"Momma sent me to pay it after I saw her. It's all taken care of, so why don't you and I put all this stuff away?" It was hard to hold the tears in.

Without noticing whether the bottles were upright or lying on their sides, she started shoving everything back under the cabinet. Knowing that the mortgage had been taken care of seemed to put her at ease. I made a mental note to come back and straighten this cabinet up. Once she was done, I walked her to her recliner.

"*General Hospital* is on," I said.

"Oh, good. I'm glad I haven't missed it." It was as if nothing else had happened that day. I turned on the television, and she settled in. I hoped she'd nod off; she looked so tired.

I got her some tea and food from the kitchen and set it on the table next to her chair. Then I kissed the top of her head. "Will you please drink some of this for me and eat a couple of bites?"

"Thank you, Lizzy," she said, scooping up some peas. "Do you want some?"

"I've had some already. That's for you. Thank you, though."

As she nibbled and got involved in the television show, I went back in the kitchen and started undoing some of the day's wreckage. I wondered what Tanya could possibly have been doing while Grandmother was tearing the house apart. I was startled to see Mrs. Culpepper peering in the window at me.

Opening the door, I said, "Hey, Mrs. Culpepper, please excuse the mess." I motioned for her to come in. "You brought mashed potatoes for lunch, didn't you?"

She looked around in amazement. "Good Lord!"

"All of this is taking a toll on Grandmother. She was used to a routine, and now that's all gone." Before I caught myself, I said, "I hope your son makes the right decision today."

Her voice was pleading. "Lizzy, I really wish I knew what was going to happen, but I haven't even spoken to him today."

"I'm sorry. It wasn't fair of me to put you in the middle like that. Please forgive me."

"Baby, it's okay. I know you only want what's best for Grace. The whole world could see that."

Mrs. Culpepper insisted on helping me clean up. Soon it was time for me to leave. My heart pounded in my ears as I headed to the courthouse. Mr. Simmons was waiting on the steps, and we went directly to Judge Culpepper's chambers.

"We have a three o'clock hearing with Judge Culpepper," Mr. Simmons explained to his assistant.

"Yes, sir. Right this way."

Even though the hearing was still ten minutes away, Tanya and Mr. Beasley were already seated at a conference table. Tanya had pulled herself together. The potatoes were gone from her hair, and she'd changed her clothes. She looked official in her blazer, skirt, and heels. Mr. Simmons directed me to sit beside him, opposite them. No one spoke until Judge Culpepper entered. We all stood.

Judge Culpepper was a robust man with a full head of silver hair and soft eyes. In a deep voice he said, "This is going to be an informal meeting to see if there's just cause to have an official hearing. I've had the opportunity to review the transfer of guardianship from Pam Wallace to Tanya Dumas." We all looked at him tentatively. "Judge Walker signed off on this transfer, but, unfortunately, he's out of town for the week. Mrs. Dumas, it's apparent that this was done on the same day your sister died. Am I correct?"

"Yes, sir."

"Was guardianship discussed prior to the progression of Ms. Wallace's illness?"

"No, sir."

"For the sake of keeping the Wallace about whom I'm speaking correct, would you be opposed to me addressing you as Elizabeth?" he asked me.

"No, Your Honor. Elizabeth is fine."

"Elizabeth, were you aware that guardianship had been transferred?'

"No, sir, not until Grandmother was removed from my mother's home yesterday."

"Mrs. Dumas, may I ask why you did not discuss this with Elizabeth?"

Tanya's face was full of sincerity when she replied, "Lizzy, I'm sorry. Elizabeth just had so much going on, and I didn't want to burden her."

My mouth fell open at this blatant lie. It was hard for me to keep from calling her on it. Mr. Simmons's hand closed around my wrist, and he gave a barely perceptible shake of his head. I clenched my jaw. My reaction had not gone unnoticed by the judge.

"Elizabeth, you obviously object to what Mrs. Dumas is saying."

"Yes, sir, I do!" Mr. Simmons's hand was still on my wrist, and he squeezed it to calm my tone. I had just snapped at the judge—not a good idea. "I'm sorry. I do object," I said more calmly.

"Let me finish questioning Mrs. Dumas, and then I'll give you an opportunity to tell your side."

"Yes, sir." I leaned back in my chair and took some deep breaths as he continued his questions.

"Now, Mrs. Dumas, how long was your mother in Mrs. Wallace's home?"

He was taking notes as she spoke. "Approximately eight months."

"Why would Mrs. Wallace feel it necessary to have guardianship and move her into her home?"

I looked intently at Tanya. Was she going to admit that Grandmother had Alzheimer's? After all, she herself didn't believe it. She'd accused us of making it up, even though Grandmother's own physician had diagnosed it.

"I believe my sister overreacted when she was told that Mother was in the beginning stages of Alzheimer's."

"Did the two of you discuss this at that time?"

"Yes, and I disagreed with the decision to move her. I told—"

He cut her off. "Without Mrs. Wallace here to confirm that conversation, we're going to leave it at that. Where is Mrs. Jenkins now?"

"I've moved her back into her home on Second Street."

"You don't believe she'd be better suited living in your home with you?"

"No, sir. She's still quite active, and I'm working to get a sitter for meal preparations and anything else she may need."

By this point, I was on the edge of my chair, and I couldn't control my reaction. "Active!" I shouted. "You think making a shambles of her house is active? Maybe it's you who's demented!" Everyone's eyes swiveled to me, but I didn't care.

Judge Culpepper arched his eyebrows. In a firm voice he said, "Mr. Simmons, please get control of your client!"

"Yes, I'm sorry, sir." Leaning into me, he whispered harshly, "Lizzy, this is not helping our case!"

I saw Tanya smirk, and I'd never hated anyone as much as I hated her in that moment. This was just a game to her. I closed my eyes over hot tears.

This time the judge's voice was stern when he spoke to me. "Elizabeth, let me remind you that you'll have ample time to speak, but I won't tolerate such outbursts. Do I make myself clear?"

I was angry at myself for getting so emotional, and I could only nod.

Mr. Simmons confirmed, "There will not be anymore outbursts."

"Okay, where were we? Ah, yes. You're getting a sitter?"

"I'm working on that. Yes, sir."

"Why do you believe you'd be a better guardian than Elizabeth?"

Tanya drew in an exaggerated breath. "My mother was born and raised here. This is the only community she's ever known. Elizabeth lives in a large city, which has more dangers than our town does. I believe familiarity will decelerate her condition. Also, her physician is here, and I'm only fifteen minutes away for anything she may need." Her response sounded rehearsed.

"Is there anything else you want to add before I begin questioning Elizabeth?" the judge asked.

"Yes, sir," Mr. Beasley said. "Elizabeth is in possession of some of Mrs. Jenkins's property, and my client would like it returned."

Judge Culpepper's face hardened. Again his voice was stern. "We are here concerning guardianship of Mrs. Jenkins. You'll have to take that issue up in court."

"But sir—"

"Don't push it, Mr. Beasley."

Sheepishly, Beasley responded, "Yes, sir."

Judge Culpepper flipped the page of his notebook. I took a deep cleansing breath to calm my nerves before he began questioning me.

"Elizabeth, I assured you that there would be time to explain your objections to Mrs. Dumas's answers, but I'm not just turning the floor over to you. I'll question you just like I did her."

Finally! I thought. "Yes, sir." I listened carefully as he began his questions.

"Have you been involved in Mrs. Jenkins's care since she's been living at your mother's?"

"Yes, sir."

He took note of my responses, too. "Do you believe Mrs. Jenkins is capable of living in her house on Second Street?"

"No, sir, I don't."

"I know you're not a doctor, but in your words, why do you believe Mrs. Jenkins is incapable of living in her own home?"

"Because her thought pattern gets scrambled. Sometimes it's like dealing with a child."

"In what ways?"

"Daily activities. She needs help with things like bathing, dressing, and even eating."

"I see," he said, scribbling down my response. "Do you think a sitter would be able to help with these issues?"

I said sharply, "Yes, sir, but I love her enough to do it myself." His eyebrows shot up, but he didn't comment on my tone.

"I don't question that you love her, or you wouldn't be here. What's best for Mrs. Jenkins is my ultimate concern."

"Yes, sir."

"Where do you live again?"

"Montgomery."

"If you were awarded guardianship, would you move Mrs. Jenkins there?"

"Yes, sir."

"Do you understand the concerns Mrs. Dumas has about that?"

My heart raced. I had genuine concerns—unlike Tanya, who was just pretending.

"Elizabeth? Do you understand the question?"

"Yes, sir. I understand the question, and yes, I have concerns. But I would never do anything that would endanger her well-being."

"Why do you feel you'd be a better guardian than Mrs. Dumas?"

"Because I've never deserted my grandmother. She can always count on me. On the other hand, *Mrs. Dumas* has never taken her condition seriously. Until today she never even acknowledged that Grandmother has Alzheimer's."

Judge Culpepper looked up from his writing. I looked straight into his eyes when I made my next comment. "If your next question is do I have anything to add, I do. I believe Mrs. Dumas has done what she's done not out of concern for her mother but because she believes she'll get something out of having possession of her." The room was silent until Judge Culpepper cleared his throat and blinked to break our stare.

He said softly, "If there's nothing further, I am going to recess for fifteen minutes and review this information." When no one spoke, he rose, and we followed suit. I watched as he went into an adjoining office.

Mr. Simmons said, "Let's step outside. I believe you could use some air." I followed him to a bench in the courtyard.

We'd barely gotten seated before I asked, "He *is* going to reverse this, right?"

He put his hand on mine. "I don't know, Lizzy. If it were up to me, there wouldn't even be a decision to be made, but I just don't know."

We sat quietly. *Why did I have to get so emotional? Will he hold that against me? What if I'd said I would move back here?* I wondered.

"Lizzy? Lizzy?" Mr. Simmons's voice snapped me out of my daze.

"What?"

"It's time."

We walked back into the conference room and took our seats. When Judge Culpepper returned, he motioned for us to be seated. He didn't make eye contact with any of us. He was looking at his notes. I saw him take a deep breath.

He raised his head. "It's sad when parents and grandparents get older and decisions like this have to be made. As a judge, it's not easy to separate love from welfare. Elizabeth, while I do see how much you love your grandmother, nothing has been brought to the table to show me that Mrs. Jenkins's welfare would be threatened by leaving the guardianship as it is."

Through tears, I saw Mr. Beasley pat Tanya's back. I was frozen.

Judge Culpepper continued, "But I do see some areas that could use improvement."

Beasley and Tanya looked at Judge Culpepper. "Mrs. Dumas, I expect you to work with Elizabeth while she's here so you'll be well equipped to take over your mother's care. I am also assigning a social worker to this case to do periodic checks on Mrs. Jenkins." He pushed a business card across the table in my direction. "Elizabeth, this is her contact information. If you have any concerns at all, you can call her anytime. She's been instructed to bring her findings directly to me."

I looked down at the card, still in shock. Mr. Simmons put his arm around my shoulder.

The judge said to Tanya, "I am not immune to the talk within this community. The way you've handled this situation, along with your sister's death, has been crude, to say the least. While I am leaving you with guardianship, I am also placing sole responsibility for Mrs. Jenkins on you. I advise you to take this seriously—there are laws protecting the elderly. Any report from the social worker will not be overlooked. Do you understand?" Tanya's face flushed, but she only nodded. As he stood to exit, I couldn't pull myself up from the chair to stand as everyone else had. My body felt heavy.

As Judge Culpepper closed his chamber door, Mr. Beasley remarked, "So, Simmons, you want to get your client to forfeit that stuff now, or do you really want me to drag her through that?" He'd barely gotten the words out when the chamber door opened swiftly.

"Beasley, my chambers! Now!" With great haste he disappeared into the chamber, and the door slammed. I heard muffled shouting coming from within the judge's chamber. Mr. Simmons helped me to my feet and toward the door. This was like suffering a death all over again.

Chapter 21

I'd forgotten that the girls said they were coming to the courthouse straight from work. When we exited, I saw them sitting outside on a bench. My face told them all they needed to know. Patricia wrapped her arms around me and held me close. I could feel her heart beating.

Rhonda sounded distressed. "Lizzy, are you okay?"

"She hasn't said a word," Mr. Simmons said.

It was hot. Patricia's heart seemed to be beating louder. Everything went black.

"Lizzy." I heard a woman's voice calling my name, and I felt something cold on my face. I heard my name again. "Lizzy."

I opened my eyes but didn't immediately remember where I was or what had happened. I reached up and touched the wet napkin on my forehead.

I tried to sit up. "Easy now, sister," Patricia said. She put her hand on my shoulder. "Just lie there for a minute."

"What happened?" I asked. I saw Rhonda and Mr. Simmons, as well as some people I didn't know.

Rhonda said lightheartedly, "You decided to take a little rest."

Then it hit me. *Oh my God! I'm on the sidewalk outside the courthouse!* I scrambled to sit up. Everything was spinning, and I felt like vomiting.

I could hear sirens approaching. "Please tell me y'all didn't call an ambulance," I said, closing my eyes to stop the spinning.

Patricia said, "Please tell me you did not decide to fall out in front of the courthouse."

I smiled, and when I opened my eyes, the spinning had stopped. I saw Judge Culpepper coming out of the courthouse.

He came over to me. "Lizzy, are you okay?"

"Yes, sir." The sirens were blaring behind me now. Once they stopped, I said, "I don't need that." I saw Mr. Beasley and Tanya coming out of the courthouse. *Or that, either*, I thought. Tanya saw me but continued walking.

"Well, you may not think you need it, but we're going to let them check you out," he said.

Everyone gave the medics room to work. No one was surprised to find out my blood pressure was high. When they recommended transport to the hospital, I replied, "Absolutely not! I'm fine. Now let me up." Patricia and Rhonda rushed over to help me.

Judge Culpepper announced, "Okay, people, the excitement's over. Move along." People began moving away. "I think you have enough support." He smiled before going back into the courthouse.

Mr. Simmons said, "I think the judge is right. Are we still on for tomorrow?"

"Yes. Thank you," I said.

After he walked away, I said, "Can we get out of here? I think I've embarrassed myself enough."

Patricia drove my car, and I sat in silence, thinking. I couldn't believe that Grandmother would not be going home with me. I'd known there was a chance, but I hadn't let myself think about it—let alone accept it. The car began to slow down—we were at Grandmother's house. Rhonda pulled in after us.

Mrs. Culpepper came rushing out. "Lizzy, baby, are you okay?"

Instead of answering, I said, "I see you heard. Did you hear all of it?"

Shyly she said, "Yes, Raymond called." It took me a moment to remember that Judge Culpepper was Raymond. Her eyes welled up with tears. "I think this is all my fault." She was so worked up that I didn't want to interrupt. "I told you I talked with him last night. I mentioned how hard I thought it would be on you to try and take care of Grace."

After this admission, Patricia and Rhonda scurried into the house.

Coldly I said, "What? I thought you were Grandmother's friend."

Tears rolled down her cheeks. "I am, and there isn't anything I wouldn't do for her."

"Did you tell him not to transfer the guardianship?"

"No, I'd never do that." She was sobbing now.

Just as Rhonda and Patricia had been Momma's best friends, Mrs. Culpepper had been Grandmother's. This was the woman who brought hats to my tea parties when I was a little girl. Even though I didn't know if this was her fault, it broke my heart to see her so upset. I put my arm around her shoulder. "Shhh, it's okay," I said. "Let's take a breath and talk about this. Sit with me." We sat on the steps. I knew it would take a moment before she could begin to explain, and I tried to be patient.

In an attempt to lighten the moment, I said, "You know, it always confuses me when you call Judge Culpepper by his first name. I'm used to hearing him called 'Judge.'" She gave a small smile; she was calming down.

She wiped her eyes and took a deep breath. When she spoke, I had to strain to hear her. "Last night when I talked with Raymond, I explained how Tanya had dumped Grace here at the house. You know, since she moved in with your mother, I hadn't seen Grace as much as I used to. Watching her yesterday, I was surprised at how much had changed." She paused. "I expressed to Raymond how unfair it was that you had to take care of your mother until her death—and then have to repeat that with Grace, even though I knew you would. You were a good daughter, and now Tanya needs to be one, too." She began to cry again.

I took her hand. I understood now why she felt it was her fault.

"Mrs. Culpepper, I don't blame you. You were a mother having a conversation with her son. We have to believe the judge made the best decision from the evidence he heard and nothing more."

"But what about Grace?"

"That's where I come in." I tried to smile. "I just have to be sure that everyone important to her knows everything I've learned over the last few months. Since you're right across the street, can I count on you to be my most important ally?"

"Lizzy, I may not be a spring chicken anymore, but I've known Grace since we were children. I'm here for both of you."

"Thank you. Now why don't we get started and check on my girl."

I brought Grandmother to the table. I wanted her to get used to having the girls and Mrs. Culpepper around more than me. Tanya hadn't called or come by. If anyone noticed, they didn't mention it. Grandmother seemed to be enjoying herself, and that was the important thing.

At dinnertime, Mrs. Culpepper brought over some food. As we ate, I jotted notes on Grandmother's routines and schedules. I felt as if I were trying to squeeze every drop of water out of a sponge. I was trying to remember everything so life could continue on undisturbed. Next to taking care of Momma, this was the most important thing I'd done so far in my life. These wonderful women sitting around the table would have to be ready when I left. *If anyone can do it, they can*, I thought.

At Grandmother's bedtime, I asked Rhonda to retrieve the things I needed for my meeting tomorrow with Mr. Simmons. She was walking out the door when I remembered the key.

"What's this?" she asked.

"The key to the house."

She laughed. "You've been living in the city too long."

I wasn't laughing. "No, with me tucked away here, Momma's house would be wide open to Tanya and Brad."

"I'm sorry. I hadn't thought of that."

"Welcome to my life."

Grandmother was sleeping soundly when Rhonda returned. Poor Mrs. Culpepper was worn out, and I'd sent her home. The girls and I talked only for a moment before we, too, said goodnight. I realized I'd forgotten to call Daddy. When I did, I wasn't surprised that he'd heard the news already. We planned for him to stop by tomorrow.

I was dreading my next call. But since she hadn't checked in about Grandmother's care, I'd have to call her. Tanya was half asleep when she answered. I tried to make it short and sweet. "Tomorrow, you need to be here early. There's a lot to go over. Come in something you don't mind getting dirty. No is not an option. See you tomorrow." I returned the phone to the cradle.

I rolled my eyes as I realized I still didn't have a key to lock the door. Again I put chairs under the knobs to lock us in. I wanted to call Spencer to vent, but tomorrow was going to be another long day. I took my place on the couch.

The next morning, we began the new routine. Mrs. Culpepper was there bright and early. Grandmother ate a full meal and was in a pleasant mood. Patricia dropped off some markers and poster board on her way to work, and I made Grandmother some reminders to let her know who would be by and at what time, as well as what time she was to eat and how much she had to eat. Since the mortgage was a big concern for her, I included on each board what day I'd be paying the mortgage for her with "Because I love you, Lizzy" written beside it.

I made a list of supplies to get for Mrs. Culpepper. Anything else she needed she'd have to get from Tanya. And yes, I'd assigned days for Tanya to come by and check on Grandmother. It was sad that I had to do that, but I wasn't sure she'd do it on a regular basis. Until I knew she wasn't blowing smoke about the sitter, I planned as if there wasn't going to be one.

Daddy came by as planned and looked at all the work I'd been doing. "You can put me in on a couple of those days, too," he said.

"I appreciate that, but you know Tanya would have a cow."

"I believe we both know that running into her here is less likely than seeing her in town."

I didn't argue and put his name on the schedule. Daddy was chatting with Grandmother when Mr. Simmons arrived for our meeting. His arrival reminded me that it was noon—Tanya still wasn't there.

We reviewed everything I needed to know about the will, filing for the estate, taxes, and a bunch of other things I could have gone a lifetime without needing to know. He put a rush on the death certificate so the ball could get rolling before I left town. The insurance money was more than I'd thought it would be; Mr. Simmons had a policy in his possession. It was all a little overwhelming. Mr. Simmons had just closed his briefcase and was getting ready to leave when the front door opened abruptly.

Tanya marched in and went straight to Daddy. "What are you doing here?" she demanded.

Without even looking at her, he said, "Visiting with Grace. How are you today?"

"I don't want you in this house. Get out."

"Tanya, it's okay. Doyle and I have been having a lovely time," Grandmother said.

"Mother, you don't know what a lovely time is," she spat. Then she turned back to Daddy and pointed toward the front door. "Get out!"

Without changing his tone, Daddy said, "Tanya, I believe we need to talk outside. Grace, please excuse me for a moment." He walked over to Tanya, and she staggered as he gripped her elbow and lifted her up just a bit. She had no choice but to go outside with him.

Mr. Simmons said, "I'll see my way out."

I watched Mr. Simmons go out the front door; he'd be walking right into Daddy and Tanya. I decided not to go outside. Tanya had brought this on herself, and it was between the two of them. We'd had a very good day, and I wasn't going to let her ruin it. Whatever Daddy said to her—and hopefully not *did* to her—might just get her in check. About ten minutes passed without any raised voices. When they walked back in, Tanya was much quieter.

Tanya took stock of the schedule I'd made up for Grandmother. I went over everything with her. At dinnertime, I showed Tanya how to get Grandmother to eat. After dinner, we walked outside and sat in the swing, while Daddy stayed in the background and kept a watchful eye over us. Eventually he and Mrs. Culpepper had a pow-wow as well, away from everyone else. I was grateful for whatever he was doing to make this easier.

Patricia and Rhonda stopped by and brought some magazines for Grandmother, who was thrilled. While everyone was there, I made a mad dash to Momma's house to shower and change. I checked the mail and the answering machine. Driving back, I saw blue lights in my rearview mirror. I wasn't speeding. *Damn*, I thought as I pulled over.

I let the window down as Chief Brown made his way to the side of the car.

"Hey, Lizzy," he said in a deep voice.

"Hey, Chief Brown. Am I in trouble?"

"No, but do you have a minute?"

I didn't, but since he was the chief of police, I surely wasn't going to tell him that. "Sure. What's up?"

"I know you hate small-town talk. Hell, Pam said that's why you moved to Montgomery. But I heard what happened with Tanya. Is there anything I can do to help you?"

"Actually, Chief, there is."

"You name it," he said.

"Grandmother wanders if she's not watched. You know Mrs. Culpepper and all these fine ladies will do their very best. Tanya is supposed to hire a sitter, but until then, they can't watch all the time. Nighttime seems to be the worst. Do you have twenty-four-hour patrol?"

"Yes."

"Can you keep an eye out and let me know if you ever happen to find Grandmother wandering?"

"That's it? That's all you need?"

"Yes, sir. It would be a huge worry off of me if you could do that," I said.

"Then consider it done."

"Thank you so much!"

He told me to drive safely and sent me on my way. When I got back to Grandmother's house, I could see that Grandmother was ready for bed, and I told Tanya to help me get her in.

"You just watch and see what needs to be done," I said.

I pulled the covers back, and Grandmother sat down. We removed her shoes. I held her hand as she eased onto the pillow. With my foot I pushed the shoes toward the head of the bed. "That's so if she gets up in the night, she doesn't step down on them and risk a fall," I whispered to Tanya. I turned on the nightlight. Before closing the door, I told Grandmother, "I love you."

She replied, "I love you more."

Patricia and Rhonda hugged me and whispered goodnight. Daddy told me he'd have his cell on and to call him if I needed him. Then Tanya and I were alone.

"Did you bring an extra key?" I asked.

She dug in her purse and pulled it out. Instead of handing it to me, she placed it on the counter. "Same time tomorrow," I said to her. "You have three more days to get the hang of this."

"I can't get this in three days," she whined.

"You don't have a choice. Same time tomorrow. Goodnight." The sooner she left, the less likely the silver would be mentioned. I locked the doors behind her. Though I'd thought I might get to sleep in a bed, I decided it was too far from Grandmother. I returned to my place on the couch.

Chapter 22

The next two days went by quickly and uneventfully. Grandmother was getting into her new routine, and all the people involved in the process were getting the hang of their roles. I was feeling a little less apprehensive about leaving.

Mr. Simmons was working diligently to get the estate matters settled and had filed the appropriate paperwork in my place since I was unable to leave Grandmother's. He brought by things that needed my signature and kept me informed about Mr. Beasley. Even though Tanya hadn't mentioned it, there was a filing in the court for us to battle over the silver service. She'd dropped everything else on the list.

When she came in, I made sure she was kept too busy to think about it. And when Grandmother went down for the night, I immediately told her goodnight and sent her out the door. Because I was spending all my time with Grandmother, I hadn't been able to get anything taken care of at the house. But I used my time well, making lists of the things I had to do before I could leave.

Friday morning, I asked Mrs. Culpepper to stay a little longer. It was my last day in town, and I had to do a few errands. She was so kind. "Honey, you've been here night and day. You don't owe me an explanation. Just go do what you need to do. We'll be fine."

I opted not to tell Grandmother I was leaving; I went out the back door. This would be a test of how well she'd do without me. I went to the house first to shower and make myself presentable, check the messages, and grab the safe deposit box key. At the bank, I ran into some of Momma's co-workers and friends. I spoke with each of them politely but briefly.

The bolder ones spoke directly about Tanya and the lawsuit we were about to enter into. Someone reminded me that the battle over the silver had been going on for years; she told me to stand my ground, that my mother would want it that way. Their words about Tanya were not kind, and I tried desperately to keep my commentary to a minimum. A small crowd had gathered around me, and the bank manager came out of his office to rescue me.

"Why don't we let Lizzy take care of her business?" he said.

"Thanks," I whispered. I showed him the box key, and he escorted me to the vault. Once I had my box, he closed the door to the privacy room. Inside the box were all the things I'd left for safekeeping. Withdrawing the mahogany box that held the silver, I remembered what one of the people in the bank had said: "Your momma and Tanya have been laying claim to that silver service for years, and it was rightfully to be Pam's. Your grandparents would have wanted it that way."

I looked down at the silver, remembering when the struggle had begun. It had started at Christmas many years ago. Grandmother had set a formal table. Holding up one of the silver forks, Tanya sang, "I can't wait for this to be mine one day."

"Yours?" Momma asked sarcastically.

"Yes, Pam, mine. I'm the oldest, and it will be mine first."

"But I was always the favorite, so that trumps your age factor," Momma told her with a smile.

"We'll see."

When we left Grandmother's that night, Momma told me, "Your grandfather wanted that silver to go to you. If for some reason Tanya outlives me, you fight for what's yours."

I'd brushed it off at the time, but now things had changed. Closing the lid on the silver, I could hear Momma saying it plain as day. I put all the items in a box I'd brought. *Tanya, if you want any of this, you're going to work for it! You've hurt me beyond the point of no return,* I thought.

With my cargo I drove to the flower shop and purchased two beautiful arrangements. Then I went to the cemetery. The flowers on Momma's grave were dead or dying; I was glad I'd gone to the florist. I spent some time removing the dead arrangements. Then I placed one new arrangement at the head of Momma's grave and the other next to Grandfather's grave. I went back to the car and got the box from the bank. I set it all out on the ground between their graves.

"Who knew the trouble this was going to cause?" I said out loud. Another visitor looked over at me; I just waved. He waved back and began moving toward his vehicle. As he drove away, I thought, *All this is why I moved away. People don't know how to mind their own business.*

I walked over to the car, let the window down, and turned the radio on to keep anyone else from overhearing me. Then I sat down again between the graves.

"I'm supposed to be leaving today, but I don't know how I'm going to make that happen. I've got so much to do at the house! I'll probably leave tomorrow. Plus, I want to pop in on Tanya after a night with Grandmother and be sure they both made it through. I think Grandmother will be okay. Mrs. Culpepper has been a godsend."

For some time I watched the clouds roll by, listened to the radio, and watched a rabbit hopping around. I saw Daddy's truck pulling in from the far side. I laughed and shook my head as it came closer and closer.

As he got out, I said, "I swear you don't have a job."

"I told you, I do what I need to. I went to Grace's, and Mrs. Culpepper told me you had some errands, and I thought I might find you here," Daddy said.

"How are they doing?" I asked.

"Great. Grace is happy as a clam."

"Good. That's one worry I can let go of now," I said.

"So what's going on here?" he said, pointing at the stuff I'd spread out on the ground.

"Not much." I didn't know what to say. I had no clue why I'd laid everything out, other than to just see it for myself.

"You seem to be doing well today," he said, changing the subject. "Is this due to the great escape back to Montgomery?"

"Partly, I guess. Now that I have Grandmother settled, it's time for me to find a new routine of my own. The past few months have been about treatments and care for others. I wonder what I'll do with myself?" This was the first time I'd really thought about it.

"I've always heard that you're not supposed to make any life-changing decisions for the first year."

I said, "Everything I do is life-changing. Nothing is ever small-scale. Haven't you noticed?"

"You know what I mean," he said, smiling.

"I have to find a house. It's something I promised Momma. She said she wanted me to have something of my own that no one could ever take from me."

"You don't think you'll move back here? Into Pam's house?" he fished.

"God, no!" The words came out fast. My throat closed up at the thought of how suffocated I'd feel being back under the thumb of all the townspeople. "I'll come back and visit and fight Tanya over this suit, but I could never move back here."

"I understand." He sounded a little deflated.

Then it hit me, and I felt like a heel. He was fishing to find out where he and I stood. It had been so long since he'd been a consideration for me. "I'll let you know when I'm coming, and the last time I checked, the roads run both ways," I added.

With a little more perkiness, he said, "Good. I'll look forward to it."

Gathering everything up, I said, "Since you don't work, why don't you come back to Momma's with me? I've got to clean out the fridge and do some laundry."

We spent a couple of hours talking while we got the house ready for me to leave; then I wanted to go back to Grandmother's. After I locked the door behind us, he put his arm around my shoulder and gave it a squeeze. It was as close to bonding as we'd ever gotten, and it felt good.

Tanya and I arrived at Grandmother's at the same time. "I hope you brought some clothes," I told her.

"For what?" she said.

"To stay the night and through the weekend. Grandmother needs to get used to you being here instead of me."

"Lizzy, I ca—"

I cut her off. "If the next word out of your mouth is *can't,* then you need to figure out how to make it *can*, because you are going to stay here. She needs to transition into relying on you instead of on me. Are you having any luck finding a sitter?" I noticed she was wringing her hands.

She whispered something I couldn't understand. When I moved closer, I saw tears in her eyes.

"What?" I asked.

"I'm scared, okay?" she shouted. "Pam always handled this kind of stuff."

"This stuff?" I raised my eyebrows at the way she was diminishing Grandmother's life. "This stuff is what you wanted. What seems to be the problem?"

"Lizzy, stop being so damn hard on me!" The tears were flowing freely now.

"Wow!" I sighed. "Where were all these tears when Grandmother was diagnosed with this awful disease? Where were all these tears when your sister was given a death sentence? You cry for yourself and what you'll have to endure—never for anyone else."

"I did cry!" she said between sobs. "I just did it in private. No one needed to know."

"Thanks for sharing. Now can you dry up this pity party?"

"I can't do this." She was sliding down the side of her car, sobbing.

"Well, you'd better find a way is all I can tell you. Now cut this out." My words were cold. I reached into her car and grabbed the keys out of the ignition. "I'm going in to see Grandmother. Work this out and come inside, please." I started toward the house.

"Just give me the silver and take her with you, Lizzy," she said. I stopped dead in my tracks.

Without turning around, I said, "I know I did not hear you correctly." So it really was just about the silver, and not about Grandmother at all. I wasn't shocked—this just confirmed what I already knew—but I was shocked to hear her say it. Everything we'd done this week—the hearing, getting Grandmother a good support system—had been a sham. I waited for a response. When one didn't come, I turned to look at Tanya. She was standing straight up now, her shoulders back; the tears had miraculously stopped. I was raging inside. I walked back over to her.

"Lizzy, we can work this out right here and right now," she said calmly. "We can pack up her things. I'll even help you."

"You made us go through all this turmoil this week when I could have been settling her in Montgomery with me. I offered this to you, and you took her anyway. You must have shown Brad the financial records I gave you."

"He has nothing to do with it," she said.

"So are you admitting you're truly this evil?" I asked.

"I won't make this offer again. You may want to think it over. I'll give you five minutes," she said snidely.

"There's nothing to think about," I replied.

"Then you are no longer needed here," she said, snatching her keys from my hand.

"Thanks for that," I said coldly.

"For what?"

"For freeing up my hand!" Without thinking twice, I punched her in the face. She'd pushed me too far; I'd reached my limit. She fell to the ground, holding her eye and truly sobbing this time. "Tanya, I'm learning your backstabbing ways. If I thought for one second you'd really let me take Grandmother, I'd give you what you want. But you want to do this in a driveway and not in front of a judge, or anyone else, for that matter—which reminds me of how untrustworthy you are. You'd just love to be able to report me for kidnapping! Judge Culpepper laid down the law to you about Grandmother's care, but now let me tell you my own requirements. If you so much as hurt her feelings, I'm going to finish what I've started here. Understand?" Still holding her eye, she nodded rapidly.

Rhonda's car pulled into the driveway. The headlights illuminated a troubling scene—Tanya crouched on the ground, with me standing over her. Patricia and Rhonda ran over to us. Neither woman reached down to console Tanya; they simply looked at me for answers.

I said the first thing that came to mind. "She fell." Both women fought hard to hold in their laughter. I had to walk away—I wanted to hit her again.

Patricia grabbed Tanya's elbow mercilessly to help her up. "Girl, I can't pick you up. You have to help." Tanya tried to get to her feet. "What did you do?" Tanya was sobbing so hard she couldn't speak. Patricia scolded her, "When will you learn not to push these Wallace women so hard?"

Rhonda joined me on the porch, and we watched Patricia dusting Tanya off. "What'd she do?" Rhonda asked.

"Told me I could take Grandmother if I gave her the silver."

Rhonda snickered. "Right here in the driveway, after everything you've been through?"

"My point exactly."

"Pam popped her once, too."

"Don't try to make me feel better." It was hard for me to believe that Ms. Cool, Calm, and Collected would have ever punched someone.

Rhonda said, "I'm serious! Tanya doesn't know when to quit while she's ahead."

Rhonda smiled and shook her head. If I'd felt the least bit sorry for hitting Tanya, that feeling was gone now. It wasn't justifiable just because Momma had done it, too, but I was relieved to know that even the most docile among us could be pushed to their limit. I'd never hit anyone before.

We watched as Patricia and Tanya walked toward us. Tanya was still sobbing. "Oh, stop it!" Patricia said. "After all you've done, you should be grateful it wasn't worse."

I could tell that Tanya would have a shiner. I went inside to check on Grandmother in the den. I knew it the minute Tanya walked into the kitchen.

A very stern voice called out, "Elizabeth Wallace!"

Grandmother asked, "Who is that?"

I sighed. "It's Mrs. Culpepper. I'll be back in a minute." When I entered the kitchen, I saw that Mrs. Culpepper had placed an ice pack on Tanya's eye.

"Elizabeth Wallace, did you do this?" Mrs. Culpepper scolded.

I stuck to my story. "She fell!"

I hadn't realized Grandmother had followed me until she said, "Tanya, I told you one day you were going to push Pam too hard."

Tanya and I avoided each other as much as possible for the rest of the evening, speaking only about Grandmother's care. Once Tanya put her to bed, I left for Momma's house. After I settled in, I called Spencer and told him everything, including hitting Tanya.

"You are too much of a saint," he joked.

I laughed. "I hit Tanya and I'm a saint?"

"Yes, because you should have just unleashed on her! You show too much constraint."

"You are not a good influence."

"Never claimed to be. What will you follow up with tomorrow?"

It was a sobering moment. "The grand finale. Coming home."

Chapter 23

I woke up early the next morning, threw on some clothes, and headed straight to Grandmother's. I walked up the front steps with Mrs. Culpepper, who used her key. The house was clean, but Tanya looked awful—she had a black and blue ring around her eye. Mrs. Culpepper just looked at me and shook her head.

"How did it go last night?" I asked Tanya.

"Fine."

"That's good. Is she up yet?"

"Yes. She wouldn't bathe, though."

"Come with me. This is something both of you need to know." We ran through the routine with the soap, tub, washcloth, and clothes. While Grandmother was bathing, Mrs. Culpepper and I chatted. Tanya sulked.

"I'm packed and will be leaving by ten. Is there anything you need before I go?" I asked.

"No, baby, I think we're all set. You've been a big help showing us how to handle Grace," Mrs. Culpepper replied.

"I can't promise this won't all change as the disease progresses, but as it does, we will, too. Thank you so much for agreeing to help Tanya out until she hires a sitter." I hadn't heard anything else about that since the hearing. I heard Grandmother getting out of the tub and went into the bathroom. Right on schedule, she looked at the tags in her clothes. "Still Grace Jenkins?" I asked her.

"Yep, still mine," she replied.

"Need some help?" I asked. I didn't want to crowd her, but offering to help was automatic.

"I think I can do it."

"You just call if you need help." I heard her humming as I walked away.

In the dining room, I told Tanya, "It's going to be a good day."

"Wonderful," she snapped.

"Before she comes out, I'm going to head back to the house and load the car."

"What? And not say good-bye to Mother?" Tanya asked sarcastically.

"I won't, for both your sakes. Unlike you, I know what's best. She won't even remember my being here. But if she asks, tell her I'm running an errand. I hope you find a way to handle all this. It doesn't matter to me whether you like it or not, but you'd better take it seriously."

To Mrs. Culpepper I said, "You have my numbers, and please don't hesitate to call if there's any change in Grandmother or if Tanya here decides to bail on you. Okay?"

"You know you'll be my first call; then I'll call Doyle," she replied, glancing at Tanya.

I gave her a huge hug and a kiss on the cheek. "Take care of my girl," I whispered in her ear, fighting the tears. Leaning back and taking a deep breath, I turned to Tanya. "See you in court." Without waiting for a response, I left.

After packing the car, I called Daddy and the girls to tell them I was leaving. I couldn't handle the emotional good-byes in person; they were emotional enough over the phone. I called the phone company to set up a disconnect date. After securing the house, I got in my car and backed slowly down the driveway, and then I watched the garage door close. My chest felt tight. I put the car in drive and then watched the house in the rearview mirror until it was out of sight. I pulled into the cemetery and sat quietly for awhile. Then I went on my way.

Though I usually drove with the radio on, today I just cried the whole way. My mind was too noisy already, filled with all the thoughts and events from the past few weeks. After I pulled into the parking lot at my apartment, I shut the car off and walked up the stairs. I fought the urge to call Mrs. Culpepper immediately; I wanted her to know I trusted her. After unloading the car, I sat on the couch in my quiet apartment. I'd believed I'd feel so much better when I got home, but now I was lonely and felt a thousand miles away from Grandmother. I busied myself with cleaning. I'd been gone for almost a month, and everything was dusty. My own fridge looked like a science experiment—I'd left too hastily to clean it out, worried only about getting home to Momma. When I couldn't take it anymore, I called Grandmother's. Mrs. Culpepper reported that she was doing well but had asked for me few times. I thought it was best that she didn't tell her I was on the phone. After we hung up, I cleaned into the early morning hours, when nothing remained untouched. *Now what?* I thought.

I picked up the phone to check voicemail but called Momma's number instead; it wouldn't be disconnected until Monday. The machine picked up. "Hi! You've reached my machine. Leave me a message at the beep, and I'll call you back," Momma's voice said. A long beep followed. I whispered into the receiver, "I miss you." I called the number so many times that weekend that I filled up the tape.

On Sunday, I spoke with "the crew," as I had dubbed them. Patricia and Rhonda had seen the aftereffects of my punch to Tanya's eye. Mrs. Culpepper told me how Grandmother was doing. Grandmother told me how Mrs. Culpepper was doing. Daddy told me how Tanya was doing. I was happy to hear that life seemed to be going well.

The phone rang as soon as I hung up. "Hello?"

Spencer joked, "Lizzy Wallace? Is this *the* Lizzy Wallace?"

"No, this is her assistant. How may I help you?"

"Well, you tell that bitch boss of yours to get on the phone."

I laughed. "What are you doing?"

"Giving you some time to get settled before harassing you."

"Well, I'm settled now."

More seriously, he asked, "How are you doing?"

"Somewhat better. I just hung up with everyone, and it seems to be going well." I heard the ER noise in the background. "You must be at work."

"You know it. You coming back soon?"

"I'm scheduled to come back tomorrow, but I'm dreading it," I said.

"I think it'll be good for you to get back to work and busy yourself with other things."

"It's not the work I'm dreading; it's the people and all their condolences. You know how that goes," I said.

"I'm sure you've had enough of those, so don't expect that from me."

I couldn't help but laugh at his bluntness. "Well, okay, I'll just take you right out of that category." I heard his pager chirping. "No rest for the wicked, eh?"

"The wicked or the wonderful. Everyone wants to see me!"

I rolled my eyes but laughed. "Yeah, yeah, yeah."

"Seriously, I get off at seven tonight. You got anything in that refrigerator of yours?"

Usually I had all kinds of leftovers and could count on Spencer to help me get rid of them, but I hadn't cooked since I'd been back. "I have to go to the grocery story. What are you in the mood for?"

"Spaghetti." I heard his pager again.

"Sounds good. See you later."

I had everything ready when Spencer arrived. We ate and laughed as he told me the latest hospital gossip. He was interested in a new nurse, but he hadn't asked her out yet. Everything seemed normal, and it felt good.

The next morning, I called Grandmother and talked for a while. She was so excited. Mrs. Culpepper was cooking dinner for Grandmother that night, at her house across the street. She told me this several times, and each time I just acted like I hadn't heard it before. Before we hung up, I said, "I love you."

She replied, "I love you more."

As I suspected, when I walked into work, several people immediately slammed me with condolences and questions. Out of the blue, Spencer stepped in and shooed them away, telling them to give me some room to breathe. In the office I shared with Spencer, I found a flower arrangement on my desk. The card read, "Welcome back. Now get to work. Spencer."

I put down my stuff, put on my lab coat, and grabbed my tray. We busted ass for the rest of the night. Every now and again someone said, "Glad to have you back, Lizzy." I walked out exhausted, crashing as soon as I got home.

The next few weeks were a whirlwind. I made regular visits to see Grandmother when I wasn't in the ER. Tanya was never around when I was there, which I considered a blessing; her absence gave Mr. Simmons and me time to work on the case during Grandmother's nap. He wanted to make sure I was unshakeable during the trial. Mr. Beasley had really touched a nerve.

I tried to stay as busy as possible; I wasn't sleeping much. When I slept, I dreamed of Momma. These dreams weren't welcome; they all featured her when she was sick, more like nightmares than dreams. I didn't tell anyone about them. I thought I was losing my mind. I just used a lot of makeup to hide my sleep deprivation.

Once Momma's life insurance money arrived, Spencer accompanied me as I began house hunting. He was very patient as I looked at house after house, taking weeks to find exactly what I wanted. I was nervous when it came time to sign all the paperwork at the closing, and I regretted not taking Spencer up on his offer to come with me. This was a huge step, but I finally had a house like I'd promised Momma I would. It was an emotional event.

As I walked out of the attorney's office, my cell rang. I tried to compose myself. "Hello?"

"What's wrong?" Spencer asked.

"I say 'hello,' and you ask what's wrong. Why?" I tried to steady my voice.

"Because you sound upset. Stop answering my questions with a question. What's wrong? Did something happen with the closing?"

I wiped my eyes. "No, I'm just being a girl." I knew I'd lose it if I told him how I wanted to call Momma and tell her all about it.

"Are you better now?" he asked, truly concerned.

"Yes."

"Good. Where are you headed now?"

It was almost three. "This took longer than I expected, so I'm going to wait until tomorrow to go to Grandmother's. I'm going back to the apartment."

"I'll meet you there."

When I pulled up to my apartment, he was already there. Spencer looked over all the paperwork as I fixed us some tea.

He asked, "So how much about this house am I going to have to change?"

"Just a few things."

"Few?"

I laughed. "We have to walk through it again so I can see where I might put what before I can tell you exactly."

"Are you going to have room for everything?"

"Spencer, I'm moving from an apartment to a house. Of course."

His voice was serious. "You have another house full of stuff."

My heart began to race, and my face got hot. I didn't say anything.

"Lizzy, I've noticed how you avoid your mom's house when we're there," he said. If our off days coincided, Spencer traveled with me on day trips to see Grandmother. He did the yards at Momma's and Grandmother's while I visited.

Softly I said, "I don't want to talk about this right now, okay."

"I'll drop it, but I want you think about how good it would be for you to have some of your mom's things."

If I removed anything, I'd be removing her. I couldn't do that.

He said, "I'm sorry for upsetting you."

"It's not you. I just need some time."

He tried making small talk to change the subject, but I wasn't up for it now. After we said our good-byes, I laid down on the couch for awhile, thinking about what he'd said. I'd have to find the strength to stop avoiding Momma's house and start going through some things.

I drifted off to sleep and had a vivid dream. Momma had just bought her house, the first house she'd ever purchased, which meant it was years before the cancer diagnosis. However, as she hung pictures on the living room wall, I saw that she had the turban on her head, the little catheter leading to the access port for the chemo, and dark circles under her eyes.

She smiled. "Hey! I didn't expect you until the weekend."

"Momma, I need to see you before you were sick," I begged.

Without directly acknowledging what I'd said, she smiled. "Of course, little one. There's a box of photos right there." She pointed to one of the boxes in the floor.

It was the box of pictures I'd gone through to find pictures for the collage for the funeral. I ran over, opened the lid, and grabbed a handful of pictures. I flipped rapidly through them, but the only image on the photos was of her lifeless body in the hospital bed. I looked up to show them to her, but she was gone. I screamed, "Momma!"

When my eyes opened I was sitting up, crying and hyperventilating. I closed my eyes and tried to rub away the image. Then I went to look at a picture of her on the bookshelf. She was smiling, healthy. Closing my eyes, I could see the same picture I'd just been looking at, but she was sick. I sank to the floor. "When will I ever remember you well?" I cried, holding the picture close to my heart. "I spent most of my life with you healthy, and now none of that exists."

Chapter 24

It didn't go unnoticed by Spencer that I made two trips to see Grandmother without mentioning them to him. He was helping me move into my new house when he confronted me about it.

"You just going to let the grass grow waist high or tell me the next time you go?"

I froze, remembering the nightmare our last conversation about Momma's house had caused.

"Lizzy, it's about the yard, nothing else. We're both off in a couple of days, and I'm going with you."

I nodded. We managed to get everything moved from the apartment in one day. Even though a ton of empty space remained, Spencer didn't mention Momma's house again.

Our next day off, he picked me up bright and early so he could try to beat the heat of the day. When he dropped me off at Grandmother's, I gave him the keys to the house as I had many times before. I'd never asked if he used them but wanted to be sure he could get in if needed.

Grandmother was getting worse. Today I had to remind her who I was. This was painful, but I knew it was inevitable. When I told her who I was, she said, "I have a granddaughter named Lizzy. She's a sweet little girl." Then she turned back to the television.

Mrs. Culpepper must have seen the hurt on my face. She placed an arm around my shoulder.

Softly I asked, "Is this getting to be too much for you? I know you said you thought it would be worse to bring in someone new, but I can tell Tanya a sitter is needed now. Even though we haven't talked much, I'll do what I have to for Grandmother."

"No, honey, but I do need to talk with you." Her voice was serious. Before I could say anything, she said to Grandmother, "Gracie, let's go outside and get some sunshine."

Grandmother asked, "Can we go to my house?"

Mrs. Culpepper had told me that Grandmother had been talking more and more about her childhood home. Rarely did she remember that this was the place where she'd lived with Grandfather and raised her family. I felt guilty that I hadn't just moved back here with her. Maybe having her family around would have slowed the acceleration.

Mrs. Culpepper didn't miss a beat. "Maybe later. Do you mind helping me pick some flowers?"

"That would be lovely."

Once we were outside, I waited patiently so as not to disrupt the routine they'd established with each other. When Grandmother was involved in her task, Mrs. Culpepper joined me in the swing. Her face was serious.

"A few nights ago, Michael brought Grace to my house. She'd crawled out the window, and he found her walking down the street."

"What?" I said rather loudly.

"Shhhh. I don't want Grace to hear and be reminded of it," she scolded.

I looked at Grandmother. She seemed undisturbed by my outburst.

Mrs. Culpepper continued, "She said she was going home. I didn't even know she could get the windows open, but when we checked the house, we found that she'd been working on one of them and had gotten it open." She pointed to one of the windows on the backside of the house.

"How did she get to the ground? That one is over my head."

"I don't know, but that's the one she went out, and we don't think it's the first time—there was a stepladder against the house."

Daddy arrived at that point; he often met me at Grandmother's when I came to visit so I could spend as much time with her as possible. Seeing my face, he said, "I see you told her."

"Yes," Mrs. Culpepper replied.

"Why have none of you told me this? When was it?" I alternated my gaze between the two of them. "Why didn't Michael call me?"

"I told him not to. I knew you'd be back to visit soon and she was safe for the time being. The girls and I have been staying around the clock. It happened three nights ago," Mrs. Culpepper said.

I was angry that I was just now finding out about this, but I was more concerned for Grandmother's safety. "Did you tell Tanya?"

"Yes, I called her." That was all she said.

"And what has she done about it?"

Daddy and Mrs. Culpepper looked at each other and didn't say anything.

I stood up and demanded, "And what has she done about it?"

"She hasn't been here," Mrs. Culpepper said sheepishly.

"Wait a minute," I said, trying to wrap my head around this. "Did you call her the night this happened?"

"Yes, before Michael left."

"When was she here last?" I asked fiercely.

"Ten days ago."

"I need you to take me to Tanya's office," I said to Daddy. "Mrs. Culpepper, are you okay here for a little bit?"

"Of course," she replied.

"If my friend Spencer comes back from Momma's, will you tell him I'll be right back?"

"Yes."

Daddy and I drove to Tanya's corporate office where she worked as a manager over sales and marketing. The receptionist welcomed us and at my request, paged Tanya Dumas; then I asked for a phone book. I'd left Grandmother's house without my purse, and I needed the number for the Department of Human Resources.

While the receptionist paged Tanya, I borrowed Daddy's cell phone to call DHR. The operator immediately put me through to Helen, the social worker Judge Culpepper had assigned us. I'd called her before leaving town to introduce myself, and I hoped she remembered me.

"This is Helen."

"Helen, this is Elizabeth Wallace. Do you remember me talking with you a few months ago about my Grandmother, Grace Jenkins? Judge Culpepper put me in touch with you."

"Yes, of course. What can I do for you?" Helen listened as I explained what Mrs. Culpepper had told me.

"Are you with Mrs. Jenkins now?"

"No, ma'am, I'm at Tanya's office. I've had her paged."

"Is she still working in that office building on Magnolia Place?"

"Yes, ma'am."

"I'll be there in five minutes."

As I hung up the phone, Tanya appeared and we stood toe to toe. "Do you want to do this in here, or would you like to step outside?" I asked her in a low, deep voice.

Without speaking, she started toward the front door, sidestepping Daddy. Once we were outside, she spun around and opened her mouth to speak—but shut it when she saw Daddy standing behind me.

"I've called DHR, and the social worker is on her way. Do you have any explanation for this?" I asked. She said nothing. "Well, you have about five minutes to get your thoughts together before Helen gets here. She's going to need to know why you haven't secured the house or checked on Grandmother since her night stroll three days ago."

We all stood in silence and waited for Helen to arrive. When she pulled into the parking lot, I waved her over. "Thank you so much for coming," I said.

She nodded at me and then directed her attention to Tanya. "I've been in touch with Chief Brown and gotten the account of the night

Grace Jenkins, your mother, left her home. Can you tell me when the last time was you checked on Mrs. Jenkins?"

"I was there a few days ago," Tanya muttered.

"Mrs. Dumas, this is a very serious matter, and if you have anything to say in your defense, I need to hear it now." Helen waited for Tanya to respond. When she didn't, she continued, "You'll need to get your purse so we can go to Mrs. Jenkins's house."

"I can't just leave work!" Tanya shouted, throwing her arms up.

"You should have taken that into consideration before I had to get involved, Mrs. Dumas, and I am going to kindly ask you to lower your voice," Helen said coldly. "I'll have Chief Brown meet us there with the officer's report."

Grandmother and Mrs. Culpepper were still in the yard when we arrived. Chief Brown pulled in behind us, but Tanya wasn't there yet.

Helen said, "Hello again, Mrs. Culpepper. How are you today?"

"Better now, Helen. Thanks for asking."

As Mrs. Culpepper approached us, Daddy stepped away. "I'm going over here with Grace so y'all can talk."

"Elizabeth tells me you've had some excitement since my last visit. Why didn't you call me?" Helen asked.

"I knew when Lizzy was coming, and I felt it would be better to let her call. We haven't let Grace be by herself since this happened."

"I'm sure you've taken great care of her."

"May I take Grace to my house while all this is going on? This might be too much excitement for her."

"Of course. We're just waiting for Mrs. Dumas." Helen glanced at her watch. Chief Brown looked up the road.

I said, "Let me help you."

"I'll get Doyle to help. You take care of this," Mrs. Culpepper said. Grandmother took Daddy's arm, and the three of them headed across the street.

I showed Helen the window Mrs. Culpepper had pointed out to me. Chief Brown went over his report while Helen made notes in her folder. Thirty minutes passed before Tanya arrived.

"I'm glad you could finally join us, Mrs. Dumas," Helen said sternly. "It appears Mrs. Jenkins's condition is progressing faster than we had anticipated. I'll be reporting this to Judge Culpepper for his review and including my recommendation that your mother be moved into a facility."

Tanya said sarcastically, "I'll work on getting a sitter for her then."

"Mrs. Dumas, it's my understanding that this is something you told the judge you were going to do at the time Elizabeth petitioned for guardianship."

"Mrs. Culpepper told me not to! She said it would hurt Mother more."

"Mrs. Dumas, she was probably right at the time she told you that, and I'm sure she was only trying to help her friend. But the current situation is not working. As I said, I'll write my recommendation in my report, but the decision will be up to the judge. For now you need to make arrangements until this issue is resolved."

Tanya was silent. Her face was red, the vein in her forehead protruding. Helen seemed unaffected by Tanya's apparent anger.

"I am aware that Judge Culpepper takes a special interest in this case, so I'm sure his decision will be swift. Do you have any questions?"

Tanya pointed at me and spat, "What's her part in all this?"

"She has no part. It's been the work of Elizabeth, along with several others, that has gotten you this far. You took guardianship, and that makes you solely responsible for the well-being and care of your mother. Any other questions?" Helen said matter-of-factly.

"No!" Tanya growled.

"Mrs. Jenkins is across the street with Mrs. Culpepper. I'm going back to my office to get in touch with the judge. When I return, you need to have a plan in place until we have his ruling." Helen closed her folder. "Thank you for meeting me here, Chief."

Tanya was quiet until Helen's car pulled away. "Why are you doing this to me?" she screamed at me.

Chief Brown was startled. "Wait just a minute. This is not Lizzy's fault."

Glaring at him, she screamed, "Of course you'd take her side!"

"I'm going to warn you against screaming at me, Tanya. Do I need to remind you that you took all this on yourself? Lizzy tried to get you to stop and think about it. I was there the day this all went down," he said.

Tanya was out of control. "I want all of you out of this house and off this property!"

Chapter 25

I left Chief Brown to deal with Tanya. I could barely hear her screaming as I thought about what would happen next. I hadn't been prepared to hear that Grandmother was ready for a nursing home. I was so deep in thought that it took a couple of seconds for my brain to register that my cell phone was ringing. It was Helen.

Immediately I asked, "Were you able to talk with the judge?"

"Yes, and that's why I'm calling."

"Does he agree with your recommendation?"

"Elizabeth, I'm having a hard time hearing you. What is all that noise?"

I ran off the porch and into the driveway. "Is this better?"

"Much. Are you still at Mrs. Jenkins's home?"

"Yes. Tanya lost it after you left. Chief Brown is in the house with her, but that's not important. Did the judge agree with your recommendation?"

"Yes and no. I'm on my way back there. Can you meet me at Mrs. Culpepper's?"

"Yes, I'll be waiting."

Chief Brown came out of the house, his face flushed. I wanted to tell him what was going on, but before I could speak he barked, "That damn woman is going to keep on until I find a reason to haul her ass to jail!"

"Maybe it's not the time to tell you this, but Helen is on her way back and wants to talk with me at Mrs. Culpepper's."

"No, no, you do what you have to. I'm going to stick around until this is resolved."

"I'm sorry you have to deal with this."

He leaned against his patrol car, shaking his head.

Before going inside Mrs. Culpepper's house, I called Spencer. "Hey, I only have a minute."

"Are you ready? I haven't done your grandmother's yard yet."

"No, that's why I'm calling you. All hell has broken loose up here. I don't have time to explain, but can you wait there until I call?"

"Are you okay?"

"Yes, we're just having some issues. I'll call as soon as I can."

"If you need me, call me."

"Thanks."

Grandmother was napping. I'd just finished explaining what had happened when Helen knocked on the door.

Mrs. Culpepper invited her in. "Can I get you some tea or coffee?"

Helen smiled. "No, ma'am. But thank you."

We all took a seat around the dining room table. I had a ton of questions but wanted to hear what Helen had to say first.

Helen said, "Judge Culpepper was surprised at the information I brought him today."

I looked at Mrs. Culpepper. "You didn't tell him what happened?"

She replied, "Lizzy, I've never forgiven myself that you didn't get guardianship. I knew you'd be here in a couple of days, and I wanted you to deal with it the way you needed to. I didn't want to make it worse."

I put a hand on hers. It was hard to believe she still blamed herself. Helen waited a minute before she continued.

"Elizabeth, I told you he agreed and disagreed with my recommendation. He believes you all have done a fine job getting Mrs. Jenkins to this point, but he has overlooked the fact that Tanya hasn't helped. We're at a crossroads now."

I asked, "Do you really think it's time for a nursing home?"

"Unfortunately, yes. She needs to be somewhere with alarms and twenty-four-hour monitoring for her own safety."

"This is an isolated incident," I pleaded. "What if I agree to move in with her?"

"Well, that brings me to why I wanted to talk with you here. She needs to be in a facility. It's only going to get worse from here. The judge believes Tanya will put Mrs. Jenkins in the first place she finds, regardless of the care she'll receive."

"I believe that, too!" I said.

"He wants to grant guardianship to you so that you can find somewhere close to you. He knows you'll go see her and be sure she's taken care of."

"Let's do it!"

"Here's the problem. His docket is completely full until the middle of next week."

I was anxious to get this started. "Couldn't he do a hearing in his office like we did before?"

"No, that was just a meeting to see if there was just cause to actually have a hearing. This really needs to be done in the courtroom."

"What are we going to do until then?"

Reluctantly she said, "We have to talk to Tanya."

Daddy had been just listening until Helen said that. "Have you heard what's been going on over there since you left?"

She replied, "Yes, I spoke with the chief, and he's waiting for us."

"Well, I hope you don't object to me going with you."

"No, but you have to remember that she does still have guardianship until the hearing next week."

I heard Grandmother in the other room. Mrs. Culpepper got up, but I stopped her. "Please, let me. I haven't had any time with her this whole visit. I'll just be a minute."

When I walked in, she smiled sweetly. "Lizzy, when did you get here?"

"Just a little while ago. You were sleeping, and I didn't want to disturb you."

She looked around. "Is this my room?"

"No, ma'am. You've been visiting with Mrs. Culpepper at her house."

"Can I go home now?" I didn't know if she was talking about the house across the street or her childhood home.

"Do you mind waiting until I get back before we go?"

"Okay."

I kissed her forehead. "I love you."

She replied, "I love you more."

Those four words meant everything to me. When I returned to the dining room, I had a renewed feeling of courage. Any apprehension I had about sharing this news with Tanya was gone. She could scream until her head fell off. This was for Grandmother.

Chief Brown said to us, "Let me go first."

As we walked into the house, I heard Tanya say, "I'll have to call you back." The moment she saw me she screamed, "I told you to get out!"

The chief's voice was firm. "Tanya, I've heard all the screaming I'm going to listen to for one day. Helen needs to talk with both of you, so pipe down."

Tanya barked, "Then it doesn't involve him." She pointed at Daddy.

Helen stepped in. "I think you have bigger things to worry about. Have a seat, and let's get started."

Tanya opened her mouth to speak, but Chief's voice was loud. "Sit down!" He pulled out a dining room chair, and Tanya sat without any more argument. "Jesus! If you'd been this concerned about Mrs.

Jenkins, maybe we wouldn't be here." His editorial surprised me. When he looked at me and pointed to a chair, I sat quickly.

Tanya snapped, "There's still no need for Doyle to be here."

I said, "Daddy, can you step outside and call Mr. Simmons for me? Please tell him what's going on here and what we've discussed."

He looked at me for a beat. I just nodded.

Once he was outside, I asked Tanya, "Can we get started now, or is there anything else Your Highness desires?" She squinted her eyes but said nothing.

Helen began. "I've spoken with the judge, and he agrees that Mrs. Jenkins needs to be moved to a facility."

"Whatever. That's fine," Tanya said.

Helen asked, "May I finish?"

Tanya's expression told us we were wasting her time. She didn't answer.

"He also wants guardianship to be transferred to Elizabeth, but the docket is full until the middle of next week. You're going to have to make arrangements to be here with Mrs. Jenkins twenty-four seven until the hearing."

Tanya asked with disgust, "Me personally?"

"Judge Culpepper feels you've had ample time to hire a sitter, and you didn't. He's not going to allow his seventy-year-old mother, Elizabeth, Rhonda, or Patricia to be responsible for Mrs. Jenkins until the hearing. He requested that I make it clear to you that, as guardian, you have to care for her."

Tanya huffed, "Fine."

Tanya's compliance made me uneasy. I asked, "Why don't you just let me take it from here, Tanya?"

Tanya smiled devilishly. "And go against the judge? Not on your life!"

Something isn't right, I thought. "Helen, I'm not comfortable with Tanya being here. She's made it abundantly clear that this is the last place she wants to be."

"I completely understand your concern, Elizabeth, and I personally will be here every day to check on Mrs. Jenkins's welfare."

Chief added, "I'll be coming by daily, too."

Tanya laughed. "You people act like I'm a criminal or something!"

Helen turned her whole body toward Tanya. Her words were harsh. "No, but neglect *is* a criminal offense. If Mrs. Jenkins gets so much as a paper cut, I'll press charges against you. Is this serious enough for you now?"

Tanya relaxed back in her chair and crossed her arms. Looking straight at me, she said softly, "Oh, yes, real serious."

Now I knew something wasn't right. My anxiety was escalating. "Could I stay here with them?" I asked.

Tanya sat straight up and slammed her hands on the table. "I won't have it!"

I saw Chief Brown lunge forward. Placing his hand under her arm, he said, "Come with me!" He took her to the back of the house.

Helen's voice was sympathetic. "I'm sorry, Elizabeth. It would be counterproductive for you two to be here together. Even the judge expressed that to me. I really will be by here every day. She'd be crazy to let something happen to Mrs. Jenkins."

Sarcastically I said, "You have met Tanya, right? She's far from the epitome of sanity."

"We just have to get through the next eight days."

Chief Brown returned alone. "Lizzy, can I talk with you outside?"

"Yes, sir." I followed him out.

Daddy was sitting on the porch steps, waiting. "What's going on?" I asked.

Chief Brown ran his hand through his hair. "Tanya's made arrangements to have some clothes brought here, so she's not leaving. But she wants you gone."

Daddy asked, "Can she do that?"

"I'm sorry, but she's threatening to file a TRO against you both. I'm trying to keep that from happening."

I asked, "What the hell is a TRO?"

Daddy replied, "Temporary restraining order. On what grounds?"

"Trespassing," he replied.

Daddy's neck reddened, and the muscles in his jaw contracted. "Funny how none of us have been trespassing before now."

"Doyle, I know. Trust me, I know. I'm on your side with this, but you know it won't look good for Lizzy to have a TRO against her next week during the hearing."

Daddy's face softened. "Lizzy, he's right."

Helen came out of the house. "Tanya wants Mrs. Jenkins brought back over. I'm going to stay for a while to monitor things."

I looked back toward the house and saw Tanya through the window, watching us. "I'll go get her. But before I do, you all need to know I have a bad feeling about this."

Chapter 26

Not long after this, back at the hospital, Spencer and I both had a lull between patients. Spencer asked, "You hanging in there?"

"I don't know yet." It had been four days since we'd left Grandmother with Tanya. "Helen says things have leveled off some."

"I still can't believe she put everyone out."

"Mrs. Culpepper has taken it the worst. She still sits all day watching Grandmother's house for a glimpse of her." I felt bad; at least I had work to keep me busy.

"Brad still being the delivery boy?"

"Yes. Mrs. Culpepper would have been happy to fix meals for them, but Tanya couldn't have that."

"Will Helen go by to check on her over the weekend?"

"Helen and Chief both said they would. I've been invited to stay with Mrs. Culpepper since I'm off."

"Are you going?"

"I don't know. I could visit with the girls. Helen says I'm halfway there, and she doesn't advise provoking Tanya."

"I know it's not funny, but I'm sure it would rattle Tanya to see Patricia, Rhonda, Mrs. Culpepper, and you all sitting around Mrs.

Culpepper's dining room window watching your grandmother's house."

"Wouldn't it, though!" I laughed.

"Seriously, have you heard from any of the nursing homes?"

"Yes, and the one I really liked has an opening. As soon as we step out of the hearing, all I have to do is call. Are you still going to be able to help me move her?"

"Yes. You sure you don't need me there Wednesday night to help you pack?"

Before I could answer, the desk phone rang. "Lab, this is Lizzy."

Madeline, one of the ER nurses, said, "Girl, I need you over here in bay four. Dr. Allen is screaming for the test results, but I overlooked them so they didn't get ordered."

"I'm on my way." I put the phone back in its cradle.

Spencer said, "We'll talk later."

I grabbed my tray and hurried over to bay four. When I pulled the curtain back, I was overwhelmed by an all-too-familiar smell. It radiated from the pores in the skin like bad cologne. Chemotherapy. My breath caught in my throat.

I looked in slowly at the woman lying on the gurney. Sunken eyes, bald head, yellow-tinted skin—she looked like my mother. This time I wasn't dreaming. I blinked several times, trying to erase the image.

A woman by the bedside asked, "Are you okay?"

I cleared my throat and tried to speak confidently. "Hi! I'm Lizzy, and I need to draw some blood."

The same woman said, "The other nurse tried and couldn't get it."

"Are you her daughter?" I asked.

"Yes, ma'am. She's really hard to get blood from because of the chemo."

Softly I said, "I understand." I looked down at the woman's armband and closed my eyes for a second to fight back the tears. "Ms. Nichols, I'm going to put this tourniquet on and just look for a moment, okay?"

She sounded tired when she replied, "That's fine, dear."

I rubbed her arm softly. The skin was dry with little elasticity. "Ms. Nichols, have you been taking in many fluids?"

"Not since this last round of chemo. It seems to have been worse this time. Everything just makes me nauseated."

I found a spot to get the blood and let her know what I was about to do. I continued talking to get her mind off what I was sure was the thousandth needle stick she'd had. "Have you tried some ginger?"

"Yes, someone told me about the tea."

"No, ma'am. Not the tea, the root itself. Try chewing on it. That way nothing is sitting in your stomach to make you vomit."

"That's one thing I haven't tried. Makes sense, though."

"It helped my mother a lot with the nausea and indigestion."

"Oh, the indigestion is the worst. It feels like pure acid in my throat."

She hadn't even realized I'd already gotten her blood. I placed a bandage over the puncture site. "It's good to pass on information. You never know what might work."

Her daughter asked, "You got it?"

"Yes, we're done."

"Thank you so much," Ms. Nichols said. "It gets so old being stuck repeatedly. You said your mother chewed the ginger? Did she take chemo, too?"

"Yes, ma'am."

There was concern on her face when she asked, "How's she doing?"

I knew she needed to hear that someone had made it through this terrible disease. She needed the reassurance that everything she was going through was not in vain.

Softly I said, "She's doing well. You take care of yourself."

Spencer saw me coming through the office door. He grabbed the tray from me. "Lizzy, are you okay? You're so pale."

Tears rolled down my cheeks. "I can't do this anymore," I said.

"What can't you do?"

"This job. Be around the sick and dying. I just can't do it anymore."

He didn't seem surprised. "You lasted longer than I thought you would."

"What?"

"You went through something very traumatic. Did you think it wouldn't affect what you do on a daily basis?"

Should I tell him about the nightmares or that tomorrow is Momma's birthday? The first one without her, I thought.

His beeper chirped. "I've got to get this, but you sit here and chill for a minute."

We both got so busy that the end of my shift came before we were able to talk again. I left a note for him. I'd decided not to go to Mrs. Culpepper's, and I'd be home tomorrow, so I invited him for lunch before he came into work.

I didn't sleep much that night. I dreamed of that dreadful night I got the call and was told Momma had two weeks to live. I made some coffee, sat on the patio, and watched the sun rise. In the silence of the morning, I thought long and hard about her, my job, and what to do next. Time got away from me. Lunchtime was approaching, and Spencer would be here soon. After sticking a roast in the oven, I showered and got dressed.

While we ate, I told him, "I'm resigning."

"I figured as much, after what I saw last night. What are you going to do?"

Proudly I announced, "Cosmetology school."

He laughed. "Well, I guess that's about as far from the medical field as you can get."

"Yes it is, and I can't wait."

"Are you going to share with me what happened last night? You went from fine to meltdown in a matter of minutes."

I told him about the cancer patient and then added, "Today would have been Momma's birthday. She would have been forty-eight." I suddenly lost my appetite.

"Oh, Lizzy, I'm sorry. Why didn't you tell me?"

The phone rang. I pushed away from the table. "Saved by the bell."

"Let it go to voicemail."

"Can't. I haven't heard from anyone about Grandmother today." I recognized Helen's number on the caller ID. "Hey, Helen. How's everything?"

Her tone was very serious. "Elizabeth, I've waited to call you until I had more information."

Panic flooded my body. It must have shown on my face because Spencer stood up from the table. I held a shaking hand up to keep him from saying anything.

She continued, "Tanya has moved your grandmother to a nursing home in Baldwin County."

Questions swirled around in my head. I was barely able to ask, "When?"

"It seems she did it yesterday afternoon."

"That's not possible. I talked with Chief Brown, and he'd just checked in on them."

Spencer came up beside me. "Lizzy, what's wrong?"

"Tanya's moved Grandmother to a nursing home in Baldwin County. Get on the extension." I wanted him to just listen in rather than interrupt.

As he went to get on the other phone I heard him ask, "Isn't that four hours away?"

"Helen, Spencer's just brought up a good point. How could she move Grandmother four hours away and none of you notice they were gone?"

She said, "It's only two hours from here, four from Montgomery."

She was right. I'd forgotten where I was. "I'm sorry. I'm not meaning to be rude. I just don't understand."

"I know, and believe me, it's okay."

I asked, "How did she move her without Mrs. Culpepper knowing?"

"Her car was in the driveway until this morning. Mrs. Culpepper got up and noticed it was gone. She called me and then let Chief Brown and me in with the key she still has. That's when we discovered that some of Mrs. Jenkins's clothes were gone. Chief Brown went to Tanya's house, and she told him what she'd done."

Spencer asked, "What the hell can Lizzy do about this?"

I couldn't remember if they'd met. "Helen, that's my friend Spencer. He's on the extension."

"Yes, I remember him. The judge is out of town, but Mrs. Culpepper has called him. We spoke this morning, and he had me find out about the facility."

"And what did you find out?"

"I've never seen it, but I know of it. They have an Alzheimer's unit, and I've heard mixed reviews about it. I've spoken to the director and made her aware of our situation. She informed me that this cleared up some questions she had about Tanya's urgency to have your grandmother admitted."

I was mad as hell but relieved that Helen knew something about this place. "What do you think we should do?"

"Until our hearing on Wednesday, Tanya still has guardianship, and she's operating within her legal rights. There's not much we can do."

"I want to see Grandmother."

I could hear Helen sigh. "Tanya has not included you on the list of visitors."

"Didn't you say the director knew our situation? Wouldn't she let me see her?"

"While she does sympathize, she doesn't want to get the facility involved. I know it's not what you want to hear, but let's not rock the boat. Wednesday you'll have guardianship, and we can make more decisions then."

"You're right. I don't want to hear that. I warned you that something wasn't right."

She was silent for a beat. "There's one more thing. I don't know if it's important, but when we were in the house we noticed that Tanya has packed all of Mrs. Jenkins's things up in boxes."

Chapter 27

After speaking with Helen, I insisted that Spencer go into work. There wasn't anything he could do for me but listen to me fume over Tanya. He told me he'd come back after his shift.

I'd just closed the door when the phone rang again. The girls, who'd just heard the news, were calling with three-way calling to find out what was going on. I shared everything Helen had told me.

Rhonda asked, "Do you think this is because y'all have court in a couple of weeks about the silver?"

I hadn't thought about it until then. "It would be just like her to do something like this for that reason."

Patricia said, "I think you need to call Bill."

"I will on Monday, but there's nothing we can do right now. No sense disrupting his weekend."

We talked for a bit longer. Neither had forgotten it was Momma's birthday, and they were going to put some flowers on her grave. They invited me along, but I declined. I told them about the patient the night before and my decision about my job. They, like Spencer, were unsurprised.

My call waiting beeped. "Daddy's calling. Will you be there

Wednesday?" They both told me they would. We said our good-byes, and I clicked over.

Before I could say hello, he said, "I just spoke with Mrs. Culpepper. Why haven't you called me?"

"I was just hanging up with Patricia and Rhonda. I haven't had a chance."

"What are you going to do?"

I explained everything again. "So until Wednesday, nothing."

"Mrs. Culpepper said everything in Grace's house was boxed up."

I'd forgotten about that. "I guess Tanya was filling her time, even though I can't imagine why she'd do it."

"I wouldn't be surprised if there was even more to moving Grace."

He sparked my curiosity. "What are you thinking?"

"I don't know, but nothing is ever this cut and dry with your aunt."

I snapped, "She's my mother's sister, not my aunt."

He laughed. "I stand corrected. Seriously, I wouldn't ignore those boxes."

"Grandmother's house is full of sentimental items. Nothing of great value."

"Maybe not monetary value, but, as you just said, sentimental. That makes them more valuable to you than to her."

"Mr. Simmons explained to me that since Momma is dead and Grandmother is widowed, Tanya and I are equals. So I don't think she can do anything without me."

"She moved Grace without you." His words stung.

I thought about Rhonda's question and Tanya's obsession. "Do you really think the silver is this important to her?"

He replied, "No, but I think hurting you is."

"Why?"

"Because Buddy loved you."

I thought about what Grandmother had said about the sibling

rivalry and what she probably hadn't meant to say about the clothes. "So you're saying all this is because my grandfather loved me?"

He backed down. "I don't know what it's about. I was just talking."

I snapped, "Don't do that! If I ever questioned Momma about Tanya, she always backed out of the conversation, too. Whether she meant to or not, Grandmother told me about Tanya shredding Momma's clothes. It's really hard for me to believe this is all because she may have felt unloved—that's ridiculous!" I waited for him to say something.

Softly he said, "I'm sure Pam had her reasons for keeping things from you."

"I'm sure she did. But, considering the circumstances, I don't think she'd mind if you told me."

He paused for a moment and then began the story. "Your grandparents, Pam, and Tanya are the only people who truly know what happened. It was a closely guarded secret within the family. I know Tanya's jealousy of Pam was off the radar. I don't know if it was a chemical imbalance or what, but she was ruthless in her attempts to hurt your mother. It got worse as they got older." I listened quietly, afraid he'd clam up if I said anything. "I didn't know about the clothes until now, and that makes me want to believe it was an imbalance. If Pam excelled in something, Tanya had to top it. Pam was popular in school, and Tanya did everything possible to destroy it. Her efforts only isolated her. Kids can be ruthless, and they labeled her 'the weirdo.' Before your mom and I started dating, Pam had been interested in someone else. Even though Tanya had been allowed to date before Pam, she hadn't. The guys didn't ask her out because she was so weird." He took a deep breath. "Are you sure you want to hear this?"

"Yes. I want to know."

"Tanya went after Pam's boyfriend. Male hormones being what they are, he didn't resist her. Then she gloated about being pregnant with his child."

I gasped. "She lied?" I thought how prim and proper Grandmother had been—this must have crushed her.

He was quiet for a moment. "No, it wasn't a lie. Pam's first boyfriend, Tanya's first husband, and Adam's father are the same person."

My mouth fell open as I thought of Uncle Darryl. How could I not have known about this? Grandfather always treated him differently. He rarely spoke to him; when he did, his remarks were short and stern. I'd never thought about it, but Adam's age would have made Tanya a senior in high school. Darryl and Momma were the same age, so he would have been a junior.

Daddy asked, "You still with me?"

I was angry. "Uncle Darryl must not have cared for Momma if he could do that to her and then marry Tanya!"

"It was a different time. They had no choice. Both sets of parents felt it was the only thing to do."

"But wouldn't that have been enough hurting for Tanya to do?"

"It was for a while. But somehow Pam found a way to forgive her—for the life of me, I never could understand why. Adam was born, and Grace and Buddy were happy to have a grandson. Everything seemed normal. After graduation, Pam and I married; a year later, we found out you were on the way. While Pam was pregnant, the sisters were thick as thieves. However, your birth seemed to start everything all over again. We were all there when they brought you in. Everyone passed you around, but when you were handed to Buddy, something inside Tanya flipped. She wouldn't hold you after that. Didn't have a lot to do with you or Pam. She brought Adam around less and less. It tore Pam up."

I thought of how Momma must have felt. "How sad."

"It was sad for everyone. Tanya ran so hot and cold. She'd love Pam and you one minute and then hate you both the next. Grace and Buddy had issues over it. Pam and I had issues over it. Ultimately, Darryl left Tanya because of it. Because you were a constant in Buddy's life, you were like his little Pam all over again. I know Adam felt thrown away by

Buddy, but Buddy kept having his heart broken by Tanya. Eventually he just gave up trying."

"But that was years ago."

"Some wounds run too deep to be healed. Your mother never gave up, though. Whenever Tanya threw her a crumb of hope, she grabbed on for dear life. I think that explains the amendment to the will. Then, during her last week of consciousness, she saw it was just another game for Tanya."

I heard Momma telling me, *Don't trust the people you think you can trust the most.* She really had been talking about Tanya.

"So do you understand why I think there's more to those boxes in Grace's house than meets the eye?" he asked.

"I do now. I'm still going to wait to call Mr. Simmons, because since Tanya has guardianship, there's nothing I can do right now. Plus, Judge Culpepper is out of town. I really appreciate you sharing all that with me."

"I think Pam would be displeased, but it's out there now. Maybe it will help you understand what you're dealing with."

"I have to admit, I never expected something like this. I can see why Momma decided it best not to tell me. As you well know, I'm less forgiving."

He laughed. "I know all too well."

I had one more person to check in with: Mrs. Culpepper. When I called, I could tell she was extremely upset. I told her what the plan was and about the facility Grandmother was in. This seemed to ease her anxiety somewhat. When Spencer arrived that evening after work, I filled his ears with everything Daddy had shared with me. He was stunned.

"And here I believed my family had some issues," he said.

I laughed. "Is your offer still out there to come down on Wednesday?"

"Sure. What do you have in mind?"

"Storing that boxed-up stuff in Grandmother's house until Tanya and I can reach some kind of compromise."

"With the trial right around the corner, I don't think she's going to be willing to do any wheeling and dealing with you."

"I know, but I can get Mr. Simmons's advice on what happens to everything with Grandmother in a nursing home."

"Are you bringing her here or leaving her where she is?"

That was the million-dollar question. "I wish I knew. How many changes can she stand? Helen will have to help me with that one."

Sunday began early. Nightmares had kept me up again, and I was exhausted. I decided to wait awhile before calling Helen. Just because I was up early didn't mean the whole world had to be. As I poured a second cup of coffee, the phone rang, startling me. It was Mrs. Culpepper.

I tried to sound chipper when I picked up the phone. "Glad I'm not the only one up at such an early hour."

She was stressed. "Lizzy, there's an auction house truck at Grace's. They're moving those boxes out."

"What?"

"The sign on the side of the truck says Gorum's Auction House. I don't know how long they've been there. I just got up."

Quickly I said, "Sit tight. Let me call Daddy and see if he can get there."

Daddy answered on the second ring. "Hello?"

My voice was panicky. "You were right. Mrs. Culpepper just called. A Gorum's Auction House truck is in front of Grandmother's, and they're loading up the boxes."

I heard a lot of noise in the background. Then he said, "I'm on my way there! Call Bill and find out your rights. I'll call Chief Brown."

"Do you think I have time to get there?"

"Probably not. Just wait for my call." He disconnected.

Mr. Simmons answered in a raspy voice. "Hello?"

I took a deep breath and tried to steady myself. "Mr. Simmons, it's Lizzy. I'm sorry to call you so early, but I really need your help."

"Sure, Lizzy. What can I do for you?"

I explained what happened yesterday and what was happening this morning. "What are my rights?"

"I need to check something before I can answer you, and I know time is of the essence. Are you somewhere I can call you right back?"

"Yes, sir. I'm at home."

"Call Doyle and tell him not to enter the residence without Chief Brown there. We don't want to create a bigger mess."

I did as he instructed. Daddy was almost to the house; he, too, told me he would call me back. The minutes seemed like hours. When the phone rang, I snatched it up.

"Mr. Simmons?"

"Yes, Lizzy. I found what I was looking for, but it's not good news. Tanya is required to pay for your grandmother's facility out of your grandmother's own money, since Mrs. Jenkins still owns land and a home. Because she still has guardianship, she's within her legal rights to sell the smaller things within the home to raise the funds for the facility's bills."

"So you're telling me there's nothing we can do to stop this?"

"I'm extremely sorry, but no."

"What about my rights as Momma's heir?"

"While I'm sure she went through and took what she wanted before packing those boxes, she really doesn't have to let you have anything. Now if she tries to include the house and the land, we can go after her for fraud."

"Do you think that's really going to happen?"

"No. I'm sure she's well schooled on her legal rights. But she should know whatever money she makes at this auction will have to be reported. Once you take guardianship, it will transfer to you for Mrs. Jenkins's care."

I felt deflated. It wasn't the money I cared about but the memories. Instead of trying to convince him to do something, I said, "Thank you."

"I'm sorry there isn't more I could do. I'll see you on Wednesday."

I called Daddy with the update—there was nothing we could do. He had to let them take the stuff in the house.

He barked, "I'll be damned if there's nothing we can do!"

Everything went silent. "Daddy?"

After calling back and getting his voicemail, I called Mrs. Culpepper. I told her what Mr. Simmons said and asked if she'd look across the street and tell me if Daddy was still there. She'd been watching the whole time and reported that he'd sped off just a minute before I called her.

Where was he going? I wondered. "Mrs. Culpepper, is Chief Brown still there?"

"Yeah, baby, he's watching these guys. Do you want to talk with him?"

"Yes, ma'am. Please. Can you have him call me?"

A moment later my phone rang. "Chief, I need someone to go to Tanya's."

Chapter 28

As I waited for someone, anyone, to call, my mind raced. Daddy was known for being a hothead, and I feared he was going to confront Tanya. I called his cell again; it went straight to voicemail. "Daddy, I don't know what's going on, but I really need you to call me," I said. Just as I hung up, the phone rang. "Daddy?"

"Lizzy, it's Michael."

"Are you at Tanya's?"

"Yes, and I don't see Doyle's truck, so I'm not going to the door. I'll wait here on the street for a little bit and see if he shows."

"Will you call me if you see him?"

"Yes."

"Thanks. I'll let you know if I find out where he is."

I called his cell again, got voicemail, and hung up. Another hour passed before the phone rang again. Without waiting for caller ID to show the number, I picked it up. "Hello?"

Daddy asked, "Lizzy, what time can you be here tomorrow?"

"Be where? Where are you?"

"I've been to the auction house. Floyd Gorum owns Gorum's. He's someone from my past who owes me a favor. The auction is scheduled for tomorrow. I've arranged for you to be able to walk through in the morning. I hope you don't have to work."

I was planning on resigning tomorrow, but I'd have to talk with Monica first thing to explain my situation. "I'll be there. I don't know where this place is."

"Meet me at Mrs. Culpepper's at nine. I'll pick you up. Lizzy, prepare yourself, because they're getting everything in the house, not just the boxes. Tanya's already sold it to them for a flat fee."

I sighed heavily. "Are you kidding me?"

"I wish I was."

I called Michael back to tell him Daddy had reappeared and to thank him for his help. If I had to be there at nine, I'd have no time to talk with Monica. I decided to call her at home and get it over with. I apologized profusely for disturbing her and then told her my decision to resign. I explained what had happened with Grandmother over the weekend.

She said, "I'll be sorry to see you go. Nobody can work the ER like you can, but I completely understand. I know you've been through hell since your mother's passing, trying to take care of your grandmother. I also can relate with what you're going through with this relative of yours. It seems every family has a greedy one. I was lucky mine didn't take it to this extreme. I know your plate is full, so what I'm going to do is unprecedented. It has to stay between you and me."

"Okay."

"With the hearing on Wednesday and your trial next week, it's going to be hard for you to work out an official notice, so I can let you opt out now."

"I don't want to burn my bridges, though!"

"Oh, no, you won't. That's up to my discretion, and I'll leave you in the system for rehire should you change your mind."

"Monica, you've been so good to me—I don't want to leave you high and dry like this."

"Losing you is traumatic enough whether or not you work out the notice."

I felt sad. "Thank you."

I called Spencer with the news. He said, "Holy hell! I leave you alone for less than a day, and this happens?"

I laughed. "This roller coaster travels fast. It's hard to keep up."

"I can't believe Tanya's already got her things up for auction."

"Daddy says she sold it all for a flat fee. I'm sure that makes things go faster."

He added, "Especially when she's just getting rid of it to spite you."

"Sad but very true."

"Are you going to stay until Wednesday?"

"No, I have to get guardianship first."

He was quiet for a moment. "You do have another house you could stay in."

"I think I've been through enough for one day."

The next morning, Daddy and I met at Mrs. Culpepper's. We invited her to go with us. The auction house was larger than I'd imagined. Rows and rows of cars were parked in the open fields surrounding the building. A big-bellied man waving a flag directed us to the next open parking space.

As I got out of the truck, several people called out to me. I didn't recognize any of them. Mrs. Culpepper waved to a few people, telling me their names, but I still didn't recognize them. I was shocked that this event was such a big thing in this small town.

Daddy led us not toward the building but to a small trailer serving as an office. When we entered, a tall, skinny man stood up from behind a desk. He wore overalls with a T-shirt; the building logo peeked out from behind the bib.

"Doyle, good to see you again. This must be Lizzy." He held his hand out to me. "Listen, if I'd known you weren't aware of what was going on, I wouldn't have bought your grandmother's things."

"You must be Floyd."

"Yes, ma'am. At your service."

"Well, sir, you've made a deal with the devil herself."

He laughed. "I like your style, little lady. You're just like your momma, and for that, we've made some special arrangements just for you."

"Arrangements?"

"Doyle, you didn't tell her?"

Daddy said, "No, Floyd. I thought I'd let you have the honors."

"In just a little bit, we're going to get started with the actual auction, but first you need to do a walk-through. Most of the people out there have been affiliated with your mother or grandmother at some point, but there are also dealers. We've assigned you a seat in the front. The people who know your family have been made aware of your seat. When the auctioneer opens the bid, people are going to look at you for what to do. If you want what's on the block, you place a bid. None of our people will bid against you. If you don't want what's on the block, look down at your lap. Follow me so far?"

"I believe so."

"Now, like I said, there are dealers out there. They're here for big-ticket items like antiques, and we can't control if they bid against you. Should you not bid and one of our people wins an item from your grandmother's house, you'll have another opportunity to purchase it for the winning bid from the person who won."

I was overwhelmed. "How did you pull all this together?"

"Phone! We're better than the PTA phone tree."

"Why would you do this?"

"I respected the hell out of your mother, owed your pops here a favor, and, basically, I can't stand for someone to be done wrong. If I can help right a wrong, I'm all for it."

"Thank you."

Clapping his hands together loudly he said, "Alright then, let's hit it!"

I walked through with him and then was shown my seat. Daddy and Mrs. Culpepper sat with me. I'd never been to an auction. Daddy explained the paddle to me and reminded me about looking at my lap if I didn't want to bid.

There was a huge stage in front of us, covered with some of Grandmother's things. As I looked at them, I caught sight of Tanya. She smiled at me smugly. I watched her for a moment, thinking how many of the people in this room knew why we were here. Without warning, I jumped up from my seat. I waved the paddle furiously and screamed, "Hey, Tanya! Want to sit with me?"

Daddy and Mrs. Culpepper burst out laughing. Hisses and boos came from behind me. Tanya's face reddened, and she ran from the building.

I plopped back down in my seat. "Damn, that felt good!"

Daddy continued to laugh. "I bet it did."

The auctioneer appeared and got the auction underway. It went so fast. I lost only a couple of items I wanted to the dealers, including my grandmother's china. After the auction, I approached the man and explained my situation to see if he'd sell it to me. He doubled the price, though, and I had to refuse.

"Did you get it?" Daddy asked.

"No, he's asking more than I can give, but that's okay." I tried not to let my disappointment show. Seeing the china at the auction had been shocking. Tanya was fighting for the silver, but the china meant nothing to her.

"A couple of people are by the truck with items to show you. I have to go and thank Floyd for his help. I'll be right back."

When he returned, he placed a box in the bed of the truck, closed the tailgate, and drove us back to Mrs. Culpepper's. Daddy loaded my car while I said good-bye.

"Thanks for going with us," I said.

She laughed. "My favorite part was when you jumped up and scared Tanya. You scared me at first, but when I saw her, it was worth it."

"That was too good!" We laughed.

Daddy came up beside me. "It's all loaded."

"Thanks. I appreciate you setting that up for me."

"No problem. You better get going before it gets late."

I couldn't leave without stopping by the cemetery. The headstone had been placed, and I saw the flowers the girls had brought by on her birthday. The beautiful blooms couldn't hide her birth and death dates. Even though her death was final the day she took her last breath, seeing the headstone really drove that harsh point home.

When I got on the interstate, I called Spencer. Hurriedly he said, "It's swamped here. I'll come by after work."

As I drove, I thought about Spencer's comment on Momma's house. Though I dreaded it, somehow I needed to come to terms with it. I felt that moving her stuff would remove her, but ignoring it was abandoning her. I decided to first see how it felt having some of Grandmother's things in my house.

I took my time unloading the car. I strategically placed something of Grandmother's in every room, remembering where it had been in her house. When Spencer arrived, there was only one box left. He appeared to have a hard time bringing it in.

He asked, "What in the world is in this box?"

"I'm not sure. I don't think I got anything that should be that heavy."

He set it gently on the floor. When he opened it, I saw it was Grandmother's china. My eyes filled with tears.

Softly I said, "Excuse me. I'll be right back."

The phone rang a couple of times before Daddy picked up. "Hello?"

"Grandmother's china. How?"

"How isn't important. That it's with you is."

Chapter 29

Driving to the guardianship hearing, my mind wandered, and my cell startled me when it rang. Spencer, driving behind me, must have seen me jump. He was laughing. "Scared?"

I laughed too. "Just thinking about this guardianship thing. Last time I felt sure they'd transfer it to me, but it didn't happen. You don't think that will happen today, do you?"

"No, it's just a formality. Don't worry so much."

I wasn't going to argue, but I was still going to worry. I changed the subject. "Tell me again what you have to do at Momma's?"

"There's just some stuff I didn't get done that I wanted to do. You let me handle my thing, and you handle yours."

"Are you sure you're not coming because you're actually worried things won't go as planned?"

"Lizzy, stop! You really have nothing to worry about. That's not what I'm doing. Is Helen going down with you once it's over?"

"Yes, we're going to check out this facility. If it's okay, I'm not going to move her." Even though I wanted her closer to me, Helen had agreed it might be best not to put her through another change.

"Well, let me know when y'all are out and on your way. My turn is coming up. It's going to be fine."

I saw his blinker in my rearview mirror. I watched as he began to slow down. "Talk with you soon."

Spencer had been right. The guardianship hearing was just a formality. After Helen's testimony, Judge Culpepper granted the transfer. I was anxious to get out of the courtroom; I wanted to go see Grandmother. This week had been the longest I'd ever gone without seeing her, and now I had a two-hour drive. Helen made the trip with me.

Once I let Spencer know we were on our way, I asked her, "Have you told them we're coming?"

"No, I want to see how Mrs. Jenkins is living on a daily basis."

Her comment made me curious. "You think we'd see something different if we announced our visit?"

"Yes, people tend to be on their best behavior when they know what's coming."

"Helen, she's okay, right?"

She heard the fear in my voice. "Lizzy, I'm sorry. I don't believe she's in harm's way. Like I explained to you before, I've heard mixed reviews about this place. I've never heard of anyone being hurt—just patients not kept as clean as they could be, not interacted with as much as needed, things like that."

"Do you know if Tanya has been back to see her?"

"She hasn't."

Now I wanted to get there even worse than before. We drove in silence.

When we finally pulled up in front of the building, I was less than impressed. The building was extremely gloomy, with peeling paint around the porch area and overgrown hedges and trees. I immediately made comparisons to the facility in Montgomery—and this place came up short. Appearance wouldn't be enough to convince Helen she should be moved, though.

When we approached the front door, Helen asked, "Is there not a lock on that door?"

I watched as she easily pulled the door open. The facility in

Montgomery had a speaker system and keypad to keep the residents from leaving at will. No one was at the front desk when we entered. Helen looked for a sign-in sheet; there wasn't one.

She was irritated now. "How would they have known if you came to visit or not?" She pulled her cell from her purse and dialed the director's number. She frowned angrily at their brief exchange. She said, "It appears the director isn't at this facility but in an office off campus. I've got the room number. Follow me."

I did as she said. We encountered several patients, which increased my anxiety. They were wandering aimlessly, with food stains covering their clothes and pieces of food stuck in their hair. We had yet to see an employee, but we heard someone yelling at the residents. "I said sit down! Look at what I've got to clean up now!"

Turning the corner, we finally saw an employee sitting at a nurse's station. Her back was to us; she was watching TV. Helen and I walked right past without her knowing we were there. At the end of the hall, we found Grandmother's room. Helen let me enter first. Grandmother was in a chair, just staring out the window.

I bent down beside her. She looked like the other residents we'd seen and smelled of urine. My heart broke seeing her in this condition. "Grandmother?" Her eyes slowly met mine. "Grandmother, it's Lizzy." She still didn't respond.

A woman in a suit entered the room. Before she could speak, Helen said, "I take it you're the director. Let's speak outside." Helen walked briskly from the room, and the woman followed.

Grandmother's hand startled me as she softly touched my cheek. "I have a granddaughter named Lizzy."

"Yes, ma'am, it's me."

"Lizzy?"

I held her hand and looked into her eyes. "Grandmother, it's Lizzy."

I heard Helen's stern voice from the hallway. "The conditions here are unfit. We'll be moving Mrs. Jenkins today."

I didn't want Grandmother to get upset and moved to close the door. "Lizzy, please don't leave," she pleaded.

I bent back down. "Honey, I'm not going to leave. I promise. Can I close the door?" Slowly she looked toward the door and nodded. "Grandmother, why don't we get you cleaned up?" I didn't see her cane, so I helped her up and led her to the bathroom. Her pants was soiled to the knees with urine. *How long has she been sitting there?* I thought. My anger grew when I thought of Tanya just dumping her in this place. It had been only a week; I was afraid to think of the condition she would have been in if we hadn't come when we did.

Helen came back into the room. She saw Grandmother's pants. "Lizzy, I'm so sorry. What can I do to help you?"

I turned the water on. "Find me some fresh clothes for her. I don't know where her cane is, either."

"I'll handle it and get her packed."

Grandmother said, "I've already had a bath." I smiled, and we went through our routine to get her in the tub. Helen returned with some clothes. Once Grandmother was bathed and her hair was washed, I asked if she needed help getting dressed.

Grandmother said, "I don't have any clothes."

"Yes, ma'am. They're right there by the sink."

She looked at the tags. "These are not mine."

Prepared to ask if she was Grace Jenkins, I looked at the tag. She was right. Someone else's name was written on the tag. I laughed, "You're right, these aren't your clothes." She smiled. Helen went through the clothes she'd packed, searching through several different people's clothes before she found something of Grandmother's.

Helen asked, "Do you want me to look for her clothes?"

"No, I just want to get her out of here. I'll get her new clothes if I have to. Did you find her cane?"

"Yes, apparently they lock them all up in a closet."

I rolled my eyes and helped Grandmother dress. She looked so much better now, and her eyes seemed brighter. "Grandmother, I love you."

She replied, "I love you more."

Helen drove, and I rode in the backseat with Grandmother. She rested her head on my shoulder and soon began snoring. I didn't move for the whole two-hour drive.

After we dropped Helen off and I was behind the wheel, heading back to Montgomery, I called Spencer. "Hey, I don't think it would be a good idea for us to come by there."

"So she's with you?"

"Yes. It was bad but getting better."

"Where are you?"

"About five minutes from the interstate."

"Do you want me to help you get her settled?"

"No, Helen's called ahead. They're expecting us."

"How is she?"

Since Grandmother was right there, I said only, "We'll talk."

"I get it. You can tell me about it later."

Grandmother talked the whole way back to Montgomery. I just listened, enjoying the sound of her voice. She already seemed to have forgotten about the facility. For me, however, the memory was vivid.

Once Grandmother was settled at the new facility, a weight lifted from my shoulders. It was a happier place, where the staff interacted with the residents. They wanted to know our routines and engaged her in the conversation. No one yelled about what they'd have to clean up now. The residents were clean and very well attended. I was welcome to come anytime—which was good, because I assured the staff I'd be there every day. Reluctantly, I added Tanya's name as one of Grandmother's visitors, should she feel inclined to make an appearance.

Spencer was waiting for me at home. I told him about the horrid facility and how I'd found Grandmother.

He was outraged. "Is nothing sacred to this woman?"

"Yes, she herself! Any doubt I had about fighting over petty things like the silver is completely gone."

"You doubted it was right?"

"Part of me did. But after what happened while Momma was

dying, finding out the full truth about what my family had to endure because of Tanya, and seeing what she just did to Grandmother, I say bring it on!"

He nodded. "You have a fire in your eyes I haven't seen for a while. Is the trial still on for Monday?"

"Yep, and it's not soon enough."

After Spencer left, I went into the dining room and opened the mahogany box that held the silver. I ran my fingers gently over the tines of the forks, along the edges of the butter knives, and inside the curves of the spoons. Tanya's voice rang clearly in my head: "You always did have a silver spoon in your mouth." This was what she'd proclaimed whenever she felt the need to express disdain for my relationship with Grandfather. I'd heard this many times.

I smiled. "No, Tanya. But I hope after Monday that I'll have twelve!"

Chapter 30

Friday night, Mr. Simmons called to check in with me. "Ready?" he asked.

"Absolutely! I'm ready to put this behind me and move on with my life," I said.

"I think we're going to be fine. Did you get Mrs. Jenkins moved?"

"Yes, thank you."

"I know Tanya didn't leave you much choice with your Grandmother's house, but what about Pam's?"

"Once we're past this, I need to go there. It's time to resolve some things."

"One thing at a time. Don't rush it, Lizzy; you've dealt with a lot more than most people could have in a short amount of time. What are your plans for Sunday?"

"I don't know. Do I need to come down then?" I asked.

"I'm not talking about the case." His voice was so low now that I had to strain to hear him. "I was talking about Mother's Day."

I felt like someone had strangled me. I'd forgotten. How could I not have even seen an ad about it on TV? I knew I'd been wrapped up with other things. Even when the TV was on, I just stared at it, lost in thought about Grandmother. I couldn't respond.

"Lizzy, I'm so sorry! I thought you would have—oh, hell, I don't know what I thought," he said apologetically.

I still couldn't speak. What kind of daughter forgets Mother's Day? The silence was deafening. Finally, I was able to say, "I'll see you Monday at nine in front of the courthouse." Then I hung up.

I'd just managed her birthday, and now here was Mother's Day. Was every first going to be so hard? Visiting Grandmother lightened my mood, but Saturday night, nothing could stop the nightmares from coming fast and hard. I hadn't dreamed of her since moving Grandmother to Montgomery, but now they were back. When I woke up, I had tears on my cheeks. I wanted to cover my head and forget about the day, but the doorbell rang. I ignored it. When it rang again, I wanted to scream at the person to go away. Then the knocking started.

"I know you're in there!" I heard from the other side of the door. "Your car is here. Open up!" It was Spencer.

Maybe he'll give up if I ignore him, I thought. But there wasn't much chance of that. He kept pounding on the door. Angry at the intrusion, I stomped to the front door, opened it, and glared at him.

He walked in without being invited. "You look like shit."

I slammed the door behind him. "Maybe because I just woke up!"

He looked at my face closely. "I beg to differ. That looks like no sleep at all, with a side helping of pity. How am I doing so far?"

"Spencer, this is really none of your business." I really wanted him to leave.

"Everything is my business! Now, go do something with yourself. You look like hell," he demanded.

"No, thank you. Hell is a good look for me today." I threw myself on the couch.

"I know you're not talking back. This is Spencer you're talking to." His upbeat tone grated on my last nerve.

"What do I need to get ready for?"

Ignoring my question, he went into the kitchen. I didn't follow. Then he went into the dining room and started measuring the wall.

I asked, "What are you doing?"

"Just getting some measurements," he said. "Look, this is your first Mother's Day without her. I know that has to be painful in itself, plus you have court tomorrow. But after we go out for something to eat, I have something for you."

"What?"

"In due time. Right now I want you to get yourself ready."

I wanted to scream at him, but I didn't. "I have to get something out of the truck," he said. "Don't even think of locking the door." I had to laugh. "Bitch, I know your ass," he added. Then he walked out. I think he was just standing outside for a minute to give me time to pull myself together; when he returned, he didn't have anything.

I told him about my conversation with Mr. Simmons. "I wouldn't let you forget, but it wasn't necessary for you to go through the whole weekend being miserable. Why don't we stop and see your grandmother while we're out?" he said.

That was enough to make me hurry to get ready. After breakfast, we visited with her for a while. Spencer had brought her some flowers, and she just loved them—even though she didn't know who Spencer was.

Spencer whispered in my ear, "Lizzy, I'm going to leave for about an hour. I'll come back and get you." I was enjoying my visit with Grandmother so much that I just nodded.

Spencer's return was perfect timing; they were just coming to get Grandmother for lunch. I watched as she went down the hall with the nurse and disappeared into the cafeteria.

I turned to Spencer. "Where'd you go?"

"You'll see."

As we pulled back into the driveway at my house, I looked quizzically at Spencer. "What in the world?"

He shut off the truck. Softly he said, "You're going to be mad with me at first, and that's okay."

"Mad with you about what?"

"Let's just go inside." He didn't wait for me to respond. He jumped out of the truck and used the hidden key to open the door. When I walked into the house, my eyes welled up with tears. Some of Momma's things were there. Pictures, knick-knacks, and the china cabinet where the silver had been were now in my dining room. I didn't say anything. I was frozen.

"Lizzy, please don't be mad. I just thought it would help for you to have some of your mom's things."

Tears ran down my cheeks. I walked through the rooms, seeing boxes in every one. Spencer followed cautiously. I asked, "How?"

"I've been working on it when I go and do the yard. Are you mad?"

I whispered, "No." I hadn't realized how much I'd missed having her things around. One box held clothes from her closet, and I could still smell her perfume. I held one of her blouses close to my face and just cried into it.

"Is it too much?"

I shook my head. "It's perfect. Thank you."

He let me have a moment. Then he said, "I'll help you put it all away if you want."

We worked together for the next few hours, putting things away and hanging pictures. I was so grateful to have Spencer as a friend. The whole time I'd been avoiding Momma's house, he knew this was just what I needed.

I asked, "How did you load that china cabinet?"

"Patricia and Rhonda had a hand in all this. I talked with them about what I wanted to do. They thought it was a good idea."

"You all were so right."

When we finished, I was exhausted. Spencer left, and I took one of Momma's shirts to bed with me. I feared the nightmares but was unable to hold sleep off any longer.

Momma said, "Hey, little one. Look at me."

"I can't." I knew she was hanging pictures, and I didn't want to see her sick.

"It's okay. Look at me."

I moved my eyes from the boxes on the floor to her. Her hand reached out for mine. I took her hand. It felt warm. I'd never touched her in the previous dreams.

"Little one, look at me."

As I turned my eyes to hers, it wasn't like before. She was healthy and beautiful. Her face was glowing with warmth, and her eyes were soft. She had a full head of hair, not a turban.

I asked, "Is it really you? Are you really here?"

"I've been here all along, and I always will be." She touched my face with her other hand. I tilted my head into her palm to soak up her touch.

"I love you, Momma."

"I love you, too." She wrapped her arms around me, and I slept more soundly than I had in months. The alarm clock woke me early, but I was still embracing her blouse. I closed my eyes. A vivid picture of my mother's smiling face was all I saw.

I showered and headed out early so I could stop by the cemetery on my way to the courthouse. Spencer called to wish me luck; he couldn't get out of work to be there. He promised to visit Grandmother today in case I was late getting back. I told him I'd call as soon as I could to let him know how it was going.

At the cemetery, I told Momma and Grandfather, "I love and miss you both very much. Today is for the both of you." After looking at their headstones for a few minutes, headed to the courthouse.

Once I got there, I had to park some distance away; there were so many cars. I met up with Daddy, the girls, and Mr. Simmons. Sarcastically I asked, "What is this, a crime-infested place? How many cases are happening today?"

"I think they're all here for this. There weren't but three things on the docket today," Mr. Simmons said.

"Excuse me?" I looked at him in amazement. Everyone started laughing.

"Not a whole lot goes on in this town, so this is big news," Daddy said. We all started walking toward the front of the courthouse.

I thought they were kidding, but as we got closer, I saw a ton of people I knew from my childhood, as well as some of Momma's co-workers. And, of course, I saw Tanya with Mr. Beasley. She smiled like a Cheshire cat as we walked into the courthouse.

Chapter 31

I was overwhelmed. There were so many people, and all of them seemed to be speaking to me, encouraging me. The courtroom was wall-to-wall people. We took our seats at the defense table. Daddy sat behind me, and Patricia and Rhonda hugged me and went back into the hallway. As character witnesses, they couldn't be in the courtroom until after they'd testified.

Judge Culpepper was supposed to be presiding over my case, but his mother's taking care of Grandmother created a conflict of interest, so we had Judge Walker. I remembered Momma talking about him, saying that he could be a hardass. I wondered what he thought of all this. We all stood when he entered the courtroom.

Once he brought the courtroom to order, Judge Walker began, "This is the case of Tanya Dumas vs. Elizabeth Wallace concerning a silver service that was in Pam Wallace's home at the time of her death. It is my understanding that the silver belonged to Grace Jenkins." He looked up from his papers. "Is there any way we can work this out?"

Mr. Beasley jumped up. "No, Your Honor. I don't feel this can be resolved without your ruling."

Judge Walker peered at him over his glasses. "Let's just see. I'd like you ladies and your attorneys to go with the bailiff to a mediation room and talk with a mediator. I'm going to give you fifteen minutes; then we'll reconvene back here."

"What's going on?" I asked, following Mr. Simmons.

"He wants y'all to talk about it first."

"Is that good or bad?" I asked.

"He's hoping one of you will give up the fight, so I don't know."

I followed him into a closet-sized room where Mr. Beasley and Tanya were already sitting. A woman in her mid-fifties came in. She asked several questions, trying to get us to agree and then sent us back to the courtroom when we could agree on nothing.

"I see that mediation did not go well," Judge Walker said. "Then let us continue."

Mr. Beasley stood. "Your Honor, I'd like to call Elizabeth Wallace to the stand."

Mr. Simmons and I looked at each other. We hadn't expected him to call me right off the bat. Mr. Simmons whispered, "Just remember, stay focused, calm, and on task." I nodded.

I was told to take the stand and was sworn in. I sat down and missed Mr. Beasley's first comment because I was looking at all the people in the room and up in the balcony.

"I'm sorry. I was distracted by all the people here," I said, looking at the judge.

"There are quite a few today," Judge Walker agreed, looking out into the crowd himself.

"Can you please repeat that?" I asked.

Mr. Beasley said, "I was saying how sorry I am for your loss, Ms. Wallace." He waited for me to respond, but I didn't. He continued, "Ms. Wallace, are you in possession of the item in question?"

"The silver? Yes."

"Did my client, Mrs. Dumas, express a desire for this item?"

"Yes."

"When my client asked for the item in question, what did you tell her?"

"The item in question is the silver service, and I cannot remember my exact words, but the gist of my answer was no," I said coldly.

"When my client asked you for the *silver service*, did you or did you not forcibly remove her from her dying sister's home?" Mr. Beasley was trying his best to piss me off. He was succeeding.

I tried to look at Mr. Simmons, but Beasley had positioned himself between us. Remembering what Mr. Simmons's words, I tried to stay calm. I focused on a spot on Mr. Beasley's tie. "Yes, I removed her from my mother's home," I said.

He asked, "Forcibly?"

"Objection, Your Honor. What does this have to do with the service?" Mr. Simmons said. "Ms. Wallace is not on trial for forcible removal. If Mrs. Dumas felt she was in danger, she should have reported it to the police."

Mr. Beasley said loudly, "Your Honor, I'm trying to establish that my client tried to take possession of her birthright and that Ms. Wallace refused her."

Judge Walker replied, "Sustained. You asked Ms. Wallace whether your client asked, and she told you she denied Mrs. Dumas possession. How she removed her from the home is not in question here. Next question."

Beasley took a deep breath, clearly irritated. "Ms. Wallace, after denying my client the service, did you or did you not remove this item from your mother's home?"

I replied, "Among other things."

"Why would you have done that?"

"Because your client's timing was inappropriate, and I felt removing the object of her obsession might snap her back into the reality of the situation."

"So you felt it was your call to decide when it was appropriate to discuss placement of this item."

"Again, your client's timing was inappropriate. She was pursuing—"

Interrupting me, "Did you make my client believe that the service was never even in your mother's home?"

"As I stated before, I removed it from my mother's home."

"In an attempt to deceive my client into believing it had never been there?" He smiled.

I snapped, "You're assuming that's why it was removed. I haven't said I attempted to deceive your client." I took a deep breath.

Mr. Simmons jumped up and screamed, "Objection, Your Honor! Mr. Beasley is harassing my client and inserting words into her testimony." I'd never heard Mr. Simmons scream before; I shifted in my chair to look at him.

Judge Walker didn't wait for Mr. Beasley to respond. "Sustained."

In a huff, Mr. Beasley said, "No more questions!"

Judge Walker asked, "Mr. Simmons, do you have any questions?"

"Yes, thank you." He stood and walked slowly toward me. "Now, Ms. Wallace, we are aware that your mother was in possession of the silver service at the time of her death. Can you tell us how she came to be in possession of it?"

"Yes, sir. My grandmother had given it to her."

"Could we call your grandmother to testify to this?"

He hadn't posed questions like this to me when we'd prepared. I wondered where we were going with this. Cautiously I replied, "No, sir. She has Alzheimer's."

"I see. Do you know when she was diagnosed?"

"A little over a year ago."

"And when did she give the silver to your mother?"

I saw now what he was doing. He wanted to be sure that Grandmother's intentions couldn't come into question. I replied, "Almost three years ago."

"So it had been continuously at your mother's home for almost three years."

"Yes, sir."

"Did Mrs. Dumas try to take possession of the silver service during this time?"

"Not that I'm aware of."

He spoke softly because I believe he knew his next question would sting. "Ms. Wallace, why did you feel it was inappropriate timing for Mrs. Dumas to ask you for the silver when she did?"

I was glad we hadn't discussed this during preparations; it would have changed the emotion I felt. "My mother was in another room in a coma, with only days to live…" Tears made it hard to speak. I looked down and tried to pull it together. Mr. Simmons placed a hand on my shoulder. I tried to finish. "Momma was days away from losing her battle with cancer, and I just didn't feel it was the right time to be picking through her worldly possessions like she was already dead." Tears rolled down my cheeks. "I removed it to get Tanya to pay attention to what was really important." Mr. Simmons handed me his handkerchief. When I looked up, I saw a number of people in the courtroom wiping their eyes, too.

"No more questions."

Softly Judge Walker said, "You can step down."

Taking my seat at the defense table, I felt Daddy touch my shoulder. Mr. Simmons leaned in and whispered, "Sorry I had to do that to you, but you did good."

Tanya took the stand next. She was sworn in, and Mr. Beasley began questioning her.

"Mrs. Dumas, how did your mother come to have this silver service?" Mr. Beasley's voice was sappily sweet.

"My father gave it to her."

"How important is it to you?"

"Extremely. My father loved my mother very much, and it is more sentiment than anything else."

"How did your sister come into possession of it?"

"Because we had our family gatherings at my sister's house, my mother let her borrow it."

"So you never knew that it had been given to your sister?"

"No, it was still my mother's possession as far as I knew," Tanya said innocently.

"Did you ask Ms. Wallace for it?"

"Yes, and she became violent with me."

"Can you explain that?" Mr. Beasley asked.

Mr. Simmons jumped up. "Objection! Again, this is not a criminal trial!"

"Sustained. Mr. Beasley, please refrain from asking any questions of that nature," Judge Walker warned.

Mr. Beasley took a deep breath and continued. "Mrs. Dumas, in your opinion, would your mother want you to have this service?"

"Yes," Tanya said.

"You're a liar!" Someone screamed from the back of the courtroom.

Everyone started talking all at once, and a few more people yelled at her, but I couldn't understand what anyone was saying. Judge Walker began banging his gavel. The longer it went on, the harder he banged.

When the noise subsided, he shouted, "Outbursts will not be tolerated in this courtroom! I will not say this again." He waved the gavel at Mr. Beasley, indicating that he should continue.

Looking at Tanya, Mr. Beasley apologized and moved on with his questioning. "Did you ask Ms. Wallace about the service?"

"Yes, on a couple of occasions."

"What did she tell you?" he asked, turning to look in my direction.

"She told me I couldn't have it the first time. The next time I asked about it, she threw me out of Pam's house. When I returned the following day, she told me she hadn't seen it and I should check at Mother's house."

"I see," he said, still looking at me. I returned his gaze. Abruptly spinning around, he asked, "And did you go to your mother's to look for it?"

"No, I'd seen it in Pam's house the night before, and I knew it wasn't at Mother's."

"Did you believe Ms. Wallace was attempting to deceive you about the whereabouts of the service?"

"Yes, I did."

"Did anyone witness this?"

"Yes, there was a sheriff's deputy I'd asked to go with me to talk with Lizzy on that same night; then there were Pam's friends Rhonda and Patricia."

"Did the deputy attempt to locate the service?"

"Yes, and he informed me that it wasn't in the house."

Mr. Simmons shot out of his chair. "Objection, Your Honor! We have established that Ms. Wallace removed the service from the home."

"Sustained," was all Judge Walker said.

Pausing, Mr. Beasley moved back and forth in front of Tanya as if he were wondering where to go now. Finally he resumed. "Did Ms. Wallace tell you what she would do with the service once her mother had died?"

"She said she'd return it to Mother."

"Has she?"

"No," Tanya said coldly, looking at me.

"No more questions, Your Honor," he said as he returned to his chair.

Before Judge Walker could even ask, Mr. Simmons was out of his seat and moving toward Tanya.

"Mrs. Dumas, on the occasions when you inquired of my client about the service, did she give you a reason why she was not forfeiting it to you?" Mr. Simmons's voice was extremely cold.

"Yes, she believed the timing wasn't right." Tanya's voice was smaller now.

"Why were you not discussing this matter with your sister, Pam?"

"She was on a morphine drip and dying." She choked up on the words.

"Did you feel it was appropriate to worry about such things while your sister was dying?"

"I was just informing Lizzy of my intentions."

"Intentions you could not discuss with your sister. Were you informing my client, or were you demanding that she forfeit the service to you?" His voice was firm, and he was standing as close to the witness box as he could get.

"I was only letting her know that I expected the service to be returned to me." She was regaining some confidence now.

"'Returned' would imply that you had at one time been in possession of it. Were you ever in possession of the service?"

"No."

"How could something be returned to you that you had never been in possession of to begin with?" Without giving her a chance to answer, he moved straight to his next question. "How much did you assist Ms. Wallace in the care of your sister while she was dying?"

"I was there when I could be." Tanya was getting angry.

"In the final two weeks of your sister's life, about how many times were you in her home? Once, twice, four times, every day?" Mr. Simmons was still standing right in front of her, and I silently cheered him on. I wanted confirmation for everyone in the courtroom.

"It was not every day, but I was there several times. Exactly how many I cannot remember."

"How many times did you say you asked Ms. Wallace about the service?"

"Twice."

"So the second time you came with a law enforcement officer?"

"No, that was after I asked for it the night before."

"So truly it was three times that you asked for the service."

"I guess so." Tanya was rearranging herself in her seat.

"Where was Mrs. Jenkins during this time?" Mr. Simmons's voice was caring now.

"Lizzy had had her moved to her room."

"So Mrs. Jenkins was in your sister's home?"

"Yes."

"Why was she there at all?"

"Mother lived with Pam."

"Your mother, who has Alzheimer's, was living in your dying sister's home?" His tone was a little higher, like this was a revelation to him.

"Yes, Pam moved Mother in with her."

"Why did she do that?"

"She said Mother couldn't take care of her own self at home."

"Your dying sister moved your mother, who needs a lot of care, into her home. Did you and your sister share this responsibility?" He was attacking her character and doing quite well.

"No, Mother stayed solely with Pam."

"Why didn't she ever come and stay with you?"

"Because I have a family of my own..." She was cut off.

"You have testified that we are all here today because of the sentimental value of the silver service. Your father loved your mother, but in her time of need, it was your sister who took responsibility, even though she was losing her battle with cancer. Does this mean you don't consider Mrs. Jenkins family?" he shot back at her.

"She's my mother!" Tanya screamed.

The courtroom began to buzz behind me. I looked down and bit my lip. I wanted so badly to smile as Tanya got caught in her selfishness.

Mr. Simmons didn't let up. He kept right on her heels. "Exactly how many people live in your house?"

"Two, my husband and myself."

"No small children?"

"No, my son is grown."

"So this family of yours consists of two adults?"

"Yes, but..." Again he cut her off.

"Was guardianship of your mother recently revoked from you?"

She cleared her throat. "Yes."

"Why?" He waited patiently, but she didn't respond. "Mrs. Dumas, why?"

Tanya's face was red, but she still didn't respond. Judge Walker said, "Mrs. Dumas, please answer the question."

Sheepishly she responded, "The social worker felt she was in harm's way."

Mr. Simmons appeared to contemplate the response by putting his hand to his chin. "I see. Who has guardianship now?"

"Lizzy."

"No more questions, Your Honor." Mr. Simmons turned and nodded at Mr. Beasley, who sat with his mouth gaping open. I guess he'd been so taken with the line of questioning that he'd forgotten to defend his client and her character.

When Mr. Simmons sat down, I leaned over and whispered into his ear, "You did good."

Without cracking a smile, he whispered back, "Thank you, thank you."

Chapter 32

Testimony from the character witnesses filled the rest of the morning. We had a list of ten. Tanya had one. The questioning of each of my witnesses was short and to the point. Each testified to seeing the silver service in the house before Grandmother moved in. The ones who'd witnessed Tanya asking me for it were asked about the timing. Mr. Simmons made sure each also testified about the length of time Grandmother had been in my mother's home and why she was there.

Eventually we were recessed for lunch so the judge could go over everything and make a ruling. We left the courtroom and walked to a diner across the street. The diner was completely full, but when we walked in, an entire group of people got up and pulled tables together, calling us over to sit there.

"Y'all don't have to do that. Please sit and enjoy your lunches," I said.

"No, ma'am, you have a seat. We're almost through, anyway." The man acted like I couldn't see the full plate in his hand.

Once we were all seated, I looked over at Patricia and Rhonda. "Please remind me to tell you something." Both looked around, taking mental notes of everything. This had been a code that Momma used whenever she wanted to say something about something or somebody at an inappropriate time. All three of us smiled.

I was anxious to ask Mr. Simmons some questions. Although the diner had been loud when we walked in, the volume lessened somewhat while we were ordering. Mr. Simmons was sitting beside me. I asked, "So what do you think?"

"Lizzy, I don't think it could have gone better. I never expected Tanya to be so blatant in her response about not really giving a shit about you, your mother, or her own for that matter." He settled his napkin in his lap. "Weasley just seemed overwhelmed. I expected him to object to my attacking her like that, but it just goes to show she's hired scum."

The door chimed, and Mr. Beasley and Tanya appeared in the doorway. Although a few people had been preparing to leave, they sat back down. I don't know whether they were expecting a confrontation between Tanya and me and wanted ringside seats or if they wanted to make sure there were no empty places for them to sit. They left.

I devoured my lunch; I'd forgotten how wonderful the food here was. It had been Grandfather's favorite restaurant, and he and I ate here a couple of times a week when I was little.

Daddy said, "Still as good as you remembered?"

I laughed. "Oh my God, yes!" Everyone else laughed, too. "Do y'all mind if I excuse myself to give Spencer a call? I want to see how Grandmother was this morning."

Several people spoke to me as I made my way outside. Spencer answered the phone immediately. "I've been expecting your call. How's it going?"

"We're waiting on the ruling now. How's Grandmother?"

Spencer laughed. "She's great! I took some pastries, and we sat on the patio. She told me stories about you."

I snickered. "Great! Just what you need is more ammunition to use against me."

"Who knew you loved 'Crocodile Rock' so much?"

It had been my favorite song when I was four years old. "You gotta love Elton John!" We both laughed. "I just called to check in and see how she was."

"She's fine, and I expect you to call as soon as you know something."

"Will do!" After I hung up, I stood for a minute, thinking about that song. Someone exiting the diner broke my train of thought. After exchanging some pleasantries, I went back inside.

"Is she okay?" Patricia asked.

"She's great! How long is the recess?"

Mr. Simmons replied, "We have another twenty minutes, but we should probably go back in ten so we can be in place."

"I want to thank you. I hate that it's come to this, but I'm glad you've been with me," I said.

"Right is right, and I wouldn't let Pam's only child be done wrong." His response was short, sweet, and to the point.

When Daddy called the waitress over to get our check, she informed him that it had all been taken care of. Daddy leaned over and told me what she'd said.

"What? I can't let them do that," I said, looking around.

"They all did it. Everyone paid over on their checks to pay toward ours," he said.

The restaurant was still less noisy than when we'd arrived, and I stood up. "Excuse me," I said. Everyone immediately stopped talking and looked in our direction.

"I just want to thank you all for your support. My mother would be proud to know that so many people care so much." I was very happy and thought I might cry.

Random comments were thrown into the air. "Good luck." "We loved your momma and miss her."

Stepping outside, I took a deep breath to keep from crying. On the one hand, I'd left this town for this very reason—this close-knit community atmosphere where everyone knew everyone else's business. But on the other hand, they'd all come together like this. My thoughts were interrupted when Patricia and Rhonda came out and both said, "Now tell us something." I started laughing.

"Do you feel like we're in an old Western and it's time for the shootout scene?" I asked. They both burst into laughter, and it became even funnier when we got to the courthouse steps and noticed the train of people we'd been leading from the diner. Tanya and Beasley were already in place. I wondered if they'd even eaten.

While we waited, several people came up to me to share memories of Momma. Then I saw a woman enter the back of the courtroom swiftly, and my heart flew into my throat. She set her eyes on me, and I feared that something was wrong. She seemed determined to get to me. As she pushed her way to the front of the courtroom, I walked over to her.

"I guess you don't remember me. I'm Kelly Arnold from City Hall." She stopped and looked at Tanya. In a lower voice she asked, "Will you please come and see me before you leave town today? It's important."

I breathed a sigh of relief. "Sure. Is something wrong?"

"Not really, but I need to see you. There's something we need to take care of." The judge entered the room. "I'll be waiting for you." She turned and left as everyone found their seats.

"What was that about?" Daddy asked.

"No clue!" I said. As I took my seat, my heart began pounding in my ears.

"All rise," the bailiff said. The room fell silent.

Judge Walker cleared his throat. "It's always a sad state of affairs when families end up in my courtroom, because no one today will come out a winner. Regardless of who walks away with what, something will forever be lost in the way of the relationship. I've reviewed the testimony carefully, and I have contradiction on both sides." He looked straight at me, and my breath stopped.

"Ms. Wallace, I do see an attempt to deceive Mrs. Dumas into believing that the silver was not in your possession, but as a human being, I can understand what you were trying to do in your deception. It was still a deception, though."

242

Looking at Tanya, he continued, "Mrs. Dumas, you started all of these proceedings, you say, out of sentiment. I believe if you'd been more sentimental about human life than material things, this could all have been avoided. That being said, my ruling is for the defendant. Court is adjourned." He banged his gavel.

The courtroom exploded with cheers. I hugged Mr. Simmons as Mr. Beasley approached. "We will be filing an appeal."

"What does that mean?" I asked Mr. Simmons.

"We're going to have to do this again, but don't worry," he replied.

Tanya was so pissed off that she stormed from the courtroom. It took time to weave through the sea of people congratulating me. Once we were outside, I thought about the woman from City Hall. Mrs. Culpepper and Judge Culpepper approached me. "Honey, I couldn't be happier for you," she said, hugging me. It was the first time I'd seen her all day. There were so many people.

"Thank you!" I replied.

"Where's Tanya?"

"She's already gone. Kelly Arnold said she needed to see me," I told everyone.

"She's from City Hall. What could she want?" Rhonda asked.

"I'll let you know after I speak to her."

Judge Culpepper spoke up. "How's Mrs. Jenkins?"

I wanted to tell him about the condition I'd found her in but figured Mrs. Culpepper would have already done that. "She's doing very well and being taken care of properly. I see her every day!"

"Good, good. I'm so glad to hear that."

Mrs. Culpepper said, "I know it's the best thing for her, but I can't help but miss her."

I felt bad. "Well, you're welcome to come and visit anytime. You just tell me when, and I'll come and get you."

"Would you?"

"Absolutely!"

She seemed touched. "I'm going to take you up on that. We're going to go. I know you have a lot to get done."

Once they walked away, Mr. Simmons explained that he'd be in touch when he had more information on the appeal. He told me to contact him if I needed anything and said his good-byes. He was in a really good mood after his win.

"What's this about City Hall?" Patricia asked.

"Don't know. Y'all want to go with me? You know I'm just dying to know. I hope it's not bad," I said. Everyone agreed to meet me there, and we went to find our cars.

Daddy and I got there first, with Patricia and Rhonda right behind us. Walking in, I said, "I'm getting that old Western feeling again. We're like a gang. Now all we need are the gun belts." We all laughed.

Kelly Arnold was waiting, just as she'd said she would be. "Congratulations! I heard you won!"

"Wow! You've already heard that?" I asked.

"My best girlfriend works in the courthouse." She reached into her desk drawer and withdrew a folder.

"I remember you now. You're the one Momma and I spoke to when we bought the burial plot next to my grandfather. I'm so sorry!" It all flooded back when I saw the folder. Daddy, Patricia, and Rhonda all knew Kelly, too.

"You were under a little stress at that time, honey. No one can blame you for not remembering everything. Yes, that was me, and that's what this is about." She opened the folder and found the diagram page. "Do you want me to discuss this with you in private or with everyone?"

"I'm just going to tell them what you tell me, so let's cut out the middle man." I smiled at her, but my mind was racing. Had I paid for the plot? Was Momma in the one she was supposed to be in?

"Well, I need you to sign off on your plot," she said.

"I don't have a plot," I said.

"Yes, you do. When your momma came in here to purchase hers, she bought two, one for herself and one for you. The day you two were here, I was so upset that she was sick that I didn't even get your signature."

"Where is my plot?" I asked.

As she unfolded the diagram, I saw that it was a map. I'd forgotten this, too. When we were here to get Momma's, I thought it was strange that you just signed your name on this diagram, and that was your plot. Add your fee and you'd laid claim to where you'd spend all eternity.

"It's right next to your momma," she said.

"That's not possible. There's a road there. Well, not a real road, but you know what I'm saying," I said. We helped her flatten out the map.

"Yeah, there's a road there, but there's also a plot. Ah, here it is." She placed her finger on a splotch of squares. "You see, here's a road, and this is a road. Your grandmother's family is here and here," she said, pointing across the top, the bottom, and to the left of my grandparents' plots. "Your grandmother wants to be buried with her family, so your grandfather bought these two. His and hers. That left these two." She pointed to where Momma had signed. "We knew no one would buy those plots because that's your family's section, so we never worried about it. But see here, this is your momma's. She purchased the last two in this block of squares. She told me the second one was yours. The only way to seal the deal is by putting your signature there, and I'll log it in this book." She held up a three-ring binder.

Looking at the diagram, I asked, "So where does that leave Tanya?"

"Don't know. Across the road, I guess, unless someone buys those plots first."

This was a morbid conversation, and I looked at Daddy, Patricia, and Rhonda, who all burst into laughter, causing Kelly and me to laugh as well.

"Your aunt is not well liked. If she caught wind of this, I'm sure she'd try suing you for this, too," Kelly said.

"Did my mother know what she was doing?" I asked.

"Yes, and she said it brought her great pleasure," she replied.

"This is so Pam!" Rhonda said.

"Classic!" added Patricia, clapping her hands.

"Let's get to signing, then," I said. She handed me a pen and I claimed my burial plot.

Once we were in the parking lot, I told everyone that we had to keep this to ourselves. Kelly was right: this would just add fuel to the fire. We pledged our secrecy and then visited with Mrs. Culpepper for a while. After I explained that my visit to City Hall concerned Momma's plot purchase, Mrs. Culpepper asked nothing more about it.

I left too late to visit Grandmother. I called Spencer, and he agreed to meet me at the house. We pulled in at the same time, and he had a pizza box in his hand. He said, "I hope you're hungry."

"I'm still full from lunch, but you eat while I tell you everything. Just let me call and check on Grandmother first." After being reassured that she'd a good day, I let go of some of the guilt I felt for not visiting. "I feel bad I didn't see her today," I told Spencer.

"I know, but you'll be there tomorrow."

We sat at the bar, and I started telling him about the day. When I mentioned the appeal, he said, "Whoa! You're going to do this again?"

"I guess so. Mr. Simmons said it was nothing to worry about, though."

"Still."

"I know. I feel the same way, but I guess her view is death for profit no matter the cost." Then I told him about the cemetery plot.

He almost choked on his pizza. "Who knew sibling rivalry could transcend the grave?"

"I have to admit, today seems like a big win, but I can't help thinking of everything we've all lost in the process."

Chapter 33

The next few months brought some big changes in my life. Grandmother's condition worsened, and she talked less and less. When she did talk, she spoke of things I didn't know anything about. Still, I visited every day, just like I'd promised. Tanya didn't visit but proceeded with the appeal over the silver.

Daddy and I saw each other as much as possible, and I was pleasantly surprised by the way our relationship was growing. My classes made it difficult for me to get away, so he made the trip to visit with Grandmother and me every chance he got. Mrs. Culpepper came with him a couple of times, but it was too hard for her when Grandmother didn't remember her.

My nightmares about Momma were gone; having her things in the house broke the spell, and I could see her as a healthy woman now. I still needed to deal with some things in her house, but for now, school and Grandmother were keeping me too busy.

I made sure to call the girls and Mrs. Culpepper at least once a week to catch up. They'd been the glue that held me together during the most trying time in my life, and I'd be eternally grateful to them for that. Mrs. Culpepper had become my surrogate grandmother. A month before the appeal, I called her for some advice.

We talked for a few minutes, and then I said, "Mrs. Culpepper, can I ask you something?"

"Sure, baby. Anything."

"Have you ever thought you wanted something, but then, when you got it, your feelings toward it changed?"

She sat quiet for a moment. "Lizzy, are we talking about the silver?"

"Yes, ma'am."

"Are you afraid you won't win the appeal? You know there's nothing to worry about."

"Yes, ma'am. But every time I look at it, I can't help but think of everything that's happened. It's like the negativity has been absorbed into the metal."

In a very matronly way she said, "Baby, you have to search your heart for the answer to this one. I know Grace and Buddy would have wanted you to have it, but I'm not sure even they would have wanted you to go through all this. You have to do what you feel is right."

Her words hung heavy on me, but she was right. "I hate being a grownup!" I said.

She laughed. "I do have to tell you, I've seen you grow so much in the last year. Your mother would have been so proud of how well you're doing."

That night, I got the silver out and thought about what Mrs. Culpepper had said. In the beginning, this had been about righting a wrong—but now it all seemed wrong. Tanya was who she was, and keeping the silver wasn't going to change her. It was just a reminder of what would never be again. I closed the box and put it away. I decided there was still time to think about it.

I focused on my upcoming midterms; then we had spring break. Spencer was surprised when I told him I wanted to use the time to move everything from Momma's house to mine.

He asked, "How many days do I need to take off?"

"A couple?"

"I know it's going to be hard."

I sighed. "Yes, it's going to be hard, but I have to do it. In a way, it's keeping me from moving forward." I looked toward the drawer where I'd put the silver. I thought, *And so is that.*

"I'll put in for the days off tonight. What are you up to?"

"I've got midterms, so I'm going to study for a while." His pager chirped in the background. "Everybody wanting to see you again?"

"You know it. They just can't get enough of me." He was laughing as he hung up.

Studying that night was hard. My mind drifted to Momma's house, the silver, and the decisions ahead. It was time to put the past behind me, but moving on was harder than I ever could have imagined.

I woke the next morning with a jolt. I'd fallen asleep on the couch where I'd been studying, and now I had less than an hour to get dressed and get to my first test. The rat race kept me focused, leaving no time to think about the silver dilemma. I managed to get to my tests on time, and then I visited with Grandmother.

She was talking a little more today than she had in weeks. It was good to hear her voice, even though it was painful to hear what she said: "Buddy will be here soon."

I never knew whether to go with the conversation or correct her. At this point in the disease, however, I didn't think it mattered anymore. "He will? Where are y'all going?"

She rarely spoke in full sentences; she just said random words that may have been in the sentences she wanted to say. "Dinner."

"Really? Is it a special occasion?"

"Anniversary."

"How nice! I know you'll have a good time."

She smiled sweetly. "It's silver."

I looked at her. While I was full of turmoil about the silver, it still brought her great pleasure to remember it. She would have been so disappointed to know the trouble it had caused. I put my arm around her shoulder. "I love you."

"You more."

As I drove home that afternoon, I very nearly knew what I had to do, but I didn't know where to begin. I still had two more tests to take, so I tried to put it out of my mind. *One thing at a time,* I thought. I prioritized my list: Grandmother, tests, Momma's house—and then Tanya.

Time flew over the next few days, and soon it was moving day. Spencer drove a U-Haul, and I followed in Spencer's truck. As we turned off the interstate, my cell phone rang.

Spencer asked, "You okay back there?"

"Yeah, I'm fine."

"You don't sound fine."

I wanted to burst into tears and then turn the truck around and drive as fast as I could in the other direction. I didn't, though. "It's got to be done. Just promise to bear with me."

"You know I will."

As we pulled into the driveway, I saw that the girls and Daddy were already waiting for us. I saw the sadness on their faces; they understood how difficult this was going to be. We shared a hug, and then I opened the door. Just inside the door was a stack of boxes already packed up, their contents written on the outside.

Spencer said, "Nothing is packed that I thought you'd want to go through."

I could tell he'd been packing things up when he'd come to do the yard. As I walked from room to room, I was overwhelmed. But I knew I couldn't fall apart if I wanted to get this done. "Let's get started before I change my mind."

We worked for hours, until every box and piece of furniture had been placed in the truck. Everyone waited outside when I walked back into the empty house. I ran my hand along the walls. I could feel Momma's spirit around me, warm and soothing. I could hear her laughter. I knew she wasn't there, but I looked for her anyway. I opened every closet and cabinet door.

I stood for a long time in her room, taking it all in. In the bathroom, I opened the walk-in closet door. I could still smell her perfume, as though she were still there. Without turning on the light, I walked inside, pulling the door closed behind me. I wanted to stay in there forever.

I was sitting on the floor when the light beamed in. My face and shirt were wet with tears. "I could smell her in here," I said simply.

Rhonda and Patricia came into the closet and closed the door. They sat down on either side of me, wrapping their arms around me. We cried together for a long time. None of us spoke. Each of us knew what the other was going through. Finally I got to my feet. It was time to leave. Patricia and Rhonda followed me out.

Reversing the path I'd taken through the house, I closed all the closet and cabinet doors. I made sure all the outside doors were locked and the garage doors were down. Spencer was sitting on the porch railing with Daddy when I walked out. I hugged Daddy and the girls without a word and then walked to Spencer's truck. They understood that words wouldn't fix what I was feeling, so they didn't even try.

Spencer got in the U-Haul, and we caravanned away from the house. I watched the house in the rearview mirror until it was out of sight. I slowed down as we drove by Grandmother's house and then headed to the interstate. Spencer followed close behind me all the way home.

In Montgomery, we began the tedious task of unloading the truck. We put they things wherever they would fit. Spencer tried to make excuses to stick around, but I asked if he'd mind just leaving me.

"I'll be back first thing in the morning to help," he said. "It's been a long day. Try to get some rest."

That was easier said than done. I worked through the night, and only when the doorbell rang did I realize it was morning. Spencer stood on the porch with breakfast.

He took one look at me and said, "You didn't sleep, did you?"

"I meant to. Time just got away from me."

There were empty boxes everywhere. "Did you leave anything for me to help you with?"

"There's still furniture that needs to be moved around and stuff to go to the attic." I'd only seen the attic once since I bought the house. I was too afraid of heights to go up there.

He laughed. "What? You couldn't go to the attic?"

"I'd have been sitting at the top of the ladder when you arrived this morning if I had." We both laughed.

He said, "Eat your breakfast."

I had Momma's dining room table now, so we sat down there. I took a couple of bites and then set the food aside. I knew Spencer wasn't going to like what I was about to say. "I've been thinking about something."

He wiped his mouth. "Sounds serious."

"It is. I've been thinking about giving the silver to Tanya."

"You're kidding, right?"

I sighed heavily. "No."

"But why? She doesn't deserve it!"

"She doesn't, but will you hear me out first?"

He pushed his food away. "You've got my undivided attention."

I pulled the silver out of the drawer and opened the lid. "What do you think of when you see this? First thought!"

"You winning the trial."

"Exactly! You don't think of the reason this came to be. The love Grandfather felt for Grandmother when he gave it to her. You remember the battle for it."

He leaned back in his chair. "I guess I see your point."

"When all this started, I was so full of anger. But I can't live the rest of my life being angry."

"So are you saying you want to make amends with Tanya?"

I smiled at him. "Hold your horses. I wouldn't go that far. I don't think the distance between us can be bridged."

He smiled back. "This was so much easier when you just wanted to stick it to her. Honestly, though, I think this is making you a better person. Have you told Mr. Simmons?"

"No, I want to be sure before I do anything. Once it's gone, I know I'll never see it again."

I knew he had more to say, but all he added was, "What else goes on in that head of yours, we all need to know?" We both laughed.

After we put everything away, we visited Grandmother. When he dropped me back at the house, I could hear the phone ringing as I unlocked the door. It was Mr. Simmons, calling to discuss the trial. I didn't tell him my thoughts about the silver, and I didn't talk about it with anyone else. The thought just stayed in my head until the day of the trial. Spencer picked me up. When I walked out of the house, I had the mahogany box in my hand.

"So you're going to do it?"

"I still don't know. Just when I think I'm sure, I'm not."

As we drove, we talked about people we knew at the hospital. Spencer loved gossip, so he got me caught up. We talked about school and how well it was going. Because we'd made this journey so many times, I only had to guide Spencer to the courthouse once we were in town.

I placed the box on the floor of the truck, and we walked up to the courthouse. There wasn't much fanfare this time. Only the people closest to Momma and me were there. I saw Daddy coming around the corner and walked toward him, away from the small crowd of people on the steps.

"Hey," I said.

"Ready?" he asked.

"Yeah, but listen—no matter what happens today, I'm okay with it."

"This is just a formality," he said reassuringly.

We headed into the courthouse. Mr. Simmons guided us to the assigned courtroom, and everyone took a seat. I looked over at Tanya. She glanced in my direction and quickly away again. I'd let her know the facility Grandmother was in, but other than that, we hadn't talked.

"Mr. Simmons, I want this to be over," I said.

"Don't worry, Lizzy, it will be soon." He started taking things out of his briefcase.

"No, sir, that's not what I'm saying. I want this to be over completely."

He stopped shuffling papers and sat down quickly. He lowered his voice. "Lizzy, what are you saying?"

"I'm saying that I'm ending this."

"I can't advise you to do that. Let's just get this over with today, okay?"

The bailiff ordered us to rise, and a judge I'd never seen before entered the courtroom. After being instructed to take our seats, I remained standing.

"Judge," I said, "can I say something?" My heart was pounding.

Mr. Simmons jumped to his feet. "I'm sorry, sir, can we have a moment?"

"We haven't even begun," the judge said, agitated.

"There's no need," I replied.

Mr. Simmons said, "Lizzy, please! Think about this."

Turning to Mr. Simmons, I said softly, "All I've done is think about this. I'm ready for this part of my life to be over."

"I know you are, but I'm here to help you win this," he said.

"Then regrettably, you're fired," I said.

"Your Honor, Ms. Wallace has just relieved me as her legal counsel."

"Ms. Wallace, what is this all about?" the judge asked.

"Sir, I can end all this right now, and I understand that I don't have legal counsel anymore. If I could be permitted to leave for two minutes, we can wrap this up quickly."

He asked, "Are you sure you're aware of what you're doing?"

"Yes, sir. May I be excused?"

"Make it quick, Ms. Wallace."

Tanya and Mr. Beasley had their heads together. The girls and Daddy were on the edges of their seats. I made eye contact with Spencer and nodded him toward the door. Daddy stood up, but I motioned for him to stop.

Outside the courtroom, Spencer asked, "Are you sure?"

I walked briskly to the truck without answering, and Spencer unlocked the door. Handing me the box, he asked again, "Are you sure?"

"I've given this a lot of thought, and nothing good is going to come from keeping the silver. It's just not how it's supposed to be." I took out one silver spoon and handed it to him. "Will you hang onto this for me?"

He knew the story of the silver spoon in the mouth, and he burst out laughing. "Absolutely!"

We walked back into the courtroom, and I headed straight to the judge with the box in my hand. "Your Honor, may I speak to Mrs. Dumas?"

"Keep it civil," he replied.

I walked slowly toward Tanya, my heart pounding. I put the box in front of her and opened the lid.

"I wanted you to see that it's in there," I said. "I only have a couple of things to say, and we can be done with all this. Will you listen?" She didn't answer. "I'll take that as a yes. Grandfather gave this to Grandmother because she was his heart and soul. What you, Momma, and I have done has tarnished its meaning completely. I can't even look at it without thinking of all the losses we've suffered. If you can take it without a second thought, then it truly does belong to you. As far as you and I are concerned, we only have one tie that still binds us—Grandmother. I suggest you take advantage of the time she has left. If you decide not to, then I'll contact you when it's over, just like I did with Momma. I can't hold onto the anger any longer—doing so would turn me into you. I hope you find some peace in your life with all of us out of it."

I waited for her to grab the box, but she didn't. Instead, tears rolled down her cheeks, and she just looked at me. I didn't understand what that was about, and I honestly didn't care. I turned back to the judge.

"Your Honor, I think we're done here," I said.

He performed the actions necessary to bring our case to a close, and I exited the courtroom with Mr. Simmons.

"No hard feelings, okay?" I asked him.

"No, Lizzy. After hearing what you said, I understand. Let me know if I can help you with anything else."

"Will do." I watched him walk away.

Everyone came over to me with puzzled looks on their faces. "Listen, all of you, I had to end this. It's been over a year since Momma died, and this just wasn't healthy anymore," I said.

"I guess you listened to your heart," Mrs. Culpepper said.

"Yes, ma'am, and I thank you for our talk that night. I just hope Momma understands."

"She'd still be proud. I'm just not sure I'm ready for you to be so grown," Rhonda said.

Mrs. Culpepper kissed my cheek. "Call me next week." We all hugged and said our good-byes.

As Spencer drove us home, I gazed at the spoon. "Can we stop and see Grandmother?" I asked.

"Sure."

We found her by the window in the day room. I pulled a chair up next to her. When I took the spoon from my purse and handed it to her, I saw the same sweet smile she'd had when talking about the silver.

She looked at the spoon and ran her fingertips over it gently. She said softly, "Buddy."

I replied, "Yes, ma'am. He loved you so much."

She handed the spoon back to me. "You, too."

Epilogue

Alzheimer's stole Grandmother from me four years later. After I left the courtroom the day of the appeal, I didn't see or hear from Tanya again, not about Grandmother, the spoon, or anything else. She wasn't even there the day I buried Grandmother, even though I'd called when the end was near. Her funeral was very small, just the girls, Daddy, Spencer, and me.

I'd always thought Grandmother would die before Mrs. Culpepper. But Grandmother outlived her by two years. The news that Mrs. Culpepper died in her sleep devastated me. I missed my conversations with her. Judge Culpepper asked me to sit with the family at the funeral. "She thought of you as one of her grandchildren," he said.

Daddy helped me when I put Momma's house up for sale. After we moved Momma's things, he'd taken over Spencer's yard work duties, and he saw that the empty house was running itself down. He treaded lightly when he suggested I needed do something. Selling Grandmother's house had torn me up.

Tanya hadn't been present for that, either. Mr. Beasley handled her portion and made sure she received her half as required by law. I put my half toward Grandmother's care and bills for the nursing home.

The girls and I stayed in touch over the years. Through them I learned that Brad had a stroke and was totally dependent on Tanya for his care. The seven-digit life insurance policy was the only reason she hadn't rid herself of him like she had her own family.

Spencer married and became a father; both roles suited him. While family life didn't allow us to hang out like we used to, our friendship stayed strong and just included more people now.

On the one-year anniversary of Grandmother's death, I sat and held the silver spoon for a long time. It was just a piece of metal, but the way she'd given it back to me was priceless. I so missed her, Grandfather, and Momma.

The phone snapped me out of my thoughts. "Hello?"

Spencer said, "Lizzy, I need you to come to the flea market on the boulevard!" He spoke very quickly.

I was startled. "What's wrong?"

"I'm not going to tell you this on the phone. You've got to see it for yourself."

I was already pulling on my shoes. "Stay right there. I'm on my way."

I tried not to speed, but I was dying of curiosity. I knew he and his wife liked going to flea markets to shop for antiques, but I had no idea what could have happened. Was it the baby? Once I pulled into a parking space, I snatched my phone from my purse and hit speed dial.

Instead of "hello," he said, "Come through the front door and go to your far right. I'm at the counter on the outside wall."

I followed his instructions. "Spencer, are you okay? The baby?"

"Yes, yes, everything's okay. I'm here alone today. Just hurry!"

I quickened my pace. The flea market was packed with things from wall to wall, and I had trouble making my way through. Finally I saw the top of his head. I called out to him. "Spencer!"

He waved me over furiously. I was out of breath when I reached him. "What's wrong?"

He was smiling from ear to ear. "Nothing. But you've got to see this."

I glared at him. "You had me all worried and you just wanted me to see something you found at the flea market?"

He yelled "Look!" and pointed to an item in a glass cabinet.

My breath caught in my throat. It looked like the mahogany box Grandmother's silver had been kept in. I bent down to look closer. "It can't be." A man's face appeared on the other side of the cabinet as he opened the door. He lifted the box out of the cabinet and put it on the glass top.

He said to Spencer, "I take it this is the young lady you were waiting for. Just let me know what you decide."

I was still mesmerized by the resemblance. Spencer opened the lid slowly. The silver was tarnished, and I could barely make out the pattern—but it was one I recognized. "Count the spoons," Spencer said.

I ran my finger down the side of each one, counting. Then I counted again. "Eleven." Spencer nodded. "But it can't be."

Spencer said, "I didn't think so either, but then I counted the spoons. The man who was just here said he bought it at a flea market in your hometown. He said he got it cheap because it wasn't a complete set. He's been unable to sell it for that very reason. Lizzy, I bet we both know where that twelfth spoon is."

I was almost in tears as Spencer made a deal with the man for twenty-five dollars. I held the box close to my heart as we walked out. He followed me to the house. I went to the coffee table where I'd been sitting when he called. I opened the box's lid and placed the final spoon on top of the others. "Happy anniversary, Grandmother."

K. T. Archer is a writer living in Montgomery, Alabama. With encouragement from her husband and their numerous pets, she writes fiction to which readers can relate. Life events, good and bad, are her inspiration.

10517431R0

Made in the USA
Lexington, KY
30 July 2011